SEAVIEW ROAD

a novel

BRIAN McMAHON

Library of Congress Control Number: 2020902897

ISBN 9780578625768 (trade paperback)
ISBN 9780578625775 (ebook)

DESIGNER: David Provolo
EDITOR: Lucy Davis

For the people that go on

"I'd known this avenue all my life, but it seemed to me again, as it had seemed on the day I'd first heard about Sonny's trouble, filled with a hidden menace which was its very breath of life."

—James Baldwin, "Sonny's Blues"

"But I reckon I got to light out for the territory ahead of the rest, because Aunt Sally she's going to adopt me and sivilize me, and I can't stand it. I been there before."

—Mark Twain, *Adventures of Huckleberry Finn*

July 5

I'll tell my side myself because I don't think anyone else will. I guess that's partially my fault. I didn't kill him. Didn't mean to kill him. But he's dead.

My hands shook last night while I was driving home because of what we did.

Shouldn't have hit him. Didn't need to. What happened after I hit him is the real problem. But I don't think any of it would've happened if I hadn't hit him. It wasn't the first time I punched him. We never got along. Which makes me a little afraid because some of the guys know that. They know I don't like him. Sooner or later they'll come around asking questions. Someone will tell them we scrapped last winter. Beat each other up pretty good. They won't mention that he started that fight. Deserved to get hit that time.

I think one bad night is probably enough to ruin someone's life and I think last night was it. For me and him and maybe the others.

    It probably won't mean a lot to everyone else but I don't think I hurt him too bad. What I mean is I don't think we made him suffer. That's what I'm telling myself at least. I didn't mean to do it. At least I didn't make him suffer.

    I've done bad things before. Violent things. Obviously never anything like this. In the past I was surprised at how quickly I got over stuff. I don't like to waste time feeling sorry for myself. This is different. I understand that. What counts as quickly for something like this.

It's the worst thing I've ever done but I don't think it was evil. If it was evil I don't think that means I'm evil.

That's what I'm telling myself.

1

"I don't remember it being this quiet," Katie Murray said to her brother, not realizing he had fallen behind, his pace slowed by his search for sea glass. He bent his neck at a painful angle as he shuffled through the sand.

"Ryan, we're almost back. I think you can give up for now."

Ryan and his mother, Beth, had spent countless Cape hours scouring South Monomo's Granger Beach for sea glass since they bought the house almost twenty years before. Katie had never been as interested in the quests, and her father, Kevin, preferred to spend his time at the beach reading or running or sitting still. He usually chose to stay up at the house observing the beach from their porch, which offered clean views of the sand and water because of its position halfway up Seaview Road's slope.

"You're just not used to spending much time here this early in the summer. Not even summer, really."

"I guess you're right. Next weekend it'll be busy."

She waited for him to catch up and flicked a piece of dark seaweed from her foot. The hairy clump flew toward the water but landed a few feet short, and a small wave brushed up against it as Ryan approached. Some people suggested he was still growing into his body, but he was by now convinced that his lankiness was permanent. He doubted that a fourth year of college-boy eating would make a difference, given the results of the first three. His bony knees and elbows matched his father's, though Kevin carried more weight in his middle age and was slightly shorter than his son. Katie also possessed some lank but wore it better than her brother, her length approaching elegance rather than miring in incongruity.

Save for two bands of pebbles and shells, one near the water and another several feet above the siblings, the sand was smooth and cool, unheated by the overcast May sky. Both walked barefoot, and Katie held a pair of tattered flip-flops in her hand, the stage of their fraying suggesting this would be their last viable summer.

"Yeah, I th—got one!"

Ryan was two steps from his sister but now squatted at her feet and scooped up an almost-jagged piece of brown glass. He rose and twirled it at eye level, running his fingers over the ridges of what was clearly the bottom of a bottle.

"What do you think?"

"I think that's just broken glass and you should throw it out. Doesn't count if you're picking up some drunk guy's trash from last night. I also think we've been out here forever and my legs are tired. Let's go."

They continued on at a faster clip, though Ryan still glanced at the ground every few paces, losing interest as they moved farther from the water. Katie guided them toward the top of a jetty so they wouldn't have to climb over sand-splashed rocks. No one sat on the beach. The only visitors were running or walking, and as the siblings stepped down a German Shepherd ran toward them, halting to inspect them from twenty feet before resuming its tail wag and grabbing a tennis ball from the sand. The owner stood closer to the rising tide and waved in their direction. Katie didn't recognize him but waved back. By the time they passed the trash cans, where Ryan deposited the brown piece and a few other borderline discoveries, the dog was flying toward them again. This time the creature zoomed past without hesitating and pounced on its ball, gripping the felt in its mouth as it tried to shake off the muck.

Katie stepped onto the beginning of the path's concrete and slipped into her sandals. Their bikes leaned against a stone wall at the edge of the mostly empty parking lot. The lot would soon be full for the summer, as beachgoers from other neighborhoods and towns flooded in to enjoy the public section of Granger Beach, which began at the jetty the Murrays had just traversed and extended sideways for about a mile that looked far longer with the sun at full blast. Ryan's sneakers, two summers past their expiration date, sat untouched between his wheels.

"I told you no one would take them." He clanged them together to dislodge their dirt and grime.

"You should be thankful no one tossed them."

Katie considered reintroducing the discussion of how vile his habit of wearing the sneakers without socks was, but she was too tired from their journey to engage. She grabbed her ride as he wrestled with one of the still-tied shoes. They walked the bikes out of the parking lot and turned right, reaching the intersection where Seaview met Squall Lane. Their house was the second up the hill on the right, rendering the mounting of their bikes unnecessary even when less exhausted. There were two cars in the first driveway but no activity to speak of in or around the house. The Simms family kept to themselves, rarely taking part in neighborhood festivities. They had two daughters, now out of college, but Katie and Ryan had never seen much of them, even in their younger years. The Murrays and their other neighbors speculated but never knew exactly how Mr. and Mrs. Simms spent their summer time or why they had invested in this place only to never, seemingly, enjoy the vistas immediately beyond their enclave.

The only time Katie could remember her parents meaningfully interacting with their closest neighbors was a night during the summer after her freshman year of high school. Beth and Kevin had been forced to invite them over to have a discussion of the Simms' concerns regarding tree work being conducted along their shared property line. Mrs. Simms believed this was one more cataclysmic step on the way to completely ruining the natural scenery of their beachside retreat. Kevin didn't help his cause by suggesting she look around at the size of the houses and their proximity to each other and decide for herself if their beachside retreat's scenery had not already been irreparably desecrated.

The sets of parents maintained a cordial relationship. Beth encouraged her children to say hello and stop for a chat whenever they saw Mr. or Mrs. Simms, but this amounted to only one or two brief encounters per summer, which they handled with ease.

"Isn't it weird that you only have one year left?" Katie spoke excitedly in case her brother had forgotten his own timeline.

"Yeah. I can't decide if it's exciting or scary."

"Definitely exciting. I'm ready for the real world after one year."

He snorted quietly. "Yeah, but you're smarter than I am. I could use another three or four."

Ryan smiled at his sister, who rolled her eyes at his self-deprecation, as they steered the bikes into the driveway and laid them to rest on the grass to its right. The lawn was full and long. Kevin had asked Ryan to cut it the day before, but he had left early to caddy at Monomo Dunes Country Club and was now too tired to comply. They walked around their father's Honda Pilot and climbed the stairs to the porch, where Ryan took his seat at the pollen-dusted table as his sister fetched lemonade. He removed his shoes again and tossed them at the mat next to the door Katie had just swung open, almost hitting his mark.

He had spent much of the previous June and July in Boston, and he was grateful to be back in South Monomo for a fuller summer, making money at the Dunes before he had to reenter the white-collar workforce with a fall-semester internship, one that carried the added pressure of being an opportunity to earn a full-time offer for after graduation, an offer that he longed for but also didn't mind waiting to pursue. The offer would be fine. It would keep certain people quiet. It would act as a delaying tactic, a way for him to avoid determining what he actually wanted to do with his life, rather than an opportunity to do, in the words of his career center's cardboard cutouts, something that "lights a fire in your heart."

Caddying and helping out at the club was sometimes too hot and too long, depending on the player and the breeze, but he cherished the mindlessness, how easy he found it to coast now that he had worked parts of eight summers there in assorted capacities.

"Are you working this week?"

Katie used her butt to push open the screened door, already half-blanketed by hot-weather bugs, and brought two glasses to the table, cradling a bowl of potato chips between them. She had explored a few summer work opportunities at school and elsewhere but eventually picked a summer at the beach over them. Some parents would question this choice for their children, but no one in her circles doubted that she would someday do whatever she wanted and do it well. The tips from driving the snack cart and working in the club's dining room added up to far more income than her other choices offered anyway. In addition, she liked having an excuse to get paid to spend time outside. She sometimes found herself driving along a fairway or idling next to a group putting out and dreaming of a job that would pay her to bike along the canal, stop at her leisure, and watch the splashing of the swimmers and marine beings.

"They told me I'll start Thursday. Said it probably isn't worth having me out there before then."

"You're going to run into some pervy guys." Ryan contorted his tongue into a look of disgust.

"I've driven the cart before, Ryan. They're not that bad."

Katie sipped her lemonade and rolled her forearms on the glass, their skin already tanned but still far from a mid-season tone, as Ryan shoveled chips into his mouth. She faced the water as he looked across the street.

"See those things? The one in front is enormous."

Two rabbits fed on the lawn across the street and down one house, looking in their direction as they chewed, on guard. The residence behind towered over the bunnies, its newness evidenced by the sheen of the driveway and the gloss of the freshly painted porch in their line of sight. A nameplate, made to look seatossed, hung over the door. *Hairston*. A trampoline sat to the beach side of the empty driveway, its safety net still in pristine condition.

Amelia Clarke, now Amelia Hairston, had purchased the house that used to stand on the lot with her husband, Nate, two years before and proceeded to demolish it, leaving in its place this recently completed structure. It fit its surroundings and setting but was nevertheless more ostentatious and less inviting than her parents' house, which sat at the bottom of the road, next to the path and parking lot. Amelia would turn thirty that summer, so for Katie and Ryan she was a former babysitter rather than a peer. She was either living or convincingly sculpting the semblance of a picture-perfect life: Harvard grad, two beautiful kids, a high-paying job in digital marketing in New York that happened to have wonderful benefits for working mothers (though she had started to work a bit less and was contemplating stopping altogether as the kids neared school age), and a slightly older husband making banking money without brandishing a full-on banker's attitude. They had been regulars at her parents' house before buying their own, and Nate's relative seniority, combined with Amelia's flexible schedule, allowed them to carve out summers spent, for the most part, here.

"Isn't it weird that Amelia has two kids? I still picture her at, like, our age."

"I followed her around all the time back then. She and her friends were so nice to me." Katie spoke in a wistful tone, which surfaced rarely, generally confined to this porch or the beach below it.

"You see their Christmas card this year?"

The question caught Katie by surprise but immediately filled her brain with images of Clarke Christmases past and the cards Amelia's parents, Jamie and Anne, liked to send out. The cards had always been professional and impressive, but they often struck the Murrays as odd attempts at making Amelia and her brothers, Jamie Jr. and Eric, look older than they were. The shots were typically highly stylized pictures of the children on rocks and quays farther down Granger Beach, sometimes in cinematic black and white. The Murrays mocked the cards each year, but Katie had always thought it was a little sweet that Jamie and Anne made sure to get as much family as possible together for a shot every summer. Ryan was quick to remind her that they didn't have to try very hard, given how much time they all spent on this block. She kept the feeling to herself now.

"No, I didn't really look through Mom's pile this year." Most years she did. The pile was reliably large, which had always perplexed her, given her parents' relative aversion to socializing outside of their deep-rooted circle.

"Ridiculous. They committed the cardinal sin of Christmas cards."

"They wrote about the family?"

Ryan nodded as he bit his nails. Multiple family members, immediate and extended, had worked hard to eradicate his habit. Those efforts failed. None had been made in years. His parents now accepted the short nails, as long as he kept the nibbling out of sight of friends and strangers.

"Like two paragraphs for each of them, which is crazy. The kids are, like, two years old. What is there to say? Plus, I don't think Nate's interesting enough for two paragraphs."

Katie wondered what her mother would write about the two of them if she created such a card, how she would fill the space, or if Kevin would be in charge of the descriptions.

"He seems nice."

Ryan shook his head halfway and cocked his brow before taking a long sip. He was generally suspicious of the entire Clarke family, viewing them as loud and showy and eager to uphold their reputation. They annoyed Katie, sometimes confounded her. Even so, she clung to fond memories of tagging along with Amelia and her friends as teenagers, college students, and young adults—at each stage striking wide-eyed Katie as quite advanced but also authentic. She understood Ryan's apprehensions about certain Clarkes, but she viewed Amelia as a caring soul, and Eric was a victim, or at the very least a product of a peculiar environment.

"They're a little boring as a couple. I think we can admit that."

Katie shrugged. She enjoyed tormenting Ryan. She found him easy to toy with and was savvy enough to stop short of truly offending him. Toeing the line was too fun to pass up. He didn't bruise as easily as he once had, thanks to her.

"You're just mad because she never even considered laughing at your Emilia Clarke jokes."

"I didn't know that uptight Harvard girls don't like *Game of Thrones.*"

Katie laughed. She had heard the line before. He had repeated the story of the failed joke more than the joke itself.

"I think they just don't like bad jokes. Do Bucknell girls laugh at your jokes?"

"I guess they're uptight, too." Katie looked away to avoid giving him the satisfaction of a chuckle, which she hid in her glass.

"Must be."

The sound of the door's aging spring alerted them to their father's presence. Kevin, his eyes in a distinctly post-nap limbo, stepped onto the porch in a pair of paint-stained khaki shorts and a shirt displaying a restaurant's logo, the bulk of which had long since faded away. What was at that point a pronounced sock tan would disappear in the weeks ahead as he and Beth embarked on their daily beach walks. His legs were already toned from the spring tennis season.

He taught high school history but didn't have to. For him, the teaching was not a calling, not a moral imperative, but it was something to do. He liked providing guidance to the kids, or realizing when they didn't need any. He had worked in finance for several years after college and had enough success to warrant promotions and offers and to unveil *options*, but he turned to teaching after marrying Beth, and he received what everyone assumed was a substantial inheritance when his father passed away. His father's side had money, though it was unclear to even Beth how much they had. The nature of Grandpa's consulting and consulting-adjacent careers was left undiscussed. The kids knew only that their family had enough and that they should not ask for more.

"Did Mom already go back?"

"She has early meetings." He stifled a yawn as he spoke.

Beth was reluctantly serving as an executive for a hospital outside of Boston. She had worked there for eleven years but was ready for a maybe-permanent break and had started to investigate other paths forward, including some that would allow her to work from the beach throughout the summer. She had spearheaded the campaign to acquire a Cape property so many years before, and she cared for the yard, plants, house, and guests with a tenderness she occasionally lacked in other locales. Her leadership position afforded her the ability to pick and choose long weekends and other time off, but having to drive back and forth left her crankier than she should have been for many of the days she passed strolling on Granger and manning the porch where the rest of her family now sat.

Katie waited for some of the sleep to leave her father's eyes. "You should just cancel your classes for tomorrow and hang here."

Kevin let out another long yawn as he inched to the chipped railing. He looked to the water and stretched his arms overhead, his back or shoulders cracking in a way fitting for a man his age.

"If wishing made it so. The students are ready for it to be over, that's for sure."

Katie tapped her fingers on the wood of the table, touching the surface lightly enough to avoid any rogue splintering. "I sort of like the end of the year. Lots of excitement. Plus you know it's almost over."

"Can't say I feel the same. My finals were brutal."

Kevin leaned his elbows against the railing and faced his son. "Ryan, don't scare your father like that. I need you to study hard so you can get out of my house someday."

"My teachers aren't pushovers like you."

Kevin was easygoing in the classroom but not a pushover, which wasn't news to Ryan. His students loved his conversational nature, and he loved pushing them, a dynamic that weighed on him as the school year wound down. He was facing the decision of whether to take the department head job that would give him control over the curriculum but would also prevent him from teaching more than a section or two. When he had agreed to his career change at the request of one of the vice principals, a friend from college, teaching was the deal. High-level decisions were for someone else. He had faced enough hard choices in the other sections of his life, or so he had reasoned with the vice principal.

"Dad, when are you and Mom coming down next weekend?"

Kevin closed his eyes in order to recall the correct information. "She'll be here Thursday, just has to take some calls once she gets in. I'll come right from school on Friday."

"It's going to be a slow week here. A lot of quality time for us, Ryan."

"Can work on my tan." He wiggled his bare toes, connected to his ghostly feet. Caddy blisters had started to form at the inner edges of his biggest digits.

"Jamie, Anne, how are you? Almost feels like summer, doesn't it?"

Kevin looked down at the end of the driveway, where the elder Clarkes now stopped. They were only a few years older than the Murray parents, but Jamie's white hair and their distinguished overtones made the gap feel bigger, as they perhaps intended, lording over the neighborhood in which Clarkes had vacationed from their compound overlooking the water since South Monomo's inception. They had always maximized the time they spent here and, now that Jamie was mostly retired—he had tested the crowd with a joke about being an advisor "emerit*ish*" the summer before but quickly aborted the bit—from the private equity firm he had founded, they were in essence full-timers. Their house in Greenwich stood mostly untouched. Both Clarkes already looked tan, the result of their springtime in the sun but also an effect augmented by their immaculate white shirts, his crisp and hers billowing gently in the breeze.

"Yes, almost there! We'll have to celebrate with some drinks next weekend."

Jamie saluted charmingly as his wife's sentence concluded. He was already moving down the hill as she smiled goodbye to Kevin and the kids, who had risen to greet her.

Kevin turned to his children again. "You two going to get bored here this summer?" He knew he would. He didn't mind occasional bouts of boredom. Long ago, he had learned to block out the cranial ringing such spells brought with them. There was splendor in the silence.

"Nope. Caddy money is easy money."

"Nothing boring about relaxation."

July 5

Deserved to get hit.

I'm trying to watch the Sox. It feels pointless. The games are too long to begin with but there's nothing else on and no one to talk to. I can see a few of the players sweating through their jerseys. It's hot in Baltimore.

That's the only park other than Fenway I've ever been to. But it was a long time ago. I fell asleep on the car ride home and I don't remember much else. We went in May but it was hot like this. They probably soaked through the jerseys that day too. I probably drank a soda as big as my head. A hot pretzel and a helmet filled with ice cream. Chocolate vanilla twist.

My hands keep shaking but I can stop them if I focus on it.

2

"Katie, wait."

She poked her head out the driver-side window and looked up to the porch. Beth rose from the table, book in hand, and gestured to the side of the driveway.

"Can you pull over a bit? Gives us more room, and I might have to run out to grab some things in a few."

Without a word, Katie backed into the street and pulled back in, this time veering toward but not reaching the lawn. She stepped out of the car, still wearing her work shirt—a lime green polo with an *MD* insignia, the same one that graced all of the Monomo Dunes shirts, hats, ball markers, and flags; the same one that had led Kevin to make a few too many remarks about his daughter studying to become a doctor at the Monomo Dunes School of Medicine to what he would characterize as tough crowds.

"You left without your brother? Does he know you took the car?"

"He got a second loop. He texted me and said they're moving slow. One of the other guys can give him a ride."

Beth held her position at the edge of the porch as her daughter climbed the stairs, happy to be outside after a longer than expected day of putting out fires from the small reading room next to the kitchen that served as her remote office. Her brown hair curled at the ends, and its disorder at the top of her head exposed the day's showerlessness. She smiled as Katie crossed the deck and took a seat, worn out from a hot afternoon spent trying to find shady loci to park her cart as perspiring men leered and joked.

"Are you done for the day? I thought you had the afternoon off." Katie spoke from a slumped position. She could see mother considering if it was worth reminding daughter of the importance of proper posture.

"I did, too. Should be done for now. Told everyone to bug off until Tuesday."

"Dad's not here yet?"

Beth didn't let it show, but Katie could sense a hint of frustration at the question, at the non-existent insinuation that this parent's presence was not enough. "No, might be a little bit. Sounds like traffic is bad, as I told him it would be. They let you out early?"

"A little. It was winding down. Much busier in the morning. Next couple days will be chaotic now that everyone's showing up."

"You want some water? You look like you got too much sun."

"Sure, thanks."

Katie watched as her mother entered the house and turned left toward the kitchen. Through the windows, she could see her pass by on her way to the fridge. On the way back, she watched her fill a bowl with pretzels from a large bag resting on the edge of the dining room table. Katie and Beth had never been especially close. If anyone in the family was forced to rank their favorites, the pairs would come out to Beth and Ryan on one side and Katie and Kevin on the other. The women spent time together, and there were spurts when they happily left the boys to be boys in front of a television or other testosteronic stimulation, but Katie tended to go to her father if she had something sensitive to share or ask, unless it centered on female anatomy, which it rarely did. She wasn't one to share or ask those things, anyway, but she meshed with Kevin. Throughout her first year away at school they had kept tabs on each other by sharing book recommendations, their phone calls regular, not usually long, and often ending with Beth's taking of the phone to check in and hang up, sometimes discouraged by what sounded like her daughter's disappointment to hear the new voice on the line.

A navy blue Audi rolled down the street. The passengers looked the other way, the driver pointing hard at Amelia and Nate's house. Beth moved to wave but noticed their inattention and turned away, taking the chair across from her daughter. The car slowed in front of the Clarke sub-estate before continuing on, pulling into the newly resurfaced driveway at the base of the hill.

"Was that one of the Clarkes?"

Beth nodded and admired the gleam of the car's exterior. She claimed to be uninterested in spending money on such a luxurious vehicle, but she wondered what it would be like to take one for a spin. Even just to own it.

"Jamie Jr. and his wife."

Jamie Clarke, Jr. was the middle child and recently married, having wed a Dartmouth classmate the previous fall. Most of his friends and family had been stunned to hear of the engagement at first, given the rambunctious lifestyle he had enjoyed in Hanover—and, it was suspected, in New York for some time after he graduated. He and his wife, Olivia, had not crossed paths at all at school. He often joked this was for the best, a sentiment the Murrays and others shared without any hint of irony. Jamie Jr. had never gotten himself into serious trouble in Greenwich, New Hampshire, or here at the beach, but he pushed the limits of what he could get away with. Multiple weekends in South Monomo had ended with one or both of his parents reminding him of some ground rules he and his SigEp brothers had to follow if they ever wanted to book another night in the house.

"Did you and Dad like their wedding? Olivia's beautiful. What's she doing with J.J. is the real question."

Beth scoffed but didn't object.

"It was nice, but you didn't miss much. A lot of fratty speeches on his side."

They had held the wedding in mid-September. Katie chose to continue adjusting to campus life rather than attend the lavish affair, held at the family's Greenwich outpost, which she had visited once as an early teenager on the Murrays' way to visit another family friend. She had been surprised by its plainness, by the predictability of its style, by the flagrant way it attempted to fit in next to its "neighbors," a quarter-mile walk to either side.

"I can't believe he got married. I hope Olivia understands what she's getting into."

Beth swatted away at the air and the implication. "Oh, Katie. He's grown up now. Don't put him down."

"If you say so."

Beth had not seen much of him, aside from the wedding, in recent years. Work and whatever else he got into in New York kept him away from the beach. He was a bright boy but had lost some of his glow over time. She insisted that calling him unmotivated was harsh. She said he had ambition or some relative of it, whatever it took to reinforce the impenetrable Eden in which he had lazed for his first quarter-century.

3

Monomo Dunes was a private country club about twelve minutes from the base of Seaview Road. The "Dunes" aspect of the club's name was self-explanatory. The "Monomo" was only slightly mysterious. The edge of the front nine was technically North Monomo territory, but the vast majority of the property fell within Worona space, including the two holes that bordered Greenstone Lake, a glorified pond. The "Monomo" branding was not so mystifying because the course was private, and the money in this area did not, save for a few exceptions, come from Worona.

The people in the Monomos weren't necessarily against spending time in Worona; there just weren't that many reasons to make the trip. The Monomians already had the beach and the ocean and the middle and high schools (for the year-rounders from all three towns) and the best supermarket.

There were, however, some Monomians, especially certain South Monomians, who went out of their way not to spend time in Worona, who encouraged their kids and friends to stay away from some of the town's hangouts and from the types of people they pictured littering them. News reports of overdoses and related activities were warning enough.

To some people, these eschewing behaviors were natural or inevitable, given the region's geography. Relative to its neighbors, Worona was contained, unmoved by the tides. It saw its fair share of the sun. Monomo land sat near the beaches. Worona sniffed the water but didn't cradle it like its neighbor did, and as populations and later development blossomed in the area, additional lines were drawn beside those that separated the plots of land. Those lines never stopped spreading, morphing.

The Monomos provided the majority of the golfers—almost all men whose wives congregated at the pool or in the clubhouse, which was overhauled in a 2013 renovation.

The Dunes ranked among the top tracks on the Cape and in Massachusetts but had not to this point established a national reputation. There were several clubs that had done so in the area, ones with names like Old Sandwich and Kittansett, and for some Dunes members this perceived second-tier status was a point of discontentment. The Dunes boasted a course design that was hard to find fault with, but it lacked the natural topographic character that propelled some of its neighbors into the spotlight. The Dunes, even played from the back tees, didn't pose a great enough challenge for the upper echelon of competitive amateur and professional golfers to host a Massachusetts or U.S. Open. The members had worked to host some qualifiers and women's events and regularly explored possible methods for purchasing more land or expanding within their existing confines so that they could host more prestigious events in the future. Work remained to be done.

Ryan knelt next to a bunker one hundred and fifty yards from the sixteenth tee, his hamstrings and back whining as he did, ready to give in after carrying two bags for thirty-three holes. He was in the proper spot, forecaddying in case a drive neared the creek and brush to his left, but his two patrons were unlikely to scare the water. They had depleted the better part of the afternoon driving the ball short but wild, typically in opposite directions, laughing about the step-count assistance they were providing for Ryan, who was forced to join in their merriment to preserve what he hoped would be generous tips.

The first shot landed in the bunker. Ryan signaled accordingly. He tracked the second as it fluttered off the club and drifted toward the right rough, thick from a combination of spring rains and an understaffed maintenance crew.

The par-three seventeenth passed quickly as both hacks somehow managed to find the sliver of green, but by the time they stood in the eighteenth fairway Ryan was seeing stars, admonishing himself for turning down the offer of a second Gatorade at the turn.

"You okay there, Ryan? We're thinking of going for another eighteen."

Mr. Wilson slapped him on the back with a level of vigor that Ryan felt would have been useful on any number of his golf swings and chuckled. Bad knees made the man almost limp his way to the finish. Ryan didn't think they were responsible for his other shortcomings.

"All good, Mr. Wilson. Too tired to laugh at that, though."

Mr. Wilson had laid up with his second shot out of the rough but still faced one hundred and eighty-four yards, according to the rangefinder he had bestowed on Ryan for the round. His back-nine performance left Ryan doubting his ability to carry the creek that crossed about ten yards in front of the eighteenth green.

"One eighty-four to the pin."

"Hmm. Give me that hybrid. Might as well try to end the day with a birdie, right?"

Ryan unsheathed the club and fed the grip end into Mr. Wilson's hand. "You're the boss. Don't need to kill it. Let the club do the work."

Mr. Wilson stood over the ball and took a deep breath, a pivotal feature in the routine he had started working on this year and had been excited to share with Ryan, who had established himself as a favorite caddy of many members thanks to his easygoing but professional attitude and competence raking bunkers, reading putts, and shooting the shit that came out of their mouths with remarkable celerity.

He glanced to the green, back to the ball, back to the green, back to the ball, and swung. The contact was solid, the sound pure, but the ball landed just a foot above the far side of the creek, taunting them for a moment before trickling down into the water.

"Damn, hit that pretty good, too." Mr. Wilson took a practice swing, which to Ryan looked far worse than the movement he had just produced.

"Yeah, maybe just a little tired. That was a good strike."

Ryan took the club from him and wandered to the right, where Mr. Strickland had just completed an optimistic assessment of his ball's lie between two trees.

A small group of caddies huddled outside the bag room next to the pro shop. Most of the Dunes' bag carriers were college kids, though some parents got younger siblings or eager others into the mix, and a couple were year-rounders looking to make extra money for the summer. Ryan dumped his bib into its bin and grabbed a bottle of water before joining the circle. Danny Moreland, a Worona kid with a chip on his shoulder and what Ryan characterized as "the accent Alec Baldwin was shooting for in *The Departed*," was bemoaning some "uptight prick" he had carried for that morning and his lackluster tip. Danny was a year older than Ryan and had a soft spot for him, having once remarked that "Murray's not nearly as bad as most of the SoMo assholes."

"Ryan, how was it out there? You guys took fuckin' forever."

The Morelands had lived in the area for centuries. Danny's inflection cut into most of his words.

"I'm dead. Should not have gone for thirty-six today."

Danny's eyes hurried around the room. "Re-fuckin' tweet, man. You comin' out? Some of us are going to Greenstone to chill for a bit."

"That's okay, I gotta head home. John, can you still take me?"

A quieter, sheepish face nodded. John was still waiting for his growth spurt. Some of the members complained about his passivity. Some liked the quiet. Ryan and John preferred the latter group.

The rest of the circle waited for Danny's reply, most looking for an escape and the others waiting for an invitation.

"Yeah, okay. Tell Katie I say hey."

Danny added no flavor to his request, but his words were enough to inflame Ryan, who managed a smile as he untucked his shirt and headed toward the parking lot. John paused to receive payment from a portly man before jogging to catch up, meeting Ryan just as their feet reached the pavement.

"When do you think Danny Moreland will leave this place? He's been here forever."

"Where would he go? No point in leaving if he'd just be sitting around getting high somewhere else anyway." Ryan looked back as he said it, part of him afraid to find out if Danny was standing there watching or following close behind.

"Good point."

A car screeched as it turned into the lot, narrowly avoiding a golfer on his way out. The boys could see the driver indicate his apology before speeding along the back row of cars and taking another hard turn to reach the bag rack to their left. The driver waved at them, but he was too far for Ryan to recognize him, so he parked and stepped out, leaving the car running. Ryan hadn't seen Eric Clarke in almost two years. He barely recognized him with shoulder-length hair and a hollow frame.

He was the youngest Clarke but two years older than Ryan. He had his share of "personal troubles"—as his and other parents termed them—before, during, and after his departure from college. He dropped out after his sophomore year and went on a trip that Ryan suspected involved rehab of some kind, but Anne and Jamie didn't publicize the details. Despite his struggles, Eric had always been the friendliest of the three siblings, close enough in age to play with Ryan and Katie and always willing to entertain them.

Eric's issues, which escalated quickly from kid-at-the-beach shenanigans to more serious offenses as he trudged through high school, led to boarding school and less time spent at the beach, but little was said about the subject other than Beth's regular early-summer check-in, usually done over drinks and met with a "Doing well, thanks for asking. Just needs to clear his head" or something of that ilk by his father in a let's-move-on tone. Eric had a bit of a falling out with his parents in the months after he decided to leave Connecticut College (Anne had joked after Eric's acceptance that "New London is almost New Haven," and it had been clear to everyone on the porch that the lack of Yale in his life upset her quite a lot more than it upset her boy). Ryan had no idea if there had been a reconciliation, where Eric was staying, or what he was doing here.

"Ryan, man. How are you?"

"Eric, uh, I'm good. What's up with you?"

Eric smiled, sensing Ryan's discomfort. "Not much. Just picking up a friend, might head to Greenstone. You work with Danny down there? He, uh, caddies. At least I think he does. Never sure with him."

Eric laughed heartily but avoided eye contact.

"Yeah, we know him."

Eric nodded and smirked, faintly aware of the shock his appearance could have on Ryan but hoping not to dwell on the reaction.

"Are you staying with your parents? What are you up to for the summer?"

He laughed again and pushed windblown hair from his face.

"Nah, it's easier to stay with some friends. My dad kind of said I could, but I've had enough fighting with him for a while."

"Well, you should definitely stop by. Come hang with me and Katie at least." Ryan's voice had climbed most of an octave.

"Sounds good to me. Just working over in NoMo during the days, but I'm around."

"Great. Good to see you, Eric. Text me sometime."

Eric shook his hand and returned to his car. He leaned on the hood and looked toward the pro shop. Ryan looked back at him and wished he would leave, along with Danny and anyone else who comprised their crew.

"That was Eric Clarke?"

"Yeah, you know him?"

John glanced back at Eric, eyes narrowed like a boy peering through a reptile exhibit's glass. "Not really, but I met him a couple times around your house I think. Before he, uh, did whatever he did."

"Probably right. We used to have a lot of fun with him."

"Sounds like you might again."

The boys laughed as they opened the doors of John's hand-me-down Land Rover. They pulled straight ahead and turned left, past Eric, who had wandered toward the putting green, which offered a view of the club's expanse, glowing now in the waning light.

"I hope not. He won't text me. He doesn't want any part of the family estate, and I don't want any part of whatever he's got."

They hadn't seen much of each other yet that summer, but Ryan and John still managed to complete their trip without saying anything of consequence. They came to Seaview having covered only the most basic of catch-up topics, with nothing said of their impending graduations or job prospects. John had his house to himself for large chunks of the summer but didn't plan to take advantage. He was quiet—not shy, but consistently unimpressed by the antics of those around him—and the hassle wasn't worth jeopardizing his medical school prospects. He waved from the car but stayed put as he stopped in front of the Murray driveway.

Ryan climbed out slowly, his legs and back locked from sitting, already dreading the early tee time the caddiemaster had promised him for the next day. He was surprised to see Anne and Jamie looming overhead. It wasn't unusual for them to be here, but Ryan sensed their visits made his mother uncomfortable, a fact she would sometimes hint at but never admit. The Murrays' house was large, warm, offered great views, and had a sizable yard, but everyone knew the Clarkes' was a step up across the board. Their compound offered a bigger yard, better views, and more comfortable chairs, so every time the Clarkes sat on her porch, Beth assumed they were comparing her property to their own and reveling in their superiority.

The Clarkes stood to greet Ryan, but his parents and sister stayed in place, Beth and Kevin seated at the far end of the table and Katie leaning against the railing to their left, her hair still wet and a new, non-Dunes sundress flowing down her torso.

"Ryan, how'd the links treat you? I was over there a few days ago. The course looks great this year, I think. Must be that handsome new head of the Greens Committee."

Beth smiled politely at Jamie. He was better than that brand of humor but employed it regularly.

"Pretty exhausting, Mr. Clarke, but the course is in good shape. The bunkers looked like a good place to nap by the end of the second round."

"Ryan, so good to see you. I can't believe you're done with junior year." Anne leaned in and kissed his cheek.

"You, too, Mrs. Clarke. I try not to think about it too much."

She wiggled a finger between the two of them. "It must be nice, you two getting to work together."

"I have the cushy job, Mrs. Clarke. Ryan's out there slaving away."

The Clarkes retook their seats, and Katie stepped behind her mother and father to go inside, her cup empty. The four parents had glasses in front of them, all filled with water except for Kevin's mostly drained lemonade. The group hadn't made much of a dent in the chips and salsa, but Ryan's body, crying out for salt, instinctively reached for a handful. Someone offered him a drink. He shook his head and mumbled something out of a full mouth.

"You have some friends caddying as well, Ryan?"

"A few. We, um, actually saw Eric on our way out. He said he was meeting up with one of the guys." He could have guaranteed the utterance would have an effect. He felt bad about pushing for it, but his curiosity surpassed the guilt.

Katie froze at the door. The four adults looked anywhere but at Ryan or each other. Jamie chose that moment to test his water. Kevin finally glanced at his son, using his eyes to signal that he had introduced a bad topic. Beth looked to Anne with undeserved pity, the latter staring a hole into the plank of wood on which her sandaled feet rested.

"Is he staying here for the summer?"

"No, Katie. You know him. Mind of his own."

Katie had heard Jamie talk of his youngest son in this manner before, and she knew it wasn't worth pushing him. She was less intimidated by him than her family was. Still, she feared angering him, and once this topic became the focus, it would take very little to set off the otherwise calm man. She had witnessed multiple fights between the Clarke boys and their father; the ones that involved Eric tended to be louder and meatier but, in her mind, overblown. It amazed Katie that Jamie Jr. had largely escaped the wrath that had forced his brother out.

Ryan followed his sister inside. She held the door and let it half slam as she turned to keep up. He grabbed a plastic cup—he didn't like using the glasses when he didn't have to—from a stack beside the fridge and poured his lemonade. He added ice, four cubes, after the first sip. Katie crossed her arms and leaned toward him.

"Sooo, you saw Eric?"

"Yeah, barely. Just said hi."

Katie slapped the sides of her legs in exasperation. "Is he okay?"

"How should I know?"

"Did he seem normal?"

"Has he ever?" Ryan seemed proud of his wit but ate his grin upon noticing the red on his sister's face.

"You're not being helpful." Katie had increased her volume with each response.

"I wasn't trying to hang around to see whatever the hell Eric and Danny Moreland were up to. Real dynamic duo."

July 6

I didn't plan any of this. I didn't expect him to be there. I wasn't looking for an excuse to hurt him. We just wanted an easy night. I wanted to get high. The wanting isn't a crime. But seeing him pissed me off. He should've avoided that place for a while. He knew what I would do if I saw him. Probably better than I did. First part at least.

He wasn't surprised when I hit him. He almost looked like he wanted to get hit. I think I might just be saying that. I'm not sure if the face I see in my memory of that night is even his. It looks more like a mannequin now. It's like the chemicals in my brain are on my side. They're in this with me. They don't want to see his face ever again. I wonder what they wanted me to do when he was dying. I wonder if I was listening to them while he did.

Even as it happened I wasn't really sure what I was doing. He was lying there and I was positive no one was watching. I lunged and did it without thinking. Before that night I understood what it felt like to hit someone but not what it felt like to break the skin. Didn't really feel like much to be honest. Which made what happened after even more surprising. Something that didn't feel like much turning into something so bad and so messy. There are probably some good sayings about that but I've never been good at remembering sayings.

I didn't know where to go. Made it almost to the city before getting off. Got a coffee and turned around. I was scared they'd be looking for me now that the sun was rising. Wasn't sure what the other guys had done.

I didn't blame them for being scared.

It felt sort of wrong to go home after all of this. I think I should've gone to work because sitting around in the empty house didn't do me any good. It turns out that watching television the morning after you killed someone doesn't work. Even when you turn away from the stations that are talking about the someone. It's hard to laugh at the channels that want you to laugh. It's hard to get sucked into the action on the others. Because the action doesn't feel real anymore. They make it look cooler than it is. They make you think some people are invincible.

The part about the whole night that got me maybe more than any other part was when I wiped my mouth with the back of my hand after we took him outside. I was already starting to flip and realize what we did. But I wiped my mouth with the back of my hand and tasted his blood. It must have been his. It got on my hands and arms when we carried him. I didn't wash it off until I got back to the house after driving and driving even though I knew that should've been the first thing I did if I didn't want to get in trouble.

He left a bitter taste in my mouth but I know I deserved worse.

4

Memorial Day weekend filled the beaches and town centers, but only temporarily. The days that followed saw an infusion of life into the shops and walkways, but they were far from the peaks that would arrive in the weeks ahead, when schools let out and the weather cooperated a bit more consistently. Many of the proprietors sat or stood at their doors, recognizing some of the passing faces and wishing there were more.

The golf course was closed for maintenance the Tuesday after the holiday, so Katie persuaded her brother to make something of the day together. By mid-afternoon, they had already walked to town, where they grabbed sandwiches from Rocky's and ice cream next door before turning back. The water was too cold to swim in—Katie opined this was almost always the case—and they had both seen enough of the beach the weekend before, all of which led them to this point, with Katie riding her bike up and down the street while Ryan begrudgingly took his from the garage and cleaned the seat, onto which a mysterious ceiling liquid had pooled in the days since he rode it last.

"What's taking so long?"

"I'm just trying to get this crap off. I don't want my ass covered in it."

She continued on to the bottom of the hill and turned left, reappearing in time to meet him as he finally rolled out of the driveway.

They rode past the parking lot, confident enough in the town's forlornness to drift into the middle of the street as they neared Canal Road. Some of the houses on the avenue towered like the Clarke estate, but sprinkled in every third or fourth plot was something smaller and almost quaint. Many of the homes had been standing since families like the Clarkes first built up the area.

To run from Seaview to the end of Canal and back could be trying in the heat at midday. By bike, under a gray sky, they reached the final houses without breaking a sweat.

Only a few cars sat in the lot in front of the canal, which would hold hundreds on the busiest days in the midst of summer. Katie led the way, the creaking of Ryan's vehicle informing her of how closely he followed. She broke after hopping from the edge of the lot onto the walkway, painted throughout its course with a white line running down the middle. A runner headed in their direction from the right but was still two hundred feet away. The trail within site was otherwise their own private playground. The ocean loomed to their left, calm, the beaches to either side of the waterway obscured by the height of its banks.

For most of the strait's first two miles, only a patch of grass several feet long, sloping down to the water, stood between it and the path, meaning this was a place of forward motion—in either direction. To stand still was to endanger oneself and anyone who might pass, unless the stopper made it down far enough to reach the small viewing deck, which was more useful as a rest area anyway, given the underwhelming scenery available to unmagnified eyes. On this day, stopping didn't pose much of a threat. Within five minutes, they saw three pairs and one trio of kayaks working away from the ocean but little else.

The views of the canal were enticing for short periods, but to look across was to see mostly shards and fragments of undefined industries and, farther off, houses that appeared as blurs to riders moving quickly. Ryan, in the first few years he was permitted to ride a bike without training wheels, often had to be reminded to keep his eyes forward and avoid drifting into the left lane. Today he kept his eyes ahead of him but still drifted as his legs tired or, more accurately, as he was reminded of his legs' preexisting fatigue, but Katie rode steadily on the flat path until they passed the viewing area. Fifty feet beyond it, she lurched to a halt. Had Ryan been riding with an ounce more verve, he would have slammed into his sister, but his dying legs saved him, as he had time to swerve around her and slow to a stop.

"What is it? A little warning next time. Katie?" He panted his frustration, sweat dripping into his eyebrows.

"You see the splashing? I think it's seals."

Ryan dismounted and dropped the bike onto the grass above the path. He looked out and saw the remains of a splash halfway across the canal but no other signs of life.

"Are you sure?"

"Definitely. At least two of them." Katie was slightly indignant. She would never misinform him on this important topic.

"Shouldn't we keep riding if they're swimming this way? Also, no offense, but what's the big deal? We see them every summer. Like a lot."

This was partially true. While they hadn't sought out the creatures in recent summers, they were not hard to find—in the canal, occasionally on the beach, around many parts of the Cape. But Katie took every chance to admire animals and their behaviors. While her brother was a danger to fellow bikers because of his wandering eyes, she was a driving risk only when there were animals in the road, known to go to great lengths to either avoid hurting them or parking her car in order to ferry the ducks or turtle or

Rainbow-Beaked Pine Dove to safety across whatever passage had brought her to them. She had remained roosted on her seat and now sped off to observe the next emergence of rubbery hide, leaving Ryan to scramble for his bike.

"See?" She yelled back and this time didn't brake or decelerate.

Two seals surfaced, still halfway across the canal's width and now slightly ahead of the bikers. The one in front quickly dunked back under, but the follower's head lingered above the water.

"What are they doing? Where are they going?"

Even if Ryan had heard his sister, whose words escaped him in the downwind, he wouldn't have had an answer, which she expected. She reveled in their ignorance, riding faster as if strong legs and patience would lead them to the hidden end of the path and the seal kingdom that marked its termination. He kept up, wheels spinning fast enough to give the illusion of standing still. Soon the seals evanesced, and the road started to veer away from South Monomo in line with the water. The bridge, ferrying drivers on to the bulk of the Cape, crossed ahead. On Murray family rides, if they even made it this far, this was usually the place to turn around. For one thing, it marked a long ride, good exercise. For another, on the far side of the bridge the land to their right opened up into a small field that had, over time, become a regular hangout for people that the kids, and more so their parents, thought it best to shun. The field wasn't much to look at. Patches of grass and sandy dirt alternated in the space between their bikes and the road that met the highway a football field away.

Ryan started to call out to his sister that they should call it a day, but she had accelerated again and was out of earshot. The shadows of the bridge passed over him. He could make out some of the brighter graffiti on the walls to his right and the stone hanging over him. He thought to himself that maybe there wouldn't be anyone in the field, and he supposed that even if a group was loitering, they would have little interest in two young bikers gliding by.

There was a smattering of people sitting in the field, close enough to the bridge that half of them rested in the shade. Ryan pedaled slowly enough to catch a fuller glimpse of the six people tarrying. There were four boys and two girls, most younger than their haggard features implied, the nearest boy likely Katie's age but closer to perishing, or at least less concerned with longevity. Most of the heads turned to look at Ryan as he passed. One of the shaded bodies stood and stepped forward to get a better view. As he did, a head of long, brown hair flopped in his face. He stroked it away. Ryan pedaled harder as he recognized Eric, unsure if the other boy was in a place that allowed him to return the favor. He looked quickly over his shoulder and saw Eric step forward again, now far enough out for the sun to meet half of his face. Riding on, he hoped the group would leave soon. He and Katie would have to pass the spot again in ten to forty minutes, depending on how long it took him to complain, so he tacitly resolved to press on until his sister stopped them, confident in her endurance's ability to outlast the crew's respite. Even if Eric had a clear idea who they were, Ryan couldn't envisage his response. But he was sure it would unsettle Katie to see him there.

Katie looked to her left, hoping her seals or others would materialize. She looked back to gauge her brother's energy level. For the next ten minutes, they saw no signs of life.

She stopped them again.

"Ew, how did this get on me?"

"What is it?"

"A tick crawling up my shin. Ew. Blegh." Katie flicked at it, flustered by the need for violence.

"God, I hate them. They're everywhere out here."

42

He was, if anything, understating his hatred for the bugs. The enmity wasn't based on any singular trauma, but he had peeled them off his person numerous times throughout his childhood. Above all else, he hated how small they were, how something so tiny had the potential to wreak so much havoc on his body, though they had never succeeded. But they wreaked havoc on his mind every single time they appeared, and today would be no different, as he sensed something tickling the back of his neck for the hour that followed Katie's discovery and subsequent removal. Katie, with her love for all things living, didn't share her brother's fears, though she showed no remorse squishing the invader and depositing it next to the path.

"They'll outlive us all."

Ryan stayed on his bike and tried to convey a look of purpose, feigning determination to ride on as Katie wiped off her leg with one hand and gripped the handlebar with the other. Her sandals were worn at the back, and her sock tan had started to fade beneath toned calves and always-skinny thighs.

"What were those guys doing by the bridge?"

The answer seemed obvious at first. Katie wasn't that young or ignorant. Then Ryan realized that he hadn't seen them in the act of anything illicit, though it was easy to guess what they had been doing before coming to the bridge.

"Don't know."

"Probably just some bored Worona kids." She rode on.

"Yeah, must be." He muttered the words to himself, afraid Katie would hear the lie if he spoke out.

5

Martha's Tavern was, according to Kevin, both an odd name and a misnomer to those who took the time to study its interior decoration and ownership structure. Martha's wasn't the most popular restaurant on South Monomo's Main Street and didn't offer the best food. Both of those honors belonged, in most minds, to Sean's Seafood (the lack of name-based creativity on the part of local restaurateurs had irked Kevin for years). But the Murrays had frequented Martha's since the kids were little. Most years, they chose to eat there to celebrate the end of school, which acted as their official start of the summer even when the June dates didn't quite align.

Kevin would have to go back the following week for some year-end meetings, but he had finished grading papers and finals, so as they walked from the parking lot toward Martha's he wore a familiar smile, one that appeared annually at about this time and would stick for the better part of the summer, until August sunsets reminded him of what was to come. He still liked the teaching. But late August to early September was a period of organization and chaos, albeit one tinged with an elation augmented by traces of fall New England air. In comparison, late June, July, and much of August were subdued. Kevin walked, biked, read, and napped.

Beth and Ryan entered first and asked for a table. Although the end of the school year coincided with more activity in the towns, Martha's was rarely full. The hostess took them to a corner booth, one they had dined in several times. A waitress came over immediately. She didn't serve the Murrays often enough to forecast their drink orders, but they rang familiar once spoken aloud.

"Are you completely done grading, Dad?" Ryan scanned the menu, though he wouldn't be branching out from his usual.

"Son, I really, truly am. Isn't it a glorious day?" He reached for a glass to raise, but they had not yet received waters.

"What did you make them write papers on?" Katie knew how much he liked to mix it up, sometimes presenting his classes with elaborate prompts that he found "exciting" and his students found "fucking annoying."

"They had a couple options. Most of them chose to read *The Red Badge of Courage* and tie it to some of our material."

"Isn't that sort of an easy book for them?"

Katie and Beth groaned at Ryan's question. Kevin licked his chops.

"Good question, Ryan. First of all, no, it is not. Nothing is easy for these students. But second, and more importantly, just because a book is hard does not mean it is good, and just because a book is easy by some oversimplified measure does not mean it's not worth your time. I would go so far as to say that anyone who suggests otherwise is a bad teacher. There are any number of ways to challenge your students. To do so by having them slog through books that fly over their heads is as useless as it is irresponsible. I would much rather have them comprehend the material in front of them so they have more time to think for themselves and to engage in high-level reflection and analysis. Would you agree?"

"Sure. So were the papers good?"

Kevin leaned back against the booth. "God, no. I could picture them boarding planes and stepping into pools as they wrote. Anything they could do to get it over with and end the year."

Katie sat on the inside of the booth, next to her father and across from Beth, and surveyed the menu's options, of which only a few were worthwhile, and she settled on the same turkey burger she had ordered on her past thirteen trips to the establishment. Ryan ordered his burger with bacon and a fried egg, prompting his mother to question whether he was planning to adopt healthier dietary habits now that he was home for the summer and had the chance to improve on his sustainable-only-for-men-under-the-age-of-twenty-two school diet. He added an appetizer order as the waitress stepped away, citing his caddying and metabolism as reasons to continue his "bulking season." Beth pursed her lips but soon laughed, her smile similar to her husband's but with a shorter shelf life. She would have to go back and forth to the city several more times before settling in for a post-Fourth of July lull, a two-week stretch she could only hope would go uninterrupted by administrative crises.

She had a hard time detaching from work, even during the vacation-like periods, always searching for ways to get ahead of relentless tasks and people. The beach was a haven, except for the conversations she fell into regarding the state of the Massachusetts and American healthcare systems and how they could be made—depending on the person starting the talk—more efficient, compassionate, or affordable. Even now, sitting at the table with her family, her club sandwich and fries already ordered, she struggled to block out the memos waiting for her weekend eyes and the questions she was sure a Clarke would raise at their next gathering, preferably away from any sort of crowd. She clawed for a reprieve.

"It'll be nice to have all the Clarkes around this summer, don't you think? I still can't fathom Anne and Jamie as grandparents. It's so sweet, watching them dote." Beth sounded for a moment like another person altogether.

"Beth, they've been grandparents for four years. I think we're going to have to get used to it."

Kevin spoke not like a man who was tired of the topic but like one who had never been interested in it in the first place. Beth's eyes warned him of how little room he had left to go before she would consider him rude and not speak to him for the rest of the night.

"You're right. I can't believe those kids are that old. I'm sure we'll be seeing a lot of them on the beach."

"That's for sure, especially if Amelia keeps letting them run around naked."

Beth closed her eyes and shook her head. "Ryan, that was three years ago. They were babies."

"Baby or not, I don't think anyone needed to see it."

All four took several pieces of calamari when it arrived, but Katie simply twirled a squiddish morsel while the others ate. Only when her mother prodded her did she sample it, blaming her reticence on another long day in the sun, made even longer by the member-member tournament that had dragged on from what felt like sunrise to late afternoon but had at least provided her and her cart partner, a college-aged girl from Worona, with ample tips.

The kids agreed with their father's claim that the squid was better than usual and refilled their plates.

The next morning was the warmest and brightest of the year to that point. Katie rose early to go for a run, unable to convince anyone to join her. She had to walk for a few minutes on her way back from Canal Road but otherwise kept up a better pace than she had in her previous efforts, leaving her mouth dry and her legs gelatinous as she climbed back up the stairs and strode into the kitchen. She filled and drank an entire glass of water in one continuous motion. Beth sat reading the paper in the dining room, and Katie stood at the end of the table after refilling, this time from an orange juice carton on the counter to match her mother's glass. After only mild protestation, she agreed to join her elder on a walk to what they hoped would still be an empty beach.

The public portion of the beach was already packed with families claiming squatter's rights on premium spots. One familiar gang, comprised of four or five families, sat close to the jetty, arm tattoos proudly displayed and their radio crackling at a midday volume. The adults sat in beach chairs, and the kids ran crazily behind them. At the perimeter of their crescent stood a pirate flag, driven into the sand in such a way that it appeared to fly at half-mast. Beth waved politely, and the couple facing them gestured back, perhaps in on the joke of it all.

The left side wasn't as full, but a few groups had marked their territories. Beth picked out Anne's traditional wicker hat halfway down the beach, a straight walk down from their balcony. Katie continued walking, but Beth swerved toward them.

"Mom, don't you want to walk? We can chat on the way back."

"Don't be silly. Let's say hi to everyone. It'll be quick."

It never was, and while Katie didn't have to work that day, she felt a need to rush away from their smiling faces and waving arms, their bone-dry designer swimsuits and carefully rolled shirtsleeves. Anne and Jamie sat with their backs to the Murray women while Amelia and Nate ushered them over. The twins worked on a hole behind their grandparents and said hello with Amelia's encouragement. Anne turned to greet them and knocked her hat into the seatback, catching and readjusting it before welcoming them to the beach, as if it belonged to her. A book rested in her lap, and the *Wall Street Journal* was splayed on her husband's, which fit his personality but still felt a little off to Katie. She wanted this place to be far removed from the world in which the contents of such papers were of enough importance to consume on a daily basis. Their aging golden retriever, Chipper, sprawled himself at Anne's feet and wagged his tail at Katie but didn't want to jeopardize his diligently selected spot, in which he had dug until he reached the first layer of damp sand. Beth had never wanted a dog around, so Katie had spent hours every adolescent summer on the Clarke porch and in their backyard playing with Chipper, now too old to do much more than lie on a beach or couch and dip in for an occasional swim. Jamie Jr. and Charlotte had one of their own, which fit what Katie and Ryan believed was the son's attempt at simulating his father in as many ways as possible, but the dog was insane and therefore only allowed on the beach at quieter times of day. "He'll grow out of it," they said, often.

"Mrs. Murray, how are you? Finally a real summer day." Katie thought it sounded like Jamie Jr. was attempting to make his voice sound deeper.

"Jamie, it's Beth, please. Sun feels nice, that's for sure."

Both forced smiles. Jamie Jr.'s seemed to require extra effort. Charlotte met his with a look that reeked of feigned admiration.

"Katie, honey, you look like you've already had a full morning. Good for you." Anne patted her on the hip from her perch. "Those legs must be able to carry you a long way."

"Not quite. I get tired after two miles every time."

Beth smiled over them all. "You guys look like a photo shoot out here. All the Clarkes in their summer leisure wear reading and laughing on the beach."

As soon as "*all* the Clarkes" escaped her mouth, Beth realized the inaccuracy but showed no sign of doing so; Katie heard it and almost spoke up but changed her mind at the sight of the squirming around her, most of which came from Amelia and her father. Anne's hands rested on, or maybe dug into, her book, and Jamie Jr. tinkered unnaturally with his feet, using one to pour sand on the other, aviator ovals blocking not just his eyes but his entire face, Katie felt.

The spouses looked oblivious or else were skilled in maintaining the catalogue-ready aura Beth's comment had threatened to disrupt.

"Too kind, Beth. I think my magazine days are over. No one wants to see these old-man legs."

"Well, don't let us interrupt y—"

"Don't be silly. Come, grab a seat. We've got an open chair and a towel, or I'm sure young Jamie would be happy to get up." Anne glared at her boy.

Katie held her place and waited for her mother to decline, but suddenly everyone was looking at her, waiting for her to take the chair Beth left vacated as she oriented herself on a striped towel, its white clean and its blue almost the same as the periwinkle of all three Clarke children's eyes. Finally she moved toward the seat. Before she reached it, the twins ran past her, almost knocking her over, giggling as they did. She babysat them from time to time but didn't seek out the work, generous pay be damned.

"Guys, be careful! That's your best babysitter," but they were already in the water, one throwing sand at the other, his motion altered by his new floaties.

"Jr. was just telling us about his hunting trip last week, though I think Anne may have heard enough."

"No, go right ahead, but I can't imagine these fine Murray women have much stomach for bloodsport." Anne looked to the ocean as she spoke, squinting at her progeny's progeny. Katie wondered if grandmothers had the power to instill virtue telepathically.

"What do you hunt?"

Jamie Jr. was shocked to hear her ask, but Katie could tell he was also happy to have an excuse to go back over the details of the trip. His open mouth curved into a smile.

Katie had been trained well. She conducted herself appropriately in any social or professional setting, but now she sensed something rising inside of her, something for which the group, least of all Jamie Jr., was not prepared. A quick glance to Beth told Katie what she had suspected: the woman who had led her training deduced something was amiss.

"Deer for the most part. A friend from school has a couple hundred acres in New York."

"His family does." Jamie Sr. didn't look up from his paper as he clarified. While the paper blocked her view of his face, Katie was pretty sure he was rolling his eyes.

"Yes, right, his family. Someday it'll be his I guess. There's some other game, but in my experience we've only gone after deer."

"How did it go?" Now the rest of the circle sat at attention, and the question hung for a few seconds, letting in the noise of the twins' aquatic smackdown, not of apparent concern to Amelia and worth a quick half-turn from Nate's brawny neck. Katie could tell from his idiotic countenance that Jamie Jr. was still the least alert. He took no notice of his brittle surroundings.

"I'm no expert or anything. My friend pretty much tells me where to stand, where to shoot."

"But did you get any?" The edge in Katie's voice suggested an imminent pounce.

Jamie Jr. was a little sheepish now, not embarrassed but wary of discomfiting his mother for the second time within the half-hour. The rest of the group looked down or out to sea.

"I got a couple. I've definitely gotten better since my first couple trips. I was hopeless at first."

"What's it feel like?"

"What part?"

"Katie, don't make him go into detail."

"It's okay, Mrs. Murray, it's kind of exciting to talk about."

Beth's eyes followed the twins chasing each other down the beach as she waited for Katie to make her move. Katie ground her teeth and flexed her jaw and blinked less than those around her. Jamie Jr. was sharp enough to be certain that nothing he said would impress or intimidate her. They rarely spoke to each other outside of conclaves like these. They had drained many summer days on the verge of clashing but had always known better than to let the other child spoil the fun.

"Which part did you mean, Katie?" Jamie Jr. locked onto Katie as he spoke, his eyes wide and white and bloodless.

"I guess the moment before you shoot. Shoot? Fire? I don't know what word you say. But before you pull the trigger, after you've found the buck or whatever you call it, what goes through your mind?" She looked squarely at him, but he performed for the group.

"It's such a rush. It's hard to even describe. Two seconds feel like two hundred, and it takes a moment to realize that this is it, this is the opportunity you've been waiting for, that you have the power to take the animal, waiting just below the tip of your finger. I can see how it would be frightening if it wasn't so thrilling. To say it makes you feel powerful doesn't do it justice. The direction of this thing's life is in your hands. You know before you even pull your finger back if you've made the shot. It's like everything is in perfect harmony—you, the gun, the wind, all of it. When it all comes together like that, the animal doesn't stand a chance."

He had waited quite some time to recite this passage. His rehearsed pauses sounded overwrought.

Katie nodded and puffed up one cheek while she considered his words. "Sure, but wouldn't it be more thrilling if the deer could, you know, put up a fight?"

"In a way, they can. They can run."

Katie met his eyes. A shiver ran down her spine at the sight of his smile, the same one that she had seen in summers past, vibrant but betraying something darker underneath. She could have guessed the gist of his answer but still found his sincerity equal parts pathetic and haunting. She picked up his disappointment as he looked to his father for a reaction only to learn his namesake had progressed to the business section.

Anne and Beth each waited for the other to steer the pack to another topic, though the former was more or less used to her middle child's grisly tendencies.

"I've got to get some steps in, but thank you for letting us stop and chat. Katie, come or stay. Your call."

The pleasantries were quieter than they had been upon arrival and shorter, partially a result of the twins' return, one boy twenty feet ahead of the other, clutching his ear and holding back tears that were, on the authority of his brother's guilty look, authentic. Amelia urged Nate to show more interest but attended to the ear herself and commanded the pair to reach a resolution, which they did almost immediately before running back into the layered waves crashing to shore.

Katie and Beth walked along the water at the latter's request, made after she had felt the wet sand and experienced the footing, solid compared to the fine grains that greeted visitors at the top of the beach. Katie waited until they were well outside of earshot before breaking their silence.

"They have such a strange dynamic."

"Which ones?"

"All of them. The entire Clarke clan."

"Just because J.J. likes to hunt doesn't mean they're bad people." No one called him J.J. to his face anymore, except his mother, and she only did so once or twice a summer, by accident. He had shed the nickname in an effort to seem more adult.

"I wouldn't say they're good people." She didn't like how she sounded even as she spoke, but it felt good to let it out. She thought of Eric.

"Well, Katie, maybe you and I just have different definitions of that phrase."

Katie had long since sussed out this disparity, what with Beth's perception always being slightly clouded by her adoration of the name and house and reputation. These were three of many factors that added up to something better than just "good" in Beth's mind, something intractable even in the face of what was to Katie the shortage of empathy that swirled inside Clarke minds to varying degrees.

The unease didn't stop them from walking their usual distance, today passing under Monomo Cliffs, a beach club that hung fifty feet over them and catered to more of a retirement crowd with its restaurant and the octogenarian-friendly golf course directly across the street. Some walks or runs stretched longer, past the rocky section that now jutted out between them and the next smooth chunk of beach, which stretched to North Monomo. Neither woman had to say a word of clarification; they turned before reaching the rocks and moved slightly up the sand. Katie's post-run feet had welcomed the cool surface by the water, but the hotter powder didn't burn. It soothed.

"Is Ryan at the club?"

Katie switched her watch back to its normal mode and checked the time. "Probably. He said he wanted to get out early."

"He better behave himself this summer. He needs to save some money and not get into trouble. Some of those kids at the club worry me."

"The other caddies? They're all pretty nice for the most part."

"If you say so. Always some bad eggs mixed in over there from what I hear." Beth had a number of sources, some members at the Dunes and others frequent guests, all on the same page.

"You mean Worona kids? Now you sound like a snob."

Beth didn't need to speak to convey her frustration. The uptick in their pace came without warning. Katie felt no need to prolong their time together.

The Clarkes were otherwise occupied when the Murrays returned. They passed in silence.

"He's a serious guy, you know, so I assume it's something bad because he's not saying a fucking thing. He's marching in front of me. No small talk or anything. Even the other partners are scared of him. We get inside. He tells me to sit down. It's ninety degrees so I'm sweating my balls off, and he goes over to the window. Crazy view. Like the whole city. Best place to work at night, you know, when it's all lit up. It felt like ten minutes before he talked. I figured he was testing me or something. But then he bends down to this little fridge. Didn't even see it when I came in. He grabs a couple beers, something I've never heard of. He's from California, so he likes a lot of California shit. Hands me one and tells me how happy he's been with my work. 'Jamie, you've impressed us these past few weeks' and all that stuff. I'll tell you: it had been unclear to me up until that point if he even knew my name. So then I'm holding the beer and waiting for him to drink his, but he starts telling this long story about some wild night a couple weekends before. He's not that old, you know. Pretty much still a young guy, which makes it surprising how intense he is. You would think he wants to be, like, the cool young one in the group. Youngest partner ever. Well, here. They've had some younger guys in London. It's all a little different over there. That's what Kelly says. She was there for a year. Don't think she's rushing back, you know . . ."

A twin cut his toe on a jagged shell. He dripped blood in the sand and, seconds later, on the edge of Amelia's towel.

6

Eric didn't like summer. Even when he was younger and didn't feel like a burden, he had a hard time with the months between responsibilities. There was too much pressure to have fun. Fun was expected or demanded. In other months, fun could be stolen, and no one batted an eye if you had no desire to take it.

He considered himself even-tempered. He had cultivated such an image after early returns suggested he would feel shame whenever his anxieties shined through. Even if the veneer failed to garner respect, even if he felt restricted or misrepresented, he would have an out. He would be able to tell himself in the quiet of his own head that he could have their respect if he needed it, that it wasn't worth the risk of receiving their pity and sideways glances into his glass enclosure.

There was no one moment in which he had decided to rebel. He learned he was a rebel, an outlaw, only when others alerted him to the fact. It didn't usually bother him to see or hear people casting him aside, placing him in categories that made them feel safe. What did hurt was his parents' belief in his lack of attention, his detachment from the world around him. They believed he was lazy and ungrateful, unwilling to reflect on his place in the world, on his luck to have been born on the right side of its tipped scales. He believed he worked hard and that they were grateful not for the power and flexibility their position provided but instead for the peace of mind and the ability to aggressively *not think*. Sure, they acted. They spoke and laughed and sang and sometimes ventured out. But they didn't think much, at least not beyond the confines of their most familiar lobes and synapses.

He never blamed them—his parents or the others. Sometimes he scorned them for little things, for his most debilitating prejudices and eccentricities, but never for his delinquency. That belonged to him, which was hard to accept because the weight was sometimes crushing. But it was also, on occasion, liberating, in that he didn't have to fear hurting anyone else as long as they kept their distance. In such a mindset, he found himself right where he wanted to be as the calendar turned to its seventh month, in most years his least favorite of all. It was hot and crowded, and his approaching half-birthday invited a phobia regarding the passage of time to resurface on an annual basis.

He had never liked the fireworks or festivities, even when he was young. The calm summer nights had always been more appealing. In this world, the one he continued to carve out for himself, he could make his own quiet. He could find solitude if he was willing to abandon the crowds that wanted no part of him.

This night was quiet and would soon yield to morning, but he would have to seek out the light. This room wouldn't let it in. Its inhabitants had enough to worry about without the intrusion of the sun. They had worlds to forge, identities to leave behind, tranquility to explore.

7

"Where's this kid play, Ry?" Kevin's question came as the pitcher dropped a toss from his man behind the plate.

"Louisville. He's a beast. Should be a first-round pick next year." Ryan held a program that listed each player's height, weight, age, and school but didn't need to check it.

"Seems like he's throwing a lot harder than the starter was."

"Oh, yeah. I think he tops out at ninety-seven. I'm sure he doesn't want to overdo it this summer."

The four Murrays sat eight rows up behind home plate in mostly filled bleachers, watching the Monomo Whalers lose to the Chatham Anglers. It was only the fourth inning, but the Anglers had effectively ended the game with a seven-run second, leaving the Whalers to work their way through a bullpen that, according to Ryan's analysis, lacked depth. The crowd didn't mind. Save for a handful of player relatives and year-rounder diehards, most of whom sat in the first two rows or behind the dugouts, the fans were there to relax on a picturesque summer evening. The unhumid air was free from nagging bugs, the obedient sun loitered even as the field lights warmed up, and the only sounds disrupting the stillness of the Rockwellian night were those for which they had come: the crack of bat on ball and the satisfying thump of ninety-seven miles per hour into the catcher's mitt.

"God, that must hurt the poor catcher's hand."

"Mom, he's prepared. Trust me. They're used to it." Ryan was familiar with her points of concern.

Beth was mostly uninterested in the Whalers and the sport they played, but she enjoyed a couple of trips per summer to Hutchinson Park, which stood a quarter mile from Main Street, near the point where the Monomos came together. She tended to wrangle Katie to her side when she looked for a reason not to attend a game or to leave one early. Katie was happy to appease her mother by simulating disinterest, but she actually liked the sport and sucking up Ryan's expertise. Kevin was knowledgeable, too, but not as knowledgeable as his propensity for emitting facts, strategies, and opinions would have one believe.

"Is Monomo supposed to be good this summer?" Katie understood the game well enough to be unimpressed with their adopted hometown's performance.

"Nothing special. They've played well, but Chatham and Cotuit are the favorites. Because of guys like this, I guess."

Ryan pointed to the mound and, on cue, the Louisville product struck out another Whaler, who didn't look that surprised to be walking back to his dugout, in which morale was low and the college minds were elsewhere.

The Whalers represented both Monomos and had been in the Cape Cod Baseball League, the country's premier summer league for top college players, for almost two decades but were yet to win a title, though they had showcased a cadre of players who later went on to MLB stardom (in a couple of cases) or longevity (more than a couple but not that many). Teams like Chatham and Harwich and Yarmouth-Dennis had more success and name recognition than Monomo, as it went with the towns themselves. Consequently, the Whalers' stadium and fanbase fell somewhere in the middle of the league's ranks: cozy and polite, respectively.

A kid in the row in front of the Murrays ate fried dough and knocked over his sister's drink. His parents sent him to the concession stand, a brick structure behind the first-base dugout, operated by volunteers, that smelled like hot dogs and microwaved cheese.

As with the other clubs, Monomo players usually lived with residents during their time on the team. The Murrays had never housed one, but some neighbors had on multiple occasions, in one case leading to a fling between Amelia Clarke and a Whaler, a fling that Ryan was quick to compare to *Summer Catch* in the years after it occurred. He assured his sister that both the real-life and onscreen renderings were largely forgettable. The player, a center fielder with a sweet left-handed swing, did go on to get drafted and even spent most of one season with the Baltimore Orioles, but a shoulder injury and his relative lack of talent left him toiling in the minors for the remainder of what ended up being a brief career. No one had the full story, and no one dared joke about the matter around Amelia or Nate—they were not full-on dating at the time but by most accounts had established some level of an exclusive relationship before the outfielder began to, as it were, play ball—but she babysat for the Murrays several times that summer, when Ryan was old enough to piece together why the young man joined them on several ice cream trips.

Another neighbor had run into some problems when her husband of thirteen years discovered her in bed with a Whaler. Upon hearing the gossip, Ryan had offered to his parents that she had good taste, having picked the team's top starter who boasted, at the very least, a live arm, but his commentary garnered a death glare from his mother and suppressed amusement from his father. The player had been quickly and diplomatically sent home, and the team did everything in their power to end the scandal and prevent future issues. Some fans argued it was the best press they'd had since the team's inception.

Hutchinson Field shared its parking lot with Monomo Regional, the high school that served both Monomos and their neighbor to the west. Most of the school building was visible through the lot that sat behind the fence in right-center. A few cars had been hit over the years, but the wood bats of the CCBL limited the players' capacity for inflicting such damage. The Regional team used the field, but the Whaler organization, small though it was, dolled it up and maintained it better in the summer. It wasn't terribly difficult to make the park look good under pink-orange skies like the one into which a ball now flew.

"Has a chance!" Kevin half-stood to follow the flight of the ball down the right field line. The crowd's roar caught in a collective throat as it hooked foul and carried over the fence, bouncing toward a playground occupied by a few sets of parents and kids with soft serve on their shirts and faces.

"He hammered that, didn't he?"

Ryan was impressed but not wowed. "Ball goes a long way when the guy throws ninety-seven."

It didn't go a long way on the next pitch or the one after that. As the Whalers took the field for the top of the sixth, the PA announcer reminded fans of the Fourth of July festivities taking place at the field before and after the holiday game against Orleans, as well as the parade, which would run from North to South Monomo the morning of the Fourth and include some of the players on what was a "float" in name only.

"Have you two made plans for the Fourth yet? I'm sure there's a lot going on for the third because it's a Saturday, but the Clarkes are having everyone over for food, fireworks, passing out on the beach, the works on Sunday."

"Yeah, Mom, isn't that the same deal every year?" Everyone tensed at the sound of Katie's attitude.

"Ryan and I are working both days, or at least I am. There's a tournament in the morning. Might even wear something low-cut for the tips."

"Katie, don't even joke about that. You'll give your father a heart attack."

Kevin had been studying something on the left side of the infield but grunted at the mention, cardiac muscles intact.

"That being said, working the Fourth's a good idea. You two keep it up and you'll have a fortune saved up by the end of the summer."

"Working on the Fourth? Seems a little unpatriotic." Kevin winked at the kids, well within Beth's range of sight.

"Kevin, let's not encourage them to slack off. Hard work never h—"

"Beth, come on. I didn't say anything about slacking off."

Katie rolled her eyes at the bickering that ensued. This debate was new to the Whaler grandstands but not to the family. Since well before either child reached a legal working age, Beth had seized every opportunity to instill in them the work ethic she believed had carried her to heights not reached or conceived of by either of her parents. Nothing Katie had ever done suggested she was lacking in determination, and parental fears regarding Ryan's future were over-blown. Nevertheless, their mother stressed over it and found fury in her husband's attitude, or in her perception of it.

His upbringing differed greatly from hers but was not as cushy as she mythologized, and he resented the implication that his world-view was essentially inferior to Beth's. Boiled down, his opinion was that there was more to life than work, a not-so-radical position that his wife had, at some point in their earliest days, shared. He feared that his children and many of his students were aware of the phi-losophy but not taking it to heart, or were in some cases having it drilled out of their brains by adults not so different from the woman whose leg was now pressed against his below the wooden bench. She wasn't the worst offender and wasn't very similar to whoever was, but every time their bedtime routine included a thinly veiled accusation of laziness in one or both of his children he wanted to scream. He pitied the man or woman falling asleep next to the worst offender.

He knew that she knew that he didn't want lazy kids, and they both understood that they didn't have any. Their disagreements, in this and all arenas, rarely led to anything that could be classified as a fight, with one recent exception a few months earlier.

On that night, with the house to themselves, both dozed off in the family room watching television, and Beth discovered her second wind in time to catch a news segment on the college admissions process, twice conquered by the Murray family but still grounds for her to rouse Kevin and spark a conversation on the topic. It went on far longer than their ballpark spat, culminating in Kevin's monologue that the people who thought working and working and working until one felt accomplished and content was the way to live were misguided and unable to comprehend their own feelings, seeing as what they viewed as a combination of relaxation and contentedness was really just *fatigue*, bone-deep and long-developing, a hindrance to any change of course until it was far too late. Beth didn't take this well, viewing it as an attack on her mindset and belief system. Kevin assured her it wasn't, at least not a conscious one.

The week following this incident would have been tense had their schedules not limited the time they were forced to spend in each other's presence. As the fight diminished into a memory alongside its few siblings, they both sort of reveled in it but said nothing, each happy to be reminded that the marriage would endure as it had always endured because of—and not in spite of—their asymmetrical intelligences.

Four boys stood on the last row of bleachers but sat down when their "LET'S GO WHALERS" chant failed to pick up steam.

"Ryan, why aren't they bunting here? Isn't this the nine-hitter? He's tiny."

Kevin reclined into the row behind them and smiled at Katie's question, for which her brother lacked a good answer. The weak-hitting second baseman from St. John's vindicated her approach quickly with a two-hopper to the shortstop. The Anglers turned the double play with time to spare.

The game had been decided for an hour and would drag on for another, but the Murrays would stay until the end, as would most of the spectators. They knew better than to abandon their perches prematurely. Life would draw them down out of the benches too soon, back toward the highway or the water or somewhere in between.

By the eighth inning, the tall, glaring lights were necessary, and the field glowed beneath them. Even on the Whalers' myriad harmless pop-ups, the ball floated starkly white against a sky that was almost dark enough to conceal its thin, staggered clouds. A volunteer hawking popcorn and peanuts paced on the walkway below the fans, but most had already indulged. Draped over the outfield fence were banners for local stores and restaurants, for which these spectators needed no reminders. The fabrics flapped in the corners where they weren't secured.

Chatham added a few runs in the top of the ninth, but no one booed or groaned, happy to have fifteen more minutes in air that refused to cool even as the breeze picked up and held, blowing out toward the sea.

"I could coach this team." Kevin spoke to no one in particular, but Ryan guessed the words were meant for him.

"It'd be nice if someone did."

July 7

One of the weird things about this whole situation is that I love the Fourth of July. It was my favorite holiday growing up. Back then we always celebrated together. We went to the Turners' down the street and watched the fireworks. Some years Mr. Turner bought us some stuff of our own. Nothing big. Nothing anyone would be able to see outside of his yard. Mom didn't like that he bought them but she let it slide because of how much fun we had with them and because we promised to be safe.

Dad and Mr. Turner made too much food every year. So when they were tired of us at the end of the night they'd get all the extra dogs and burgers and offer twenty bucks to whichever one of the kids could eat the most. It didn't matter who won. The number always grew by the next morning and even more by the time we told the other kids in the neighborhood or at the fields.

Anyone's guess what the Turners do for the Fourth now. Mr. Turner's still in that house. Ricky's away at school I think. He works there during the summers and I was never close to his brother or sister.

My parents were taking it easy that night because they were leaving to go see my mom's friend in Delaware the next day. I don't know how her friend ended up in Delaware. She was born near here. My mom says the beaches are good there. Different from ours.

The Fourth might still be my favorite even though we don't do the kid stuff anymore. I think it confused the other two because I was in a good mood at the beginning of the night. Not for long though.

Maybe now I can't say the Fourth is my favorite anymore but I'm not sure what I can put in its place. Christmas by default I guess. My parents used to go all out for Christmas even when they shouldn't have and even when they really couldn't they still made it look good. They liked watching us tumble down the stairs. My dad used the same crappy camera to film us every year.

We cut down the tree together a few times in a spot in the woods by the playground where you weren't supposed to. He made us say a prayer before we chopped it every time. He knelt in the snow and did it but I kept my eyes open and smelled the tree. That sort of felt like a prayer.

Christmas is always quiet around here. The whole winter is. In a way I think that's how this all started. It was kind of easy to get into trouble when we were little because they were busy and there wasn't that much to do. They left us alone a lot. We did the rest.

8

In a sixth-grade discussion, one Katie had thought was fairly dumb even at the time, her teacher had asked the class to debate what day on the calendar best embodied the *meaning of America*. Memorial Day, Veterans Day, and Presidents Day all had their defenders, but Katie's classmates had quickly reached a consensus that the Fourth of July was the choice.

Now older and wiser, Katie figured the answer depended on how an individual celebrated these days, as well as how they defined the so-called *meaning of America*—someone who sang "God Bless America" to start the Fourth thought of it differently from a Gold Star parent who visited their fallen child's grave, and both of them were approaching the holiday with access to weightier emotions than the people Katie saw wearing American-flag swimsuit bottoms or planting an actual flag in the sand outside their plot on the beach, sharing their country radio with the people in adjacent packs. She knew that none of these displays necessarily had moral authority over the others, though she found it difficult to convince herself that the man in stars-and-stripes shorts with koozie in hand had a greater claim to his Americanness than the mother who slumped six feet above her son, running her hands over the stone marking his grave, some small part of her wondering if tracing the engraved letters might awaken the dead, another part unsure if she should want to. Katie didn't usually think like this in the cart. She worried the sun was getting to her.

"You girls look like you should be lounging on the beach on a sunny day like this."

"Quite a tan you've got. I can't do it. I just burn out here. Like a goddamn lobster. Irish genes."

Katie recorded their member numbers and purchases while her cartmate, Cassie, absorbed their indiscretions. The pair walked their half-covered, messily shaved legs back to the fairway. Their caddie waited next to the balls, resting on one knee between their bags in the shade of the trees the players had narrowly avoided.

"Some of these guys are such creeps." Katie watched them walk off and grimaced as one adjusted himself out of a wedgie.

"For sure. It's not always so bad, though. Devin's pretty cute."

Katie coughed while Cassie exaggerated biting her lip.

"Cassie, he's like forty-five. He has a kid in high school."

"He could have me, that's for sure." Cassie elbowed Katie and winked.

Cassie's flirtatiousness and liberal interpretation of the Dunes dress code were more a declaration of her true self than a clever ploy at receiving higher tips, but Katie did find her pockets fuller after the shifts she covered with her full-bodied coworker. Cassie was sometimes ignorant but not completely naive. She was self-involved but still pleasant to talk to about the insecurities of the men hacking away around them, the ones that spoke to her too fast, for too long, and held up play.

Both men missed the green and glanced over, hoping the cart had moved on. Cassie scrolled fast, liking friends' Instagram posts indiscriminately, commenting on every third one, unbothered by Katie's lack of interest.

"They definitely didn't need both of us today."

"Katie, don't complain about them paying us more than they have to."

"Good point. What are you doing for the weekend?"

Katie knew more about Cassie than Cassie would have thought, though she was used to people muttering about her parents and her family. Had she taken the time to think about it, she would have suspected that Katie had access to some parts of her story. Katie associated with enough people from the area to glean a thing or two that Cassie would have preferred to keep under wraps.

Cassie grew up in the area and moved to Worona during high school, and she had two older brothers at one point but now only had one. Katie hadn't heard the whole story, but she was correct in thinking that the younger of the brothers, there when the older one died of an overdose, had been thrust out of the way by paramedics in their futile attempt to revive his sibling. Someone in the bag room had told her the story the summer before. Cassie's parents were in the picture but only its periphery, pushed closer to the edge, or rather fleeing further from its center, ever since they buried their boy and turned away, so as to escape blame for whatever vicissitudes awaited the other two. Katie had no idea what Cassie thought of the situation or if she ever talked about it with anyone. They weren't all that close, though they enjoyed each other's company. She wondered if Cassie was in control of her life or if she wanted to be, based on the people she spent time with and the places in which they let it pass. Katie sensed that she remained close to her brother, but who knew if they would be better off apart. She was pretty sure the siblings rarely saw their parents, who lived in their mutated version of Worona, one that must have belonged to another world.

Another group approached the tee. The first man launched a ball with his driver and yelled "FORE," but the dimpled sphere bounced softly twenty-five yards in front of them.

"I'll probably take it easy today. More action tomorrow. You think you'll come to Greenstone?" Cassie awaited a no.

"I don't know. Seems like there's always trouble there every year."

Cassie sipped from an iced coffee and drove them slowly away from the twelfth hole. "Not real trouble. Just the kind of trouble people our age are supposed to get into in the summertime."

Katie looked over at the selfie Cassie pressed her to inspect but didn't investigate closely other than to note that the poster's breasts were not as large as she had been able to make them appear.

"We'll see. Probably stuck at the Clarkes' anyway. Maybe if Ryan wants to we can slip out."

Cassie had never come this close to convincing Katie to go out. "You should. I think Mark would be happy if you were there."

"Mark? Mark Hunter? I don't think so."

Cassie planted them between the thirteenth green and the fourteenth tee box. A foursome walked away from the former, and another group approached the latter, halting to watch as one player deposited a short approach into the bunker ten yards to the girls' right.

"Would I lie to you? I've known him forever."

Katie didn't mind the company of young men of or around her age, and Mark Hunter was more handsome and thoughtful than the majority of her coworkers, but she hadn't envisioned her time at the Dunes leading to love or whatever someone like him had in mind for someone like her. She wasn't the type to be persuaded to attend a dubious gathering with information like this, but she still liked to hear it. She blushed as she watched Mr. Levinson splash out of the bunker; the ball refused to check on its way through the front tier of the green.

"Isn't that Mr. Clarke right there?"

Jamie leaned on his putter and stood next to his caddie at the front of the green. His ball sat eleven feet to the right of the pin. Katie thought of him as a true golfer—he talked about the sport unobnoxiously but often. He was one of the best players at the club, but never, based on the names adorning the club championship trophy, the best. He was always among the top finishers but never higher than second. Recent years had pitted Jamie against a handful of worthy competitors, a few of whom had won the title, including Jack Hampton, a New York banker with whom he often played.

Jack's ball sat farther from the hole, but Jamie's look of focus suggested his competitor had enjoyed an easier go of it in the round's first two thirds.

Katie found many of the members' hole-by-hole accounts interminable, but Mr. Clarke's contained a little poetry. Kevin played some golf but not at Jamie's level, so he savored listening to stories of his rounds, travels to other courses, and second-place finishes, about which Jamie managed to speak politely even as his face turned red at the memory of close calls—the most painful being a choke on the eighteenth hole in 2008 against Jack, who considered his runner-up a friend and thus lifted the trophy with slightly less enthusiasm than he would have under other circumstances.

Jamie gave his birdie putt an aggressive go but missed below the hole. This time he avoided any embarrassment as he cleaned up a par and made his way to the cart.

"Katie, good to see you out here. Oh, and good to see you reading."

Katie always brought a book in the cart but rarely read it, especially on days Cassie joined her. The top half of her current selection's cover was visible underneath her sunglasses in the compartment in front of her. Cassie got out and strutted over to Katie's side, where most of the beverages were stored.

"Cassie, how are you? I'll just take a yellow Gatorade, please."

His smile lacked the dirtiness many of his fellow members displayed, but his eyes did wander as she reached past the beers for his selection.

"I'm looking forward to tomorrow. It's supposed to be a perfect night for fireworks."

"Ah, Katie, that makes one of us." He took his bottle and dropped a bill into Cassie's hand, not letting his own brush up against her unblemished skin.

"You don't like the Fourth?"

"I don't mind it. I prefer the quieter summer days. Less noise, less to do. Until then."

He raised his unopened bottle and backed away, turning and opening the drink as Jack bent over to put his tee in the ground. His apprehension ahead of the next night didn't surprise Katie. She wouldn't want to be responsible for a pack of drunk, pyromanic revelers in close proximity to a body of water either. Anne was the true hostess and eager to play the part. For all his success and storytelling and social prestige, Jamie was a quiet man when he was allowed to be and, Katie thought, sometimes when he shouldn't be. It was clear to her and others that people had always found him captivating. Sometimes she felt the pull, too, despite herself. But at his core he was introspective, so he picked his spots and was perfectly content on the sidelines. Usually that meant perched on their deck with a drink and a book in the dying light, the dark an hour away from hiding the world from him, or vice versa.

"Text me about Greenstone."

"Okay. Probably a no."

Katie added enthusiasm to punctuate her answer and snapped her fingers to emphasize Cassie's failure to entice.

"I'll put you down as a yes. It'll be fun to see each other in something other than these stupid shirts."

"Put me down as a maybe. What are you going to wear?"

"Less than you." Cassie smiled and twirled away and flashed

a peace sign toward the cart.

For Katie, there was nothing to look forward to on the third of July in South Monomo, nothing state-sanctioned. That it fell on a Saturday this summer would add to the depravity, she was sure.

As darkness crept onto the beach, the drinking was ongoing but tapering down, having started when the previous darkness first slunk away. The smell of meats grilling lingered even where the machines no longer ran.

The night beach crowd always skewed younger than the surrounding neighborhood's demographics. On this night, it was even greener than usual, with just a smattering of nostalgic middle-agers sprinkled throughout the crowd, clinging to a hint of life before parenthood, to a feeling they convinced themselves they once had, one they were sure went unappreciated by the next generation.

This day and the ones around it left Katie disappointed most years. She avoided eye contact as she wove through the blobs of teenagers and recent grads, increasingly frustrated with her brother for not answering her texts. Without warning, someone in a group to her right announced the beginning of the unsanctioned fireworks show with a poorly aimed blast, one that missed his friend's nose by the length of the snapback hat on his head.

Fireworks were illegal in Massachusetts, but the unwritten rules of South Monomo encouraged them for the holiday, as long as things didn't get out of hand. The random beach displays served as demonstrations of creativity or buying power or some combination thereof. Most were short and disorganized, but every year one or two people raised their game and produced something close to professional, long and loud enough to let their audience extrapolate how much effort and money had gone into transporting their goods, likely from New Hampshire, all for four to six minutes of what was in their minds glory and in everyone else's mild amusement.

Katie liked the smell but preferred the sounds from a distance and thus favored the morning after, when the scent hung in the briny air and remains of the blasts rested on the shore and in the shallow waters. Each fireworking group waited their turn for the most part, sometimes overlapping as the concluding troupe's supply dwindled. Fuller shows could be seen in the distance, the Cape's tip visible on the right side of the horizon, faintly illuminated under defective finales.

"Gotcha!"

She jumped at her brother's touch, and he wrapped an arm around her that she quickly pushed away. His bare feet jogged back to their circle. A healthy fire raged at its center. Katie recognized some but not all of the group from the club and neighborhood. In the flickering darkness, most of them looked alike, equally afraid of each other's silent examinations. They held beers, some bottled but most in cans, and the smell of a joint drifted over the group, its source the smaller faction behind them, closer to the water.

"Ry-guy! What's up, man?"

Danny Moreland greeted Ryan on the far side of the circle with a rough embrace, flanked by two unlit faces. Katie couldn't hear Danny over the pops in the sky and the murmuring pre-adults, but it was clear he was mocking someone, maybe Ryan. After a moment, he looked straight at her and simpered but quickly turned away. She walked toward her brother. Danny was gone with a hard pat on the shoulder and a jeer to the crowd by the time she reached Ryan. She watched the white hat fade as he stumbled down the beach.

"What were you guys talking about?"

"Don't worry about it. Just Danny being Danny."

"You better not be hanging out with him." Katie jabbed him in the side and felt a little like her mother.

"Not if I can help it."

"Do you know those other guys he was with? One of them looked really familiar." She looked down the beach, but the boys were concealed.

Ryan had thought the same thing when Danny first arrived but hadn't been able to place the pale, gaunt figure behind him at first. His brain had churned as Danny heckled, and soon he remembered where he had seen the sunken face: in the group by the bridge along the canal. It didn't surprise him and wouldn't have surprised her to learn Danny was hanging with such a crowd, but he saw no benefit in telling her of his realization, so she maintained her suspicion, partially directed toward her brother.

Overhead, someone carried on, their fireworks purple, green, and shimmering. Those close to the men setting them off didn't say much, and when they spoke it went unheard beneath the fanfare. The men lighting them, two brothers, didn't possess the loudest or highest-climbing bag of tricks and didn't need to. They preferred to last the longest, into the darkest section of the night, to be the reason the crowd hummed a minute longer and looked back as they walked past the porta-potties and the full lot on their way up the hill to haphazardly parked cars and trucks.

As the lights went out, the bugs crept back onto a beach that smelled largely of repellent.

July 8

It never got more fun than when we started smoking pot. There weren't a lot of us at first because we were young and the rest of the kids were scared. The older kids let us go with them so we appreciated them and when we saw them start doing the other stuff we figured we would try it when we were older too. And we did. We didn't rush. We knew what it could do. Most of what it could do.

When we messed with the other stuff there were more of us than there had been before. Strength in numbers I guess. Or just a shit ton of weakness maybe. Weakness looks like strength sometimes if there's enough of it and you stand by your choices.

We had a dog when I was little. My parents had him before I was born and he was slow and lazy by the time I was old enough to remember him. He liked to lie next to me on the couch while I watched cartoons or the Sox.

Sometimes he had bad dreams. I assume that's what was happening because he whimpered and shook until I woke him up with a cough or by petting him on the head.

I always got worried about him. I asked my mom what dogs had bad dreams about and she didn't have an answer. Being alone I think. I think he dreamed about being left behind somewhere. Maybe wherever my parents found him. I don't usually remember my dreams but I think the bad ones are mostly about being alone. At least they used to be.

I was always nicer to the dog than other kids. One time my dad told me I should treat everyone in my class like they were Manny. But I liked to fight.

I still don't remember my dreams now but I'm pretty damn sure I get what the bad ones are about. And I'm positive I have them. Lately it's taken me a long time to fall asleep. Most mornings I wake up sweating and I'm on alert.

When Manny died I started to act out more.

It hurt my mom and dad all the time. Not being able to make me act better. I don't know when I broke them.

9

The morning of the Fourth in South Monomo played to its audience. The parade down Main Street started almost promptly at nine every year, so tired or hungover parents sat on shaded grassy humps or in well-loved chairs, the young kids bustled along the street when the high-candy-volume carfloats passed, and most of the post-adolescents stayed home or arrived late.

At a young age, Katie had been quick to point out, to her parents' chagrin, that Fourth of July parades usually possessed few ties to the holiday's history except for the colors plastered throughout town and the accessories festooned on the storefronts and passing vehicles. The Murrays didn't like to watch the parade anymore.

This one was mercifully short, snaking along for about two miles at a healthy clip. Most of the town's small population was present. Many of them had walked to their roadside spots, and more than a few kept their seats long after the final car—which held South Monomo's oldest resident, centenarian Barbara Mullens, who looked remarkably spry, if a little sun-baked—some to stay cool, some to continue visiting with neighbors they barely knew, and some to look wistfully out at the stores and candy wrappers before them, wondering how another year had reached this point so soon.

Four Whalers sat in their car, driven by one of their host mothers. They wore their jerseys on top and shorts and flip-flops below, and three of them hurled candy at higher velocities than Barbara

Mullens was able to generate. The fourth had pitched the night before, so he tossed Tootsie Rolls gently with his left arm and barely reached the children.

Restaurant and store owners draped signs over the sides of their cars and waved to their regulars. Tom, from Tom's Bait and Tackle, threw candy while his second wife drove but also mixed in some tassels, which was at first a disappointment to the youngsters but soon became a source of great excitement when one caught in a boy's fingertip, drawing blood. Anne and Jamie rested behind their grandchildren. The twins hopped up and down at the sight of each car.

South Monomo's leaders were veterans when it came to scheduling the day's activities. Field games followed the parade and often devolved amidst the onslaught of sugar rushes taking place throughout the town green. The festivities began with an egg toss. Every year, cheating abounded: some teams simply carried on as if their eggs weren't broken, other pairs stayed closer together than their competitors, and the cleverest allowed themselves to be lost in the shuffle for several rounds, saving their actual throws for when the spectators and judges paid better attention.

Cheating was harder to pull off in the three-legged race, though some of the older, more clueless kids tried. What the event lacked in rule-bending it made up for in anarchy. One race seeped into the next. After a few minutes, a girl sat in the middle of the course and screamed, blood gushing from her nose. That blood only started flowing at this juncture was an improvement on the year before, which had seen not one but three ugly collisions take place during the egg toss. Someone eventually removed the wounded child, and the heats proceeded until a winner was crowned.

"I think the girl who smashed her face had the right idea. Early exit. They're probably lounging on the beach by now. Maybe we can bribe one of ours to run into the other."

Anne didn't laugh at her husband. "You're lucky the twins are too far away to hear you say things like that."

"Honestly shocked we haven't had one of them bawling their eyes out. Braden's usually good for a tantrum on the Fourth."

"Plenty of hours left in the day."

The boys who won seemed a little too big to be competing, but the parents didn't complain. There was no formal prize. The thrill of crushing younger competition wore off quickly as the applause faded.

The final official event was a foot race that started near a gazebo in the center of the green. Jamie questioned how "official" the race really was, given its thrown-together appearance. He thought it was very possible that the race was in fact a last-minute addition by parents hoping to have restful afternoons that had morphed into something larger as kid after kid crowded behind an arbitrary starting point. Refreshments were available, but the lines at the carts mostly consisted of hellions who were quickly reprimanded and told to join the race. They stuffed their crinkled bills back into their pockets and ran over. In and around the gazebo, parents watched and held their too-small-to-race children, trusting that someone else had instructed the kids about where to run and for how long.

It took only a minute or two for the fiftyish kids to break into more distinct groups, but for the first few hundred feet they moved as one, and they yelled at no one and nothing in particular. Most wore at least two of the day's three colors. Those without shoes were smart enough to run on the grass next to the scorching pavement.

As the elite group distanced itself, a few stragglers looked back to see the gazebo still in reach and opted for honorable discharges. The middle groups flailed, but a pack of four emerged as the race reached the far end of the grounds and turned back for the home-stretch. Two of the boys, joints sharp and legs longer than they themselves comprehended, led the way, but a scrawny boy kept pace two steps behind, and a girl, the smallest of the four, strained to match his strides, her short legs taking three steps for his two, her feral blond hair sweating against a bedazzled shirt. The path straightened two hundred feet from the finish line, conjured into existence by two adults and a piece of string dangling between them.

Anne nudged the twins and told them to look up ahead as the little miss surged. She passed the third-place boy with ease. He grimaced as she did and puttered out quickly, slowing to a near-walk. Her burst had her a step behind the leading pair. The one on the left's legs wobbled. The girl recognized his exhaustion. She had almost caught up to him when he zagged to cut her off. His left elbow struck her right shoulder. She stumbled but regained her speed and settled a step behind in the middle of the path. The boy on the right turned back to see her, but their eyes didn't meet. The girl pushed forward to the leader's right. He peeked back and saw the other boy cross into her path. The punk's flared elbow pressed her side, and she tripped, now straddling the grass. The leader slowed to let his left heel drag, occupying his follower's landing space. The boys' legs tangled, and the leader braced himself for the choreographed fall.

The girl hadn't seen the plan in motion. By the time she gathered herself, she was unimpeded, jogging the final thirty feet as parents and kids cheered with newfound brio. She stopped just beyond the crude line and looked back at the boys. The feisty one yelled at the former leader, who looked toward the finish with dry eyes and a thin streak of blood inching down his leg.

Anne strained to see the girl, but parents and friends swarmed around her. One of the twins wandered back toward his grandmother.

"Grandma, what happened? Did someone get hurt?"

"I don't think so, sweetie."

Jamie was already on his way back to the road, waving them along so they could beat the traffic.

10

The Clarkes' Fourth of July party lived in cycles. What had once been a gathering of parents and their high-strung kids was now a more adult affair and would remain so until those kids had children of their own. Some did already but not many, so the party was a little drunker and less focused on fireworks than it had been in Katie and Ryan's first years of attendance. Parents were less concerned about their special little guys and girls drowning or going missing, though the kids behaved worse than ever. Amelia's offspring were the only third-generation attendees. They stayed inside, supposedly napping in one of the guest rooms so that they could be retrieved when the time for fireworks came. Katie was, as far as she could tell, the youngest and clearest-headed person on the deck, from which tables and chairs had been removed to allow for the large crowd, comprised primarily of the hosts' neighbors and friends but also containing some of their children's peers.

Most of the latter stratus carried on conversations with each other but dressed and postured like their elders: upright, eyes constantly scanning for their next partner. They moved quickly between conversations and often in pairs, some platonic and some anticipating pyrotechnics of their own, to be set off in bedrooms they had vacationed in for many years or in little suites someone's parents had included in their modern beach design with the hope that their heirs might visit.

Katie didn't have to socialize to extract the topics they covered.

They spoke of their school days, city lives, and past indiscretions, of which they all remained quite proud. They didn't all know each other, but they all connected to somebody—from Andover or Choate or Deerfield or from one of the acceptable schools into which such preps fed. Once in a while, an adult entered one of their circles, and positions changed. The young men tightened up and strained for eloquence, and the fathers did their best to remember the language of the young and burdenless.

What stood out to Katie, not just on this night but every time she visited or even passed this house, was its light. The grays and whites of the sides and doors glimmered on cloudy days, and the living room with its tall windows pulsated whenever the sun filled it. Even now, without the assistance of those rays, the deck beamed, the white railings freshly painted and the brown of the wood brighter than she would have expected. Light cascaded down from two fixtures adorning the back side of the house, revealing how much time each guest had spent in the sun that week—and validating those who had taken extra time to prepare themselves for the night. The Davises both dressed for these lights, outshone only by their teeth; Mrs. Adelston went through this effort regardless of an event's illumination; Mr. Lynch had no marriage to worry about, but his summer suit's fit threatened three of four other partnerships when wives and husbands gripped his fabulously tan hands and took in his rejuvenated, Crossfit-sculpted frame.

Without looking too hard, Katie could find one of the most disturbing sights available to human eyes: the lonely adult partygoer, the well-dressed aristocrat unable to find the proper conversation. He or she didn't look so different from the teenage version; the party itself tended to resemble a high school dance. The women managed their unpopularity better than the men. They projected cheer and entered powwows; they waved to an ally across the deck, someone who understood their predicament. The men were lost. The savvy ones hung near the drinks, inspecting labels or finishing one off so they had an excuse to stick around and wait for whichever friend found his glass empty and struck up a conversation.

Kevin and his kind tended to float through nights like this, preferring their sangfroid to the formality of such celebrations, unimpressed by the detailed accounts of families' past years that awaited them in any given huddle or at the bar, manned by a rotating cast of talkative gents. Beth sometimes joined in their sardonic analyses, but they took for granted that at least a part of her luxuriated in the festivities. On this night she fully basked in them. She wore a green sundress that had lived for years in her closet, and her coiffed hair made her look seven years younger rather than the twelve or fourteen for which she had hoped.

Mr. Davis didn't work in the health care world himself but had numerous friends who did, in Boston and Washington and at high levels, so he listened intently and commented now and then as Beth spoke while his Mrs. focused her attention on the drink that had been poured for her almost an hour ago, now watered down by melted ice. Mrs. Davis perked up at Mrs. Ledingham's arrival but soon withdrew as her neighbor—both next-door here on the Cape and down-the-street in their central Massachusetts hamlet—entered the fray, asking Beth questions regarding the treatment of drug addicts in her hospital, the questions more philosophical and their follow-ups more intellectual than anyone in this quiet corner of the party had foreseen.

Kevin made some rounds and spoke as infrequently as possible. His wife had found a new cranny and four new sparring partners by the time he happened upon her, drink in hand mostly empty and clearly not her first, her words not quite slurred but delivered a touch goofily to an equally sloshed audience. She wasn't rude when Kevin approached, but the arm she placed around him lacked warmth. She spared no time introducing him. This circle spoke of overdoses and of a Cape different from their own, minutes and worlds away, down the road. Kevin knew these stories and some others closer to home, but he kept quiet and absorbed the conjectures of the group.

Beth offered opinions slightly misaligned with those they had discussed in private, blighted with the aloofness of the others taking part in this unmoderated debate. Kevin thought he was the more sentimental of the pair. It had been that way since they first met. But in moments like these he always waited for Beth to sound off on the unfeeling takes of the moneyed. But she wouldn't. She liked to avoid disruption, avoid upsetting these ostentatious people. Or so she said. Maybe he was the one she tried not to upset. Her current role was too administrative, too dependent on operational efficiency, to demand the level of compassion he fantasized that people in her field carried with them. She let her arm fall from him. A minute later, he slipped away and wandered toward the beer.

The stairs down from the deck led to a flat surface from which one could view the water or supervise children in said water before resuming their descent to a sandy path, one surrounded by brambled grass and head-high bushes until it spit travelers onto the beach.

Katie and Amelia sat above the flat surface, just three steps below the rest of the party. Other than a few of Jamie Jr.'s friends who had ventured down to the water for some heathenous purpose, they were the lowest to the ground of anyone in attendance. Amelia looked up as if she expected the show to start early. Katie held a drink that felt more comfortable in her hand than it had the summer before and wondered what proportion of people ended up drinking with their babysitters, giggling internally at the thought of sitters getting their wards drunk before thinking maybe it was a little dark, even for her private contemplations. For a while, they didn't talk about anything of substance. Katie recited her takeaways from a year at school, and when Amelia struggled to process how old they had gotten, Katie savored the moment—this revelation that the Amelia she had lionized for so long was there, at least for now.

"If I sit here long enough and stay quiet, maybe the kids will just sleep through the night."

"I think you got pretty lucky. They seem way better behaved than most of the kids we see out here on the beach. Little monsters."

Katie still spoke quickly in her presence, conscious of taking up too much of the older girl's time.

"They're the best. Any time you hear me complaining or see me looking annoyed, just know that I know they're the best."

"That's sweet."

"Too sweet, isn't it? I'm such a loser now. I have no life besides them." Amelia stuck out her tongue at herself. Katie remembered the motion well from hundreds of past instances.

Katie looked up from her step, one below Amelia's, and their smiles joined. Most of the natural light had ebbed away, and the deck's fixtures didn't reach this far down, but Katie saw in Amelia the same face she had esteemed all her life. Amelia looked Katie's age, and Katie felt like a child, suddenly jealous of the tots sleeping inside. Amelia's svelte white dress fluttered over her feet. Katie was reminded of what a beautiful bride she had been.

The wedding had been gaudy, the manifestation of Anne's visions and self-assurances. Two hundred and fifty guests on a sweltering September afternoon, decorations and the space itself evoking the type of pastoral life no one in attendance had ever lived. But Amelia had been beautiful, her dress simple despite its cost, her flawless skin unaffected by the heat. She was always comely but was on that day breathtaking. When she took the time to dance with Katie, after the crowd's buzz had started to dim, she whispered, "This will be you someday, with the luckiest boy in the world," and Katie had hugged her, wondering even then if a hard-enough squeeze could transport them to another life, one that looked a little bit like the world in which the day's constructed atmosphere professed to exist.

They could hear the ocean if they let their ears focus in that direction, and for a few minutes they did, until Amelia was almost asleep. Katie rested her head on the wood behind her and inhaled the salt of the air, her mouth drier with each breath. A few houses away, pre-teens blasted the songs of that summer. They screamed the choruses.

Jamie Jr.'s voice carried down to them as he searched for his wandering guests, but some unheard messenger convinced him not to go check on them, and his playful indignation vanished as he turned back. Amelia's eyes had opened at the sound of her brother's voice. They rested upon learning of his retreat.

What did Amelia think of her brothers? Katie was afraid to ask. Amelia was too polite to answer honestly anyway. Amelia could befriend anyone, tolerate any interaction. But Katie assumed she acted differently when it was just family around her, or maybe she didn't. Maybe she just kept them comfortable. She saved them from the most disturbing confrontations.

"Do you think we need to go back up there? I feel like I should be socializing more."

"Maybe. I'm all set. Everyone will just assume I'm inside with the kids. I'm also pretty sure no one's paying close enough attention to notice that we're hiding."

Amelia's face was more expressive than her parents'. Her darting eyes suggested a willingness to make a run for it.

"Yeah, and I think I've done my college is fun spiel enough for a night."

Amelia's tongue shot out again. "Whoops. I sort of made you

88

do it, too, didn't I? Bleh. My parents' friends are all a bit screechy when they're this drunk, and J.J. and his pals are a bit much no matter what."

"I didn't think you guys still called him that."

They didn't, not often, and never to his face. They knew it bothered him because he had told them several times—most notably at a dinner around the time of his college graduation. A few classmates and their parents had joined them for a friendly meal to celebrate their boys. After the third or fourth instance of "J.J." at the table, Jamie Jr. lashed out. His parents and siblings accepted the change in due course, for at a previous, Clarkes-only meal he had made his general desire to act like an adult clear by way of a titanic fit, thrown after he accused Anne and Amelia of condescending to him about the best way to remove a ketchup stain from his tie. Katie had experienced none of this, but the Murrays had caught on quickly when "Jamie Jr." became the preferred nomenclature. Even thinking "J.J." to herself flooded Katie's mind with impressions of him playing on the beach or running home from it, making and evading trouble at the hands of his parents, stopping short of full-on bullying Katie and Ryan and others not out of pity or sporadic empathy but because he understood what he could get away with, a dangerous tool for any kid, one he hadn't lost hold of, one his sister never wanted, one about which his brother had never learned.

Amelia didn't respond. Katie learned from her silence. She could read in her eyes that for J.J. there was still hope for change or maturation. While Jamie Jr. was set in stone, set in his ways, still abusing his power, J.J. would someday think better of it and stop pushing, stop his consequenceless experimentation.

Katie wondered if Eric lived somewhere in his sister's silence or if he ever had. She thought she saw a touch of him. She wanted to ask where he was and why it wasn't here, with them, on the steps.

89

But she was afraid of losing this Amelia, of scaring her back into her shell at the mention of his name, at the first sign of disturbing this little peace that had formed in the shadow of the sea. When would she have the opportunity to speak with this Amelia again if she let or forced her to escape now? But this was, for all intents and purposes, her only chance to remind a Clarke about their pariah, her chance to investigate if they were confident in his well-being or just too uncomfortable to ask.

"I thought I might see Eric here tonight. Ryan has seen him around this summer."

Amelia's affectless response confirmed the family's malaise. Of course Katie hadn't expected to see her brother, and they were both aware that "around" didn't mean close to them or here. Clearly Amelia had been aware Eric was in the area, and sensed what kept him here. She looked down. Katie hoped she might cry and reveal years of discomfort and fear. She had been Eric's babysitter, too. Sometimes she monitored them all together. She let them stay up late, watch movies they shouldn't have watched at such young ages, ask her questions their parents wouldn't answer. Katie searched her eyes for a desire to help, to run and scour the streets for him.

"I don't think my parents wanted that. I doubt Eric does either."

"But how do you know?"

Amelia's discomfort was clear and bordered on visible agitation. Her tongue stayed in her mouth.

"Sorry, I shouldn't pester you about him."

Someone's impractical shoes clacked messily and paused halfway between the top step and the girls. Katie could smell her perfume but didn't recognize her even as she moved out of the way of the light behind her and revealed a face not worth the effort she had poured into it for the night.

"Amelia, there you are. Your mother is looking for you. She

wanted you to meet the Lewises. I think. Something about a college classmate of yours who went to Delbarton. Squash player. Some of the specifics are, um, well. She sent me on a search and rescue mission for you. Or maybe search and destroy your evening."

She slurred the final words and mumbled the last before returning to the party, latching onto a conversation between two men who eyed her approach skeptically. Amelia rose fast and reached out to help Katie up.

"Millie, I'm sorry. I shouldn't have said anything."

"It's okay. He'll be alright, Katie. I'm sure of it."

She lifted Katie and climbed the stairs in one motion. Katie watched her go, then glanced back at the water. Inaudible fireworks danced in the sky, rising from some other town's shore.

Katie climbed the stairs and found herself walking an empty path through the middle of the deck, which was more crowded than it had been all night. A throng, now condensed into rows, pressed against the railing, staring up at the Monomo show. The sound only registered for her upon looking at the crowd, which didn't meet her gaze. These fireworks were of a different kind from both the prior night's and the other towns', paid for by a few private, over-zealous citizens.

The opening caught the attention of everyone on the Clarkes' deck and dozens like it, some filled with adults and others with kids or families but all of them full and looking to the sky. The benefactors had prioritized variety this year, and the show dragged a little in its second act due to a prevalence of fizzing and popping and a dearth of thunderous bangs, for which even the adult decks longed. Katie had stepped forward as the pyrotechnics began but paused ten feet shy of the house and watched them alone, the parted way leaving her three feet from any warm body. The finale put the rest of this and other shows to shame, its reds and blues cacophonous. The crowd around Katie started to mutter, checking if the exhibition was done, but their whispers were soon drowned out by the encore.

They all looked up in expectation of something hard to describe, something they were yet to see. Some returned to the earth faster than others who, resisting gravity, reached and strained to stay where the light was, where the burning was encouraged and, after the last pops diffused, applauded.

Katie wasn't surprised to find her brother and father keeping to themselves in a corner of the deck, the latter listing on the railing and the former sitting on it, each with a near-empty beer in hand. Ryan raised his to welcome her. Kevin's stayed put as he pulled her in with the non-leaning arm. Ryan smiled and pushed himself off the ledge.

She wondered why he would give up his spot, but he tapped her on the shoulder and moved past her, greeting a boy she didn't recognize who had just stepped out from the house.

"Who's that he's talking to?"

"I don't know, Dad. Probably from the club or something."

Ryan's friend texted and talked animatedly. Ryan stole a glance at his father, but he and Katie had turned to look over the barrier, the angles of their leans mirroring each other, racing away from this place.

The friend finished a text, stuffed the phone into his pocket, and handshake-hugged Ryan, holding it until Ryan nodded and held up his hands to suggest he would make his best effort.

"Dad, you mind if I head out?" Ryan bobbed up and down on his toes, flexing his calf muscles.

Kevin didn't even turn, but Katie flipped herself to listen to him cut down his boy. "Probably not a good idea, especially if it's to go get in trouble at Greenstone."

"That sounds like something Mom told you to say."

Now Kevin turned and inspected his son. He placed his bottle on the railing and used the freed hand to pull Katie in for a side hug. He was a cautious father at times but trusted them both. Neither one ever let things get out of control, not like their classmates, not like some of the kids he taught. His parents had never paid much attention to where he was or when he got home, which had been nice at times. He had been allowed to follow his impulses, to indulge in whatever he and his friends found most alluring on a given night. For a long time, he gave in without thinking. He gave in so often, so routinely, that it became difficult not to. To resist an urge was painful, a feeling reserved for the old-fashioned, the imprisoned. He couldn't remember how he had escaped the cycle. He recalled drifting apart from some friends, growing tired of the constant exhaustion and the haphazard sleeping arrangements. By the time his parents sat him down, he had already turned, but he didn't mind their help or its tardiness. It gave him an excuse for when the friends tried to bring him back along, to ignore his trepidation.

"If your sister goes with you, I'll turn a blind eye. That way you two can keep an eye on each other. Or I suppose she can keep an eye on you and drag you out of there if she has to."

Katie groaned and pulled away. "What? Why? This isn't *Taming of the Shrew.*"

Kevin clasped her tighter and laughed while Ryan searched for the humor in his sister's reference.

"*10 Things I Hate About You*? C'mon, Ryan, you're better than that."

"Okay, okay, relax. I get it. I knew what you meant."

"You're the dumbest smart person east of the Mississippi." Katie had used the line many times before. Ryan embraced it. Sometimes he felt it was generous.

He wiped his nose and coughed and flashed her the middle finger of his left hand.

"Katie, don't say that." Kevin feigned an austere look.

"Yeah, Katie, do—"

"He's smart for a dumbass is all."

Father and daughter kept laughing and reclined. Ryan joined in but grew silent as his eyes jetted between them.

"So are you coming?"

"Convince me." She crossed her arms and waited.

Before he could try, she remembered her conversation with Cassie. She would enjoy Mark Hunter's company but would have preferred to make it somewhere other than Greenstone, which she was certain would be crawling with drunk numbskulls looking for a fight at the slightest provocation.

"I don't know, Katie. It's summer, and we're young. Let's have some fun, and we can leave right away if it's a bad scene."

"Bad scene? Is this *Grease*? Whatever, I'll drive you at least, but no promises on me socializing with anyone."

She pushed herself off the railing. Kevin warbled, "*Summer lovin', had me a blaaasst.*"

Ryan spun his arms in an attempt to shush him, but he only hummed softer. "Works for me. Dad, I'll make sure I bring protection and everything."

Kevin stopped humming. "Not funny. Not even in the neighborhood of funny."

"Let me just run to the bathroom."

They left Kevin in the corner, and he looked around for his wife, not overly concerned with finding her. Ryan found his friend and talked quietly on the opposite side of the deck while Katie turned to go inside, her path now refilled with guests. She reached the inside of the house without being pulled into any conversation, which she considered a victory. The bathroom was a sharp left turn away. As she took it, she saw Amelia's profile in the doorway to the kitchen.

Amelia led the conversation, laughing and gesturing to what must have been the Lewises, the white of her dress shining in the bright room, her smile radiant, or maybe radioactive, glowing outward and searing her from the inside.

July 10

If I could do it again I wouldn't leave him there. If I could do it again I guess I wouldn't have done it at all but I definitely wouldn't leave him where I left him.

He moved here in middle school and we weren't mean to him. He was quiet but he wasn't a pussy. High school was worse for him and me. I tried not to be around him.

I didn't expect the blood. It made me feel sick in the dark because it didn't even look like blood and I wasn't fucked up or anything but for a second I thought something else was coming out of him. A spirit or demon. Something that had been trying to escape for a long time.

If things were different in high school for him and me this wouldn't have happened. We might've been friends back then if Lauren Ryder hadn't blown him at a party. That was the first time I punched him. Lauren came running in and told me not to and I thought about hitting her too but my brain didn't make me.

He told me that night and later that week that he didn't mean to fuck with me. I didn't believe him then. But I didn't mean to kill him either so maybe we're even now.

Something that feels like nothing. A little thing that turned into a big thing. Out of my control. That's what I'm telling myself.

11

Katie found Greenstone Lake quite pleasant in the daytime. The water was warm and clear. The beachy area stretched only a few feet up from the pond but was more than wide enough to accommodate four dozen people, and the crowds never got much bigger than that. The parking lot was smaller than it should have been, so people got creative when they needed to, leaving their cars on the edge of the grass or double-parked behind someone familiar. There wasn't anything more exciting than a hawk or deer in or around the water, and even those sightings were rare. Mosquitoes and unremarkable fish were abundant, as were the dogs, but those weren't indigenous.

In Katie's mind, the less populated it was at Greenstone, the better, though even a mess of splashing kids could do little to tarnish the lookout from the sand. When the sun reached a certain point in the sky, its light danced in cartoonish patterns through the trees, leaving shadows on the ground that taunted the dogs. The scenery was best experienced in the fall. The water chilled quickly in autumn but stayed still. The squirrels and birds, before they fled, ran freer once the summer dogs and their people returned home to other ponds, to other trees and leaves, where the sunlight jigged less in shorter days.

On this night, the darkness weighed down the pond and its trees and the people skulking among them. The fireworks were finished. Only a few clouds checkered the canvas, but one settled in front of the moon, which on most nights bathed the water. In these conditions, one wouldn't find the pond until they felt it around their ankles, and the best plan for locating the path was trial and error or a phone flashlight, brightness high.

The path was easy to follow once found. The humans who walked it usually didn't stray, so the dirt was firm and its sidelines well-defined. Most of the roots and thorns fell outside the walk-way. People picked up after their dogs or trained them to go in the denser brush or, as needed, found a stick to flick what needed to be flicked into a bush. A rugged path popped up every few minutes where runners or hooligans had blazed a new trail. The half-paths, easy to avoid in the daylight, were tricky at night, though even if someone started down one they usually realized sooner than later that their walk was no longer following a Parks and Recreation Department-suggested route.

The humid air had let up around the time the fireworks started, so Katie and Ryan rode with their windows down and the radio off, the sound of the occasional car driving in the opposite direction their only conversation. Ryan's friend and inviter, now disclosed as someone named Ethan, had driven his own car. Katie had tried to insist that he ride with them as they chatted in the Murray driveway, at first out of courtesy and then out of a desire to reduce the al-ready-high number of patriotic drunk drivers in the area by one, but as they approached the parking lot she was thankful for his refusal, sure that one tipsy, male twentysomething was enough on her plate.

Katie pulled into the parking lot, its tenants a blend of the three towns that fed it, if the bumper stickers and car types were any indication. She passed two full rows before settling for the grass at the end of the first, the one closest to the water.

Ryan climbed out and waited. Katie didn't move. The car still ran. He tapped on the passenger window. She opened it halfway.

"You're really just going to sit here and wait?"

"I think so. What do people even do here?" She looked straight ahead, keen on expediting his departure and subsequent return.

"Smoke and drink. I think other stuff, too, though. Bonfire, s'mores, I don't know."

"You think someone's making s'mores over there?"

Ryan rolled his eyes. "I don't fucking know. But I'm sure you'll recognize lots of people. Cassie and all them."

"Tell you what. I'm going to stay here. If Cassie's over there making s'mores, you let me know, and I'll go over."

Ryan walked in a small circle and raised his arms. "Have you ever seen a night nicer than this? No way to get in trouble when it's this nice out."

"Just make sure you have your phone on."

She abandoned her pose to stretch toward his window, making sure he heard her and that she shook off any trace of liability for his actions.

"What are you even going to do? It's probably safer to come with me."

"Read, listen to music, abandon you. I have a lot of options."

He turned theatrically and walked toward the water, swaying his hands overhead. Before he reached the path, Katie could see him greet someone she hadn't seen until that moment. She didn't like that she hadn't noticed him. She locked the car again and surveyed the lot for any other surprise entrants.

Katie was cautious to an extent, but more than anything she was skilled at picking the right moments for exercising her independence. "Better safe than sorry" wasn't her mantra, but she did seem to be better at identifying "safe" and recognizing a potential "sorry" than her fellow college students. She didn't fear the dark or the people out there in it, and she didn't even fear getting swept up in whatever nonsense they were producing. Her apprehension came from a place of uncertainty, unfamiliarity.

She wasn't concerned with being cool but also knew she wasn't. At school, she had found friends who shared her social perspective, though she was sometimes pressured to attend the cool event of the day and performed well in such circumstances. At Greenstone, on that night, the cool thing to do was apparent, but without anyone there compelling her to do it, she was free to choose safe over sorry.

The problem, though, was this: although Ryan's words had not been cogent in his sorry attempt to get her to join him, his absence was. He was a level-headed boy but was also not too hard to push around. Katie had been guilty of doing so on a few occasions and had been witness to others doing so on more than a few. He never got into much trouble, but he was also not quite as adept as his sister with regard to distinguishing between the safe and the sorry. She had little interest in dragging him home or hiding his deviant behavior from their parents the next morning. To her knowledge, he didn't drink that often and had only smoked pot a few times at the behest of friends. Some of the Dunes staff members were interested in heavy-hitting materials, and she worried that Ryan might be unable to avoid them if the collective demanded he inhale, ingest, or inject.

Concern was already chipping into her resolve to stay in the car when curiosity smashed it to pieces. Katie grasped what parties looked like in frat houses and at places like the Clarkes', but she wondered what was so appealing about a hangout like Greenstone, not so removed from the world but mysterious enough to keep the unwanted away, too alluring for someone as mild as her brother to resist, tempting enough for her to not abide by the rules she tended to follow. On the other side of the pond, a ten-minute walk away, was something either new or nostalgic, high-octane or Zen. As the seconds ticked away, she realized she wanted to learn more, in either case. She didn't want to be Cassie or the others, but she wouldn't mind at least experiencing whatever feelings they were chasing, the ones that at times seemed so much lighter than her own.

She got out of the car and slammed her door and locked it without looking back. Then for several seconds she stood there, at the top of the miniscule beach, and listened to the wind, waiting for a sign.

The elements refused to impart anything. Katie walked gingerly and turned right toward the path. She checked her phone's battery three times before putting it back in her pocket. She considered using the flashlight but decided the terrain was familiar enough, despite its invisibility. Past family trips had instilled an understanding of Greenstone's fauna: there was nothing to fear unless she smelled skunk. On a night like this, she figured the odor could just mean she was approaching her destination.

The first few hundred feet of the path, the still-sandy ones, ran slightly away from the pond. A creek trickled along to her right in the direction she was walking. She heard only bushes shaking and then, when they quieted, the stream's circulation.

Katie wandered from the path without realizing it, the ground at her feet hard-packed dirt as expected but not cleared. She found herself drifting to the right instead of turning gradually back toward the pond, which her memory calculated was the proper way around. She stood still and squinted into the black, trying to make out the best way forward. The trees convulsed in a reinvigorated breeze. Despite the air's temperature, she let herself tremble. Running back the way she had come didn't sound so bad, but her directional confidence was now low enough to make retracing her steps sound like a chore, at best.

She pulled her phone from her pocket and swiped on the flashlight, but suddenly hushed voices breached her ears, and she clumsily turned it off, dropping the phone in the process. She squatted and swept her hands over the earth, feeling for the device, finding it next to a small rock, its screen intact with a minor crack running diagonally across the top. She waited for someone to come running after her, but the voices continued without any sign of unease. The spot where Ryan and the others were supposedly congregating was still several minutes away, so Katie assumed this was a cabal that had split off from the pack. She didn't want to find out why. But when she heard another voice, now slightly louder and clearly panicked, she crept closer, inching behind a boulder until she could make out hunched silhouettes and the perturbed words they were failing to stifle.

"Don't call him 'it,' man."

"What are you talking about?"

"It's not like a doll or something. It's Tim. It was." The voice shook.

"Okay, fine. We need to focus. We've fucked up enough already."

Katie recognized the last voice and peered around the rock to see if she could confirm its source. Sure enough, Danny Moreland's jagged features matched the accent she had heard and ducked so often at work. He stood tall and paced, his eyes glued to something on the ground, over which two others knelt, their backs to Katie. She smothered a gasp as she realized it was a body.

"Danny, you sure this is the best spot? We're not that far from the path."

"That's the point. This isn't that complicated. Focus."

Danny started to cloak the area around the body, waving to his conspirators to do the same. They rearranged brush as if they were expecting the Viet Cong. Each boy seemed to have differing endgames in mind, one action countering another. Danny scanned the scene again and again, constantly wiping sweat away from his eyes, dirtying his face until it looked like war paint. One of the henchmen sniffled loudly and spat. The other carried a stick aimlessly, letting it drag through the dirt.

"This isn't going to work. He can't look hidden. We need it to look natural, like he, uh, passed out over here. Is his phone in his pocket?" Danny ran his hands through his hair, letting his baseball hat dangle from his left pinky.

One of the crooked figures patted the body down and pulled out a phone. Even in the dark, Katie could sense the queasiness with which he touched the legs and pockets.

"Good. Put it next to his hand there. It'll look like he fell or something."

Danny stepped away from the body and walked in Katie's direction. She dipped low behind the rock and held her breath as sticks crunched under his feet on the other side of the boulder.

"You guys sure no one saw you? Parking lot looked pretty full."

"Definitely. Waited in the car until a couple kids walked away." Danny's associate spoke with more confidence now, but the effort it took to convince himself and his boss was still evident.

As Katie's mind raced, she realized her breaths had become heaves, and she held them again. "Tim" didn't ring a bell. She ran through her options: call the cops or Ryan or her parents, or she could simply make a run for the car and drive until she found someone worth telling. Danny had killed this Tim, or at least watched him die, and he would have no issue adding her to the pile. The magnitude of his crime stunned her, though she couldn't measure it well. She had assumed he smoked and drank and maybe stole and got into situations for which she had no useful schema, but she wouldn't have guessed he was someone who allowed himself to end up standing over bodies in the woods.

She tried to reassure herself. It was an accident. Danny didn't know what he was doing. But he didn't sound afraid, at least not as afraid as she would have liked. Compared to his friends, he was composed, a leader. He knew what had to be done. He seemed ready to adapt to his mangled circumstances, to live well within them. She glanced at the rock and its neighbors, unsure if there was a way to escape unseen.

"Won't his family figure out he's missing like right away?"

"His dad has no fuckin' clue. Probably hasn't seen him in weeks." Danny chuckled at the convenience of this estrangement.

"His mom will figure it out. She knows what he gets into."

"But she won't be surprised. It was just a matter of fuckin' time."

"Shit, man. I can still see him shaking. I just sat there. Danny, why didn't we call someone? They could've done something. They deal with ODs every day. Danny, what the hell are we doing?" The figure fidgeted and waddled away, his silhouette quivering.

"Shut up. Someone will hear you. It's too late for any of that. We've gotta make sure we're covered and get the hell out of here."

Only now did Katie let the fact that she was crouching so close to a dead body wash over her, and she cringed as she pictured a faceless, lifeless boy. She had consumed stories of boys her age succumbing to this fate, stories that fed perceptions of Worona and its people that she tended to believe were misguided. She was normally able to separate her distaste for Danny from the town he happened to call home, but in this moment she was furious that these Worona boys could find no better way to live out their summers than fulfilling every bad stereotype of their hometown. For a shameful moment, Katie experienced a haughty pride in her summer borough and yearned to venture back in time and deride her brother's offer to accompany him here, to the no man's land between these two worlds. She played out every other way this night could have progressed—for her, for Ryan, for the dead boy in the dirt with his phone discarded beside him. He looked younger with each iteration of the image that refused to dissipate in her mind.

"Where do we go now?" One of the henchmen sounded on the verge of tears.

"You guys gotta get back to the car without seeing anybody or anything. No one else knows we were with him." Danny's tone softened as he gave the instructions.

"But then what? Eventually the cops will find us or something."

"What if we went to your parents' thing? If people see us there, that could give us some cover, right?" His voice shook.

"I don't think so. They'll think something's up if they see me." The third voice was softer, tinged with gloom.

"Okay, whatever. We'll figure it out. Just take a quick look around and make sure you didn't leave anything. Then get out of here."

Katie shivered at the croak of Danny's now-rasping voice. He didn't sound wise or hardened anymore; he sounded like a child. This didn't reassure her. He sounded like a child but one racked with a fear strong enough to make him reckless, new enough to make him unpredictable. She tried to visualize her escape: back away slowly while they surveyed the scene, keep quiet until she reached the path, sprint along the path until she was sitting in her car—or maybe lying on the floor of the back seat, where these accomplices wouldn't see her. She would call Ryan or maybe leave without him, and she would speed back to Seaview and wait for morning, or for the kickstart telling her this was all part of some bad dream.

The first step of her plan worked. She was a coordinated girl, and the adrenaline coursing through her focused her movements as she stepped precisely backward, a foot at a time. After eight steps of progress, she felt the swampiness of the air return, and the soundtrack of mosquitoes enveloped her. She swatted indiscriminately to shoo them away, but as she resumed her tread one flew into and past her barely parted lips. She suppressed a gag, but the suppression distracted her from her main task. As she covered her mouth, she toppled to her left. Her arm broke the fall, but her momentum carried her into the beginning of a leafy bush, which rustled at her touch.

"What the fuck was that? Did you see someone?"

"I don't see anything."

"Someone's there. We gotta fuckin' find them. Go. Go now!"

Katie scrambled to her feet and lit out in what she prayed was the direction of the trail, clipping roots and twigs but maintaining her balance as the boys took off from their site in separate lines, oblivious to the exact source of the disruption. She made it to the path but stepped into a hole, only inches deep yet uneven enough to bring her to the ground once more. Five feet to her right, a crepuscular figure stepped out from between two bushes and slunk toward her. She pushed herself backward and crawled, but he walked faster and soon stood over her.

"I didn't see anything I swear I didn't just let me run out of here I pro—"

"Katie, be quiet. Shh, Katie, it's okay."

He squatted to her eye level. Much of Eric's long, curious hair stuck to a face covered in sweat and dirt, but she could see his eyes clearly in the slivers of moonlight that fought their way through the treetops. Her breathing slowed while her heart kept up its tempo. The eyes were too blue to belong to an adult. Once, Katie remembered, one of Anne's friends had passed by on the beach while she and Eric chased Ryan. Anne called her boy over, so the chasing stopped. He shook the friend's hand, a reintroduction, a "My, how you've grown" anticipated but instead replaced with "Look at those eyes. Those will break some hearts when you're older," which even young Katie had marked as bewildering.

"Katie, listen to me. You gotta get up quietly and get out of here. Go to your house or ours and stay there. Danny doesn't know what to do, so he'll do anything. He's freaking out. You understand?"

She nodded weakly and looked closer. Beneath the crud, his face was smooth, as if he had shaved that morning. The teleplay was comforting: him craning in front of the mirror, razor in hand, the closed door protecting him from whatever stood beyond it. She found it hard to imagine him shopping for razors, scanning his options in a CVS aisle or quickly finding his go-to brand, but she liked the picture. She let it move; she watched him pay, leave the store, drive off. But Danny's face soon appeared, and her breath sped up again, jolting her.

"Eric, what happened? You can't—you've got to run with me. I can hel—"

"Katie, run. Go now. I'll be fine. I'm sure of it. Go. Go."

She muscled herself up and brushed off the front of her shorts. His eyes widened as she hesitated, and finally she took off with tears in her eyes and dirt in her shoes, which barely made a sound as her strides became full and less desperate.

Eric let her run for fifteen seconds before jogging back into the trees. He simulated being out of breath and caught Danny's attention with a grunted "Hey" and two loud spits.

"I think I heard them, but I can't see shit. They must have run toward the clearing, toward everyone else."

"We gotta find them, man. We don't know what they saw or what they think they saw."

"We can't. Right now it's one person who maybe saw something. They're probably just confused, Danny. It's dark, and they were probably hammered."

Danny balked at Eric's logic but took a moment to think it

over. "Fine, but we gotta leave. If this person brings us all down, it's your fuckin' head."

He traipsed back to Tim's body and glanced around it one more time before advancing into the thickening forest. In the distance, voices echoed and rose but were thrust back to the ground by the uncaring canopy.

Eric considered running off toward Katie and the cars. Maybe she could cover for him or get him into his house. How would that conversation go? How would his parents and J.J. and Amelia react? He didn't know how the conversation would start but he remembered where it ended—in the same place it always did, only now with greater confidence that his cause was a lost one, that any opportunity to teach him a lesson or show him rock bottom should be seized.

But they couldn't identify his rock bottom. Their version of it involved him slumped on the floor of a dirty room in a strange house with his eyes rolled back and his blood infected. While he had lived out this vision or most of it, it didn't describe his bottom. His lowest place looked much different. Its rock was far harder, which is something they and most people didn't consider because they were so busy talking about how high he had to climb to make it back to them that they never stopped to measure the force of the impact, the damage that would linger when the climbing started and then ceased, when it turned into a newer, faster fall. He wasn't sure if the night he remembered was his rock bottom, but it was certainly low. He had spent it on the beach in front of the house that was now hosting a party, high for some of it but mostly empty and unable to sleep, even when the water had calmed and tried to swaddle him.

He had taken care to park at the far end of the lot upon their arrival. They liked to think he was somewhere far away. He did, too, sometimes. Maybe he was. Distance and proximity didn't matter so much given the devices in their pockets, the ease with which they could track him down. In a way, they would have to travel far to reach him. The tightness of their bubble amplified any movement that ventured beyond it. The bubble traveled with them to pre-approved destinations. It didn't allow for deviations or changes of course. What the bubble allowed shouldn't have mattered, considering their ability to overpower it, to burst it, but they hadn't used that ability in a long time. They feared what would happen if they tried to unleash it now.

To him, far just meant out of reach, so he was far, and they weren't to blame. Something larger than they were was responsible, some amorphous cloud facilitating their apathy, their redirection of attention. He could blame it, and ruminate on its presence, but he wasn't sure how to stop it, or where to find it. It was out of reach.

Katie felt stupid lying on the back seat, resting her head beneath the lock of the door, but she was afraid of Eric's companion, and Ryan hadn't answered her calls or texts. She wanted to leave him but couldn't shake the image of him lying in Tim's place. It made her want to sprint across the water to find him and hold him and bring him home. She called him again and punched the seat at the sound of his pubescent, recorded-eight-years-ago voicemail. She sat up, ready to maneuver to him, but heard voices approaching, their words slipping through the cracked passenger window she had forgotten to close. As two specters crossed in front of the car next to her, the one she used to romp with pointed to something on the water, and they passed without a wayward glance. Katie peered through the slit under the driver's headrest. She could tell they were getting into a car, Eric on the driver's side. The car started but didn't budge. A scream rose in her throat. She wanted to shove the passenger out and tell Eric to flee, to lie low, but they inspected something under the car's overhead light. Katie muttered incantations that had no effect. Three taps on the passenger window startled her, but she muffled her yell before it could escape the car.

"Katie, what are you doing back there?" Ryan smiled dumbly as he peered inside.

"Uh, napping. Trying to rest."

"Unlock the door."

Her shaking hands dropped the keys as soon as they left her pocket, but on the third try she pushed the right button, and Ryan hopped in at the sound of the double-click. He didn't notice how gently his sister opened and closed first the rear door and then the driver's, but her stare once she was seated disturbed him.

"Is something wrong? I probably smell." A few drinks had dulled his speech.

"No, nothing. How is it out there?"

"Kind of lame actually. Not as much going on as you would expect."

She smiled at his artless irony and at his being here, next to her, safe. He seemed no worse than drunk. She had feared belligerence or incoherence and the attention that either would have attracted, but this state appeared manageable. He was nearly asleep. The weight of what it seemed she was still witnessing pressed on her skull and shoulders; the words she wanted to spill needled her. Their disclosure would be permanent and their consequences unknown, so she closed her eyes and resolved to tell him in the morning.

"Why aren't you starting the car?"

"Sorry, zoned out. I'm really tired."

"Isn't that Eric's car?" Ryan looked over his left shoulder as a sedan sidled past, and Katie stared at his straining neck, afraid to see the vehicle in motion. Finally, she allowed herself a glimpse of the car as it reached the road, edging out straight forward, as if the driver wasn't sure whether a right to Worona or a left toward home would be safer. Katie understood that one might be a better choice than the other but that neither way could extricate him from his role in the funereal woods. He turned right and quickly gained speed on the empty road. The car disappeared from view.

She felt some relief at the thought of the car and its passengers receding into the night and put hers in reverse, only to have a petrifying notion slam into her. If Ryan recognized Eric's car, did so despite his state, surely someone else would be able to recall seeing it at the pond that night and tell the police, who would pursue Eric, though she was still unsure of his crime. She backed up slowly and looked behind her, but her eyes played a different drama, one in which Danny was taking matters into his own hands and eliminating his witnesses: Eric's car was splayed on the side of some shrouded Worona road, the two bodies inside lifeless, still warm.

"How could you tell that was Eric's car? Did you see him out there?"

"When I, uh, saw him at the club last month he was driving one that looked like it. I doubt that was actually his. Plenty of guys around here drive their daddies' cars . . . " He snickered and burped in place of punctuation.

Katie waited for more, but he was drifting off with his head against his window, yawning over and over and giving off the impression that he might forget any questions she asked him by morning.

"Did you see him tonight? Out there? Ryan?"

"No, um, I don't think so. But there were a lot of people, and I wasn't really paying attention. We should tell him to come hang at the, uh, beach this week."

"Did you see Danny out there?"

Ryan yawned again, opened his eyes, and stretched his arms into the back seat. "Moreland? No, thankfully. Why? Did you?"

"I don't know. Just seems like his type of place."

"Mmm."

Katie accepted that she was giving a bad performance. She played dumb and did an amateurish job of it, but Ryan was too woozy to effectively interrogate, coherent enough to approach the truth but too sleepy to suspect it lived behind his sister's words. The dark and the drink left him unobservant, or else he might have noticed the dirt on her face, the stray leaf in her hair, and the dismay in her eyes.

As they drove off, farther from Eric with each revolution, Katie wished he would sober up. The weight had partially lifted but only to morph into ropes that tightened her hands on the wheel. She thought maybe she would just keep driving. Once she got out of the car and climbed the stairs and crawled into bed, the sun would rise and make this night real. Each night from there on out would be longer and darker until the transgression detonated a blast that would light the skies over Seaview Road with a contaminated blaze. The resulting fire would persist for generations, until the houses and the beach for which they outstretched their arms became altogether uninhabitable.

12

Katie didn't sleep but stayed in bed until someone called her down for breakfast. She wished she had waited longer when she reached the bottom of the stairs and saw the local news covering a developing story. Kevin and Beth sat at the small kitchen table reading different sections of *The Boston Globe*. Ryan sat between them, eating a bagel with no regard for those who had to listen to him chew.

"What's this they're talking about?" Ryan put down what was left of the bagel.

Thirty seconds into her morning, Katie already regretted not telling him what had happened. He upped the volume on the television, and both parents lowered their papers.

If you're just joining us, early this morning the Worona Police Department was called to Greenstone Lake, where a woman and her dog discovered the body of a young man. Police have released the identity of the victim. The deceased is 22-year-old Tim McNamara, dead of an apparent overdose. Much remains to be learned about the situation, and we will keep you updated as we receive more information. Another sad entry in what has become an alarming trend here on the Cape.

Thank you, Lauren. An alarming trend indeed and heartbreaking for the friends and family of young Tim McNamara. We will stay on this story throughout the day as we learn more. Back after this.

Katie's first response wasn't fear or despair. She was stuck on the woman and her dog, which was supposed to be on its leash around the pond but must have been roaming free in order to smell and find the body. She didn't know whether to be thankful or angry at the rule-breaking. She could no longer picture the clearing without Tim's corpse, though she understood they must have removed it by now and allowed the sunlight that squeezed through the leaves to take its place, splotchy wherever the arborous shadows paused. The woman with the dog probably hadn't even hesitated to call it in once she realized what was sitting there. Katie questioned why she hadn't done the same. But what she would have been calling in other than a death sentence for Eric and Danny and the other boy, all guilty of things that she couldn't enumerate? Eric's presence had affected her, softened her stance, prohibited her from dialing the phone.

"Katie, did you guys know about this? Kevin, I told you they should—" Beth's eyes darted around the room. She smacked Kevin lightly on the arm.

"Mom, nothing happened when we were there. I promise."

"Katie, is that true? You're sure you guys didn't see anything or hear anything?" Beth blinked rapidly.

"Nothing. Ryan's right. And I was napping in the car the whole time."

The lying came to her easily. The measured delivery felt natural, the dulled tone believable. She closed her eyes. Eric's face flashed in front of her, but she held steady as the broadcast returned and captured Beth's attention. Katie lied on occasion but never when the stakes were high, not that she had ever encountered stakes as high as the ones she had stumbled upon hours before. This lie felt right. She didn't want her mother to have access to information that she could so easily misconstrue. She was better off lying. The truth would have given Beth permission to act, to become lead witness for the prosecution of boys conducting themselves in just the way she expected—and on some level wanted—them to.

"God, his poor family. Imagine those parents waking up to this news."

"I wouldn't feel so bad."

All three of them turned to Katie. Lack of sleep combined with the insights of the night made the remark come out cold and short, ripe for any number of misinterpretations. The news anchors saved her from further suspicion.

Again, if you're just joining us, a sad morning after the holiday. 22-year-old Worona resident Tim McNamara died last night of an apparent heroin overdose. His body was discovered three hours ago in the woods around Greenstone Lake. This would be the twelfth documented opioid casualty in Worona since the beginning of last year. Worona police are still gathering information, and Tim's parents, Peter and Meghan, are expected to release a statement shortly . . .

"It's so sad to see places like that struggling so much. It's almost a lost cause. I think people at the hospital feel like we're running out of options."

"It's not like Worona is cursed. It's not just a Worona thing, Mom."

Katie wanted to unleash herself, to reveal everything, not to get the weight off of her chest, but so she could bring the world crashing down on top of her mother. Eric's place in it would be too close to home, too immediate to ignore.

"Katie, you know what I mean."

"I'm not sure I do."

They butted heads on a variety of topics. In Katie's mind, most of the conflicts stemmed from attitudes like the one her mother now expressed—generalized, pessimistic, more bureaucratic than empathetic—and an absolute certainty that Katie's rebuttals lacked validity. On this subject, Katie had listened to Beth spout unfair claims and statistics relating to their western neighbor, as if the towns were closed off from each other, South Monomo in a hazmat suit looking down at the petri dish containing the bungled Worona experiment. She had reminded them more than once about being careful at the club and to stick together if they "consorted" with coworkers they "didn't know as well." She didn't seem to mind the shitty breakability of her code. She wanted them to break it so that she wouldn't have to speak in plain terms. The irony was that her greatest desire was to be like the neighbors at the end of the road because she assumed they lived rich, fulfilling lives that never rubbed up against the coarseness of these news stories. Beth wasn't the only one who spoke in codes. Katie heard it at the club, on the beach, back home in reference to other Woronas. The codes avoided controversy, spoken in various dialects depending on the region but always with the same tone and diction, in short sentences that trailed off. The listener was supposed to infer the idea that had been deciphered a hundred times before, the hidden message delivered again and again, purposefully obtainable.

Kevin hadn't spoken this whole time, and no one expected him to break his silence. A promising student of his had died a few years before after an overdose, someone neither he nor anyone else at school had been concerned about, and he had withdrawn to some dark place after the shock. He had taken a liking to the boy. The parents had reached out to him in the days after he died. They learned he was one of the first people on the gruesome scene, tucked away on a third-floor bathroom after school had ended for the day. They wanted him to know how highly the boy had spoken of him, how much he had enjoyed debate practices in Kevin's classroom. Tim's death had reopened a wound in Kevin, stitched together but inflamed.

Beth turned her attention to her son. "Ryan, did you know this boy? Did he work at the club?"

"No, never met him. Sounds a little familiar, though. I think he might be friends with Danny Moreland."

"Who's that?"

"Just one of the guys at the club. From around here." Ryan wasn't putting anything together, unable to recall any of his sister's peculiarities from the night before. That someone in Danny's circle had met such a fate failed to unsettle him.

. . . *Worona Police are asking anyone with information that could be useful to call the number below. Car tracks found at the scene suggest a vehicle drove into the woods. Police now believe Mr. McNamara's body was moved to Greenstone from an undetermined location after an overdose had occurred. Greenstone is closed to the public today. Again, Commissioner Morton has asked for anyone with information regarding suspicious activity at Greenstone or in the area between midnight and six this morning to report that information. You could be doing both law enforcement and the McNamara family a service. More to come.*

"What does that mean? They think someone was hiding the body?" Gears started to turn in Ryan's mind as he asked the question, but for now their motion stayed beneath his threshold of perception.

"Sounds like they didn't mind someone finding it as long as they found it there and not wherever he OD'ed." Beth's disgust reached a new high as she considered the lengths to which the degenerates had gone to carry out the act.

"So is this a criminal investigation?"

"Not sure, Ry. If someone went to that kind of trouble, they were worried about something serious."

"Katie, did we see anything suspicious that we need to call in? I'm a little fuzzy on the end of the night." He laughed, and Beth smiled, and Katie did what she could to join in, her attempt valiant but imperfect enough for Ryan to detect a flaw somewhere in her manner. She saw a glint in his eye that she was sure was one of recognition, but if it was he didn't confirm it. His laugh died out unnaturally fast.

Katie glided to the fridge and poured herself a glass of orange juice. Her stomach growled, but she didn't trust any food to stay down. She leaned on the counter and sipped while her brother continued to eat. Kevin watched the television silently for another moment before rising and heading outside to embrace the sun's salutation.

"I think we did see someone leaving at the same time as us. Right, Katie? Didn't we see someone acting sketchy or something?"

He looked to her for an answer, and Beth turned without looking at her daughter to better hear the reply. For once, Katie was grateful that her own mother didn't know her all that well, that her role was closer to stepmotherish than friend. She had always been around, present but busy to the point of seeming unapproachable, and though she was never cruel or neglectful, Katie resisted opening up to her. Beth had no counterattack. It stung at times, not having a mother waiting with open arms to bounce questions and problems off of. It didn't sting now. The lying was barely even lying. Katie spoke forcefully into the ear Beth had positioned to better listen.

"There was another car that left right when we did, but it was just a couple guys who had been hanging with all the other people like you."

"Did we know them?"

"I couldn't tell. They seemed normal, like they were having a good time. Maybe not as good of a time as you were."

Katie delivered this line of her script credibly and laughed at her brother, who blushed but smiled. Beth shook her head while her shoulders heaved in a short bout of repose, both mother and son happy to hear that he had enjoyed his night without causing any trouble for himself or his sister.

. . . That's Lauren Cranston reporting from Greenstone Lake, where police continue their search for evidence relating to the death last night—or early this morning—of Worona resident Tim McNamara, the latest in a series of opioid-fueled tragedies on the Cape and in Worona, specifically. Every year, dozens of young people flock to Greenstone on the night of the Fourth, and last night was no different. We've spoken with several children and young adults who spent time at the pond last night. They all agree: Tim McNamara was not among the crowd there. Police believe his night began somewhere away from Greenstone and ended in a clearing in the woods there. They want to know where it began and what transpired in the hours leading up to and following his death. They are asking for your help, whether you were one of the people at Greenstone last night or if you have information regarding the whereabouts of Tim and known friends and associates in recent days and hours. We have the end of this story, and it is a tragic one, but here's hoping we can get the full picture in short order so that this family and community can grieve fully and properly. A sad day for Worona, for the Cape, for the state of Massachusetts, and for the McNamara family. They've lost a son and a brother. Our thoughts and prayers go out to them today. Back after this.

Only then did Katie grasp Tim's cause of death. It wasn't surprising. Danny and the boys had mentioned it. How else would a boy like Tim find a way to die in a place like this? But it hit her then. She had known before. Maybe it was obvious but too painful to consider:

Eric was using, too. She had held out hope that he was living clean or close to it in his exile. She hadn't seen him use or heard him admit anything, but now she knew, and she steamed at the thought of how easy it might have been to pull him away with her. They could still be driving. By now they would have been out of reach.

July 11

I like getting high alone but I don't like waking up without someone to talk to. Makes the timing hard. Depends on how high you want to get too. Sharing weed is fine. Sharing a pot high is natural I think. But the other stuff I like alone.

I didn't like when my mom said we could get high together in high school even though she knew I smoked pot and sold the stuff. And she still did it from time to time. It wasn't that bad when we did it but she was so quiet and then she never said anything about doing it again. She just told me to be careful.

She and my dad were together when they were young. I never asked them how they ended up together or why they stayed together and now I don't think I ever will. I was saving those questions for when I had a girl that I thought was worth asking them for advice about. A girl at the club or something. Someone easy to get along with. That's all my parents wanted was to get along with each other. They're better at it than they used to be. I never would've guessed they'd still be together now. Not sure what together even means now. I think they pick their spots. Choose their battles. They said that a lot. Choose your battles. Not everything's worth fighting over. Some things are. They agreed with me. Just not on what those things were.

The girls worth asking them about don't want to be around me. By now they've all moved or found guys. I'd have a hard time getting them interested. They'd be able to see the darkness. I don't know if I can hide it.

We assumed someone would find him. We didn't talk about it while we put him in the woods but we guessed it wouldn't be long. Still it happened so fast.

I swear one of the local news guys was smiling while he talked about it that next morning. About the lady finding him with her dog. I guess the dog started barking.

The other two need to be smart. Can I trust them to be. Not with something like this. They're sensitive. If I didn't like both of them I'd call them something worse.

It's not that what I did hasn't hit me. It's more like some days it hits me and some days it lays off. I've had feelings like that before. Fixes.

It didn't hit me today until she asked about Eric. She's quiet. I don't think she acts like she's better than me but I guess now it's pretty clear she is. That's not that tough. But it felt like a confrontation.

I don't think this is going away quietly and I don't think I can either unless I want to go away like go away for good. They pretty much told me the same thing the night we did it. When we were driving. Before we switched him to the other car. That night I wasn't listening. I was acting. Does it make it better than I didn't have time to really think about what was going on.

I don't know why she wants to talk to Eric. She doesn't seem like a threat. She doesn't seem like she ever gets into any trouble at all. But more people talking to Eric means more chance that he tells someone about what we did. More chance he falls apart. If he hasn't already fallen apart.

I can't have that.

13

The first few days without Tim McNamara in the world passed quietly for those who didn't turn on the local news, which had nothing better to cover. The week after the Fourth was always a little quiet. This year was hotter than most. For some reason the sea breezes hibernated, and for a few afternoons rainstorms promised to cut into the unabating humidity but backed off in the gloaming.

The Murrays had no air conditioning in the house, so no one slept well, least of all Katie, who woke each morning that week with a headache and her shirt clinging to her while she stuck to the bed. She was able to separate herself in order to get water and to see her brother combating the heat by dressing down to his boxers as he roamed the halls and staked his claim to the right end of the couch, next to a large fan.

Katie detected South Monomo slowing down as the days passed. People settled in for the heart of the summer. Most of them were too worn out from their lives and families to devote energy to Tim McNamara. He came up in passing conversations here and there, usually prompted by the television screen or the smaller-every-day section of newspaper running updates on the case. Some beachgoers noted the details of his story more than others, either out of boredom or attempts to connect their beach reads to this real-life mystery. The majority didn't pay much attention to the local news while they were on the Cape, and the neighbors and friends who did weren't enough to motivate them to change their comfortable ways.

If ignorance was blissful, disconnection was heavenly. Something like that, something that would make for an amusing bumper sticker, if they would even consider putting one on the Audi. A fridge magnet, perhaps.

On Thursday Katie read in her cart, unpartnered and uninterrupted. She missed Cassie's distractions. The weather made for good business but also kept some players away from the course entirely, especially those over the age of sixty who deemed themselves health risks whenever the mercury crept so high. She was surprised to find this Thursday morning that, as she slid her bookmark into something she had only skimmed the first time around when she read it for school, only a third of the book remained. She looked up to see if the three women walking down the seventh hole had picked up the pace as she sipped from an Arnold Palmer that had lost its cool.

One of the women waved but only to say hello, and Katie pulled away. She drove for a few minutes. In the ninth fairway, two of the men chatted by their well-struck balls while their partners stood on opposite sides of the short grass, shin-deep in sand traps. Katie recognized the man in the bunker on the right but couldn't remember his name. He smiled at her after advancing his ball, motioning that he would grab a drink later in the round. The man in the left bunker was flustered by the position in which his first attempt at escaping the sand had left him. He hacked again and this time made it to the fairway. Katie drove ahead to the green while the group carried on, anticipating a break in the cool bag room now that she had offered her services to every group on the front nine. All four men ordered beers and Gatorades, a combination she silently judged, and two left tips, their bills crinkled and damp.

A mess of carts and caddies loitered outside the bag room, which was bordered on one side by the pro shop and on the other by a small concession stand that went largely unused. If the cart malfunctioned, Katie or her equivalent would do their work from the stand, but this was an inconvenience for many members and an absolute annoyance for a handful, the same handful who three years ago had ensured that enough money was available to purchase a cart of significantly higher quality than its predecessor.

The caddies came in all shapes and sizes but usually looked more sunken after a summer of carrying bags, which at the Dunes were often oversized and filled with the members' keepsakes from well-known courses around the country. On days like this, sweat hid the scripted MD logo on their green bibs. Graham, who ran the caddy program, let anyone over thirteen give the job a shot, so most seasons the troops included a dozen eighty-pound waifs whose eyes bugged at the sight of their fifty dollars at the end of each round. The young caddie corps thinned by this time every summer. Ulysses S. Grant's face wasn't as exciting the eighth or ninth time around when the days were warmer, the rounds longer, and the players less interested in your life story. The caddies who did stick it out worked their way into Graham's good graces and learned many life lessons from the older loopers about how to make the most of one's summer on the Cape as a teenager with limited responsibility and lapsing supervision. On July days like this one, the younger ones lingered as they waited for rides or cooled off before hopping on bikes toward the next great adventure.

Katie didn't mind the wandering eyes of the younger caddies, who were hormonal and easily intimidated. The braver ones squealed "Hi, Katie" when she passed them, and they all knew to avoid Ryan's wrath, which on two previous occasions had come in the form of a report to Graham leading to a swift removal from the program. The gazing of the older caddies was harder to take but also more difficult to confront, so she mostly kept away from them and snapped at them once in a while to keep them honest.

She had never snapped at Danny, not that he wasn't sometimes deserving. He was dangerous, had been even before she saw harrowing proof. She assumed most of them would never hit back at her, would never persist once she spoke her mind, but she quailed at what Danny might do, at how he might react. How sure was he of his invincibility?

Six or seven caddies, some still bibbed, stood at the high-tops next to the concession stand, and another one stepped out of Katie's way as she pulled the cart into the bag room. She parked, already dreading her return to the course. To the right of the carts sat Graham's desk, its surface covered with tee sheets, notes for club cleanings and tee-time cancellations, and a small lost-and-found bin. Graham was outside chatting with a member by the putting green, laughing dutifully at a story about a match played the week before in Brewster. Ryan sat at the desk wearing his bib, his hat turned backward and marked with spikes of sweat, and talked with Danny, who leaned against the table and swung a sand wedge someone had left behind, letting his wrists act as a pendulum, keeping the club half an inch from the floor.

Ryan didn't consider Danny a friend, but he was at home in the bag room. In there he was sure of himself. In there Danny's tales and threats sounded harmless. Danny had acted the same as long as he had known him, simultaneously superior and sticking his nose into everyone's business as an excuse to share his own stories. When they were young caddies, the stories had been hyperbolic, sometimes entirely fabricated, in an effort to impress the others. Now they were grisly and meant to intimidate. Danny liked Ryan, Ryan thought. Regardless, he was used to the antics and vulgarity by now. But lately Danny had been quieter than ever, almost subdued for the last few days. With someone else, Ryan would have considered probing, checking if everything was okay, but he was sure that would set Danny off. He inferred Danny had some problems, family and otherwise. They would blow over, and Danny would be back to harassing everyone soon. Sometimes he pocketed younger caddies' money, just a portion of it, if they had carried bags in his group. "Instructional fee," he called it. "You gotta pay to learn from the best." Two members yelled playful jeers at their opponents from the doorway.

"No, I gotta go. You doing another loop?"

"Yeah, Mr. Blair and his son. I don't think the son plays at all. You sure you don't want it? Extra cash for the weekend." Ryan leaned back in the chair, pushing his words toward the ceiling, where the crusted pipes looked untrustworthy.

"Hard to say no, but I have to run. There's a service or, uh, reception thing I'm not fuckin' sure at the McNamaras' house."

"Oh, geez, of course. So sorry to hear about that, Danny. Sounds like he was a good friend."

Danny shrugged off the condolences. "Thanks, man. It's nothing big. I knew Tim, but we weren't close or anything. Didn't see too much of him to be honest. Just going as a courtesy."

By now Katie was close enough to hear them clearly, and she flared at Danny's lie. Visions of the night in the woods had gnawed at her for three days, but until this point she had quashed any urge to tell the police what she had seen. Now she thought of how easy it would be, of how quickly she could step outside and call the cops without Danny even noticing, of how she could do so and then step back in and distract him until the squad cars pulled in and took him away. She pressed her hand against her phone in her pocket and imagined dialing the numbers, but she doubted how smoothly her plan would work. Reporting Danny would drag Eric back in.

She didn't know what trouble awaited him or whether he was on some level deserving of it. She wasn't even sure she herself was all that innocent, given her indirect harboring of a fugitive or two or three. She had the names of two of the people who were presumably among the last to see Tim McNamara alive and were possibly responsible for his death and were definitely responsible for it playing out in such a loathsome manner.

Three young caddies bounced a ball between the clubs they held low to the ground. It squirted away. Katie rolled it back to them with her foot.

"Hey, Katie, how's it going?"

She smiled at him. "All good. Sorry, I should've said something sooner, Danny. So sad about Tim. I never met him, but it sounds like he was a wonderful person."

He hung his head at the sound of the name, and for a second she forgave him.

"Yeah, it's okay. A lot of guys around here just get pulled into that life. Really sad. He's had some struggles from what I hear."

"Had you seen him at all recently or anything? Must be hard to have him just, um, go." She tried to study his face, but he looked straight down.

"Nah, been a while. He's always been a nice guy, but I try to stay away from a lot of that crap. Tim didn't run with the best crowd, if you catch my drift."

"I think I do." Katie spoke with an uncareful edge but masked it with a somber nod, and Danny stood up straight, using the club as a cane for a moment before leaning it against the desk and slapping Ryan's hand goodbye.

"It's just crazy to think. Like we were there that night, at Greenstone, me and Katie. Just like a regular night, but meanwhile all that shit is happening to Tim in the woods."

Danny's hand stayed in Ryan's a second too long before he stepped back and alternated glances between the siblings. Katie held a stoic gaze, arms crossed, drink dangling from one hand and its cap from the other.

"You guys were there on Sunday? The night it, uh, happened?"

Ryan spoke with a mix of excitement and misplaced pride. "Yeah, for a bit at least. I'm honestly a little fuzzy on it, don't remember much. But I don't think anyone had a clue what was going on. Seems like it must have happened after everyone left. I'm not sure. Katie probably knows the story better than I do."

Ryan's lack of detail reassured Danny, and he turned to leave, stopping short of meeting Katie's eyes as he said "Later, Katie" and moved through the shade.

"Hey, Danny." She squared herself up.

"Yeah?"

"Random question, but do you have Eric Clarke's number? I'm trying to get him to come to this dinner with our family and his, but I'm afraid to ask his parents or J.J. They don't get along so well. Ryan said you've seen him."

Katie wasn't sure why she asked. It would make her look suspect. Danny would play dumb. She could get the number from someone else, likely Ryan. But she did want to talk to Eric, and she wanted Danny to feel some heat, just for a split second, even if he then decided her question was a coincidence. She didn't want him to identify her as a threat. But she wanted to see him vulnerable. She wanted to make sure she could bring him down if it came to that.

She thought he would spend the rest of the day wondering if he had covered his tracks, if there were any loose ends remaining. She liked the idea. Who knew what Danny had done, if she had witnessed all of it, or if he was hiding something more grotesque?

"Sorry, don't think I have it," and he walked away, his khaki shorts stained with the morning's perspiration and the backs of his calves burned where he had failed to reapply.

Ryan spoke to her back. "Katie, I have Eric's number. Why do you need it?"

"I need to talk to him."

14

The Murrays and those like them had little reason to visit Bayside Beach, which sat a couple of miles down the canal and was covered in rocks. The distance and terrain made it appealing to Katie. She had told Eric to meet her there.

She hadn't been to Bayside in years. Their uncle, Kevin's brother, had liked to fish there before moving on to better spots. Kevin humored him. Sometimes Katie tagged along to make sure they threw the fish back, but they never caught anything worth keeping.

To reach Bayside, Katie rode her bike—Ryan had left early for work with the car—on streets she didn't know well, passing people who didn't recognize her as she skirted their driveways, many of them dirt or gravel in front of houses that were camouflaged by their similarity to one another. The heat hadn't subsided, but clouds filled the sky, to which the parched brown grasses and wilting flowers looked in desperation as she rode.

It was still light enough to see when she reached the beach, but darkness waited on the edge of the visible spectrum. She hadn't devised an excuse for getting home so much later than normal. Both parents had texted her within the past few hours, but neither had expressed concern regarding her whereabouts, and Ryan had gone out with John.

She sat on a large, smoothed rock, her bike resting next to her on a sandy patch, and wondered if Eric would even show. She had been vague in her messages but hoped she had still managed to convey urgency. This avatar of Eric was an unknown. She had no idea how he had spent the days following his friend's death, or if he considered him a friend at all. The entire basis of this rendezvous, of her attitude toward him and the situation, was the twenty seconds they had spent scrabbling around in the woods five days before, when he could have handed her over and didn't, when he had maybe been high or close to it but had still seen clearly enough to protect her. Everything she surmised about him now came from the family members who ignored his existence, so she knew very little, she realized, and she had no reason to trust him to insulate her or himself other than the tone of the voice she had heard in the forest, the voice that belonged to someone who wanted out of whatever he was caught up in. The tone had sounded strained but—and she now hoped this was a veracious memory and not an edit made by her brain—resilient.

Still sitting, she closed her eyes. The recollection came without warning; she let it proceed. The images were fuzzy at their edges, but Eric came into focus as he approached her. She sensed Ryan next to her, but he looked away and wandered to the edge of the parking lot, steps from the beach, while she waited for their neighbor. She had seen Eric linger at his front door, seen him listen to someone out of sight, but she hadn't heard a thing. He tried to walk past her, to signal that they should catch up with Ryan. She watched him avoid her gaze. He turned slightly away, but she could still make out a fresh cut on his lip and a smudge of blood below it. He called for Ryan to throw a football his way. The throw forced Eric to pivot toward Katie as he made the catch, and she took in the full view. He bit his bottom lip to obscure the cut, but he couldn't hide the redness around his eyes. She was young, maybe eight, but she recognized when eyes had cried, when hands had tried to rub away the evidence. He sniffled and swallowed before he looked at her and blinked.

"Are you okay?"

"Yeah."

He threw an awkward spiral back to Ryan but slowed down to walk beside her. She figured he must have fallen or taken some roughhousing too far. His parents hated when his siblings goaded him into bolting around the house.

"Do you believe me?"

"What?"

"Do you believe that I'm okay?"

She nodded and watched her toes wriggle against the straps of her flip-flops, almost ready for retirement after a summer of wear and tear.

"I'm strong, Katie. I can stick up for myself."

She was sharp enough to notice the tone he took on, the effort he made to sound convincing, but too young to make anything of it. The football flew toward them again. This time she caught it and quickly punted it back in the direction of her brother. It flew over him and into a circle of chairs.

"Nice one."

"I didn't know I could kick it that far."

"You're strong, too."

She still wasn't sure what to think, what to make of his tone or the words inside it. But he seemed to believe what he said, and that was enough.

He jogged ahead and took a sharp left turn to chase Ryan. At first Ryan evaded him, tiptoeing away from a tackle. Eric stumbled but regrouped, and within a few seconds they were colliding, then falling into a heap in the sand. Katie watched them get up and race to the water.

The more she chewed it over, the more she trusted Eric's ability to look out for her, but she doubted his ability to monitor his own well-being. He had always been that way. As the youngest in his family there were times when no one else needed protecting, or when no one thought of him as the one to look to for protection. Those were the times when he was lost, when he idled, responsible only for Eric.

Katie stood by the water, each sneaker on top of a jagged peak, when Eric arrived twenty minutes after they had planned. They hadn't discussed what to do if someone else was around, if another car rolled into the lot while they talked, but for now his was the only one. He smiled as he wove through the rocks toward her, his face unshaven, the beard uneven and denser in the neck, his hair unwashed but recently brushed.

"Thanks for meeting me. I thought it would be good to talk face to face."

"I was pretty surprised to see who the message was from. I thought you might just keep running after Sunday night. Wouldn't have blamed you."

He sounded wistful. He looked unaffected by his surroundings, like he hadn't listened to a new song in years and was better for it. He walked like he had already made up his mind about his future, about his complicity in the events at Greenstone.

"What did you three do after you saw me?"

He knew why she had texted him. Still, he had hoped she had somehow forgotten that night. "Nothing. That was the end of it."

"Have you talked to the other two?"

"No, we agreed we should all lie low for a bit. Figured it's better to stay out of each other's way, avoid freaking each other out. I don't know, might be a shit plan."

Eric kept his sandals on as he walked into the water, letting it reach his knees. He looked pale next to Katie's bronzed arms and legs. His long-sleeved tee's logos were worn out. It clearly didn't fit him as well as it once had, and he had pushed the sleeves halfway back on his forearms. He didn't mind the water splashing the fabric and clinging to the blond hairs on the backs of his hands. Two seagulls jousted over food on the beach. He looked their way while Katie spoke.

"Why don't you just tell the police? You didn't do anything wrong, right?"

"I don't think it's so simple, Katie. I think that might get us into trouble."

She was afraid to pry but could sense him holding something back. He was protecting someone, maybe her. She hoped it wasn't Danny, or if it was that he had a good reason. The water's undulations crept up to the middle of his Under Armor shorts. He dipped his hands and ran them through his hair.

"Why do you even hang around with those guys? They were bound to get you into crap like this eventually."

"You sound like my mom. Or your mom."

He was right, and she hated it, but she also hated what she had seen in the woods, and she hated how gaunt his face looked, how its color matched that of the overcast sky. She hated how sure she was that the long sleeves were there not for warmth or style but to hide track marks. She found herself more upset with him hiding them than with their existence. The hiding was clear evidence that he was ashamed, and he didn't deserve to be.

"I don't mean they're trashy or anything. It's just, well, Danny's a bad guy. I've been pretty sure about that for a long time."

Eric tripped and splashed as he jumped out of the water and toward Katie, grabbing her by the shoulders and scanning the beach beyond her, as if Danny waited somewhere in the dunes, his hair blocking one eye until he brushed it away with a well-trained hand.

"How do you know Danny? You saw him? How do you know his name?"

"H—he works at the club. I know him. I, uh, recognized him. Ryan sees him all the time."

Eric let go. He shuffled his feet back to the water, retrieved the stray flip-flop that had come off as he scrambled.

"Right. Shit. I don't know how I didn't think of that." He let the water reach his feet but went no further.

"Katie, I think we just need to move on."

"Maybe, but I can't just go home thinking that you're still in trouble. I need to know you have a plan."

"I'm not in trouble. Look around when you get home. Everyone is moving on. Tim's a—he's a distant memory. No one's out there looking for anything on it anymore. He's just another dead junkie on the Cape. It's not some crazy mystery. I'm not America's most wanted man."

Hearing the dead boy's name from these lips reactivated every morsel of guilt and shame she had tried to tuck away. "You knew him well?"

"Yeah."

He looked her in the eyes, through her. She remembered a birthday party at the beach, eight or nine years before, what must have been Ryan's given the summer celebration. Some invented game in the sand, Eric tackling Ryan but taking Katie down with them. Anne's voice, level but piercing. Eric helping her up, apologizing without being told to.

"What happened?"

"They've pretty much got it right. Friends get high. One overdoses, so the other guys panic and move the body. People find body. Town mourns. Town moves on."

He picked up two rocks and weighed them against each other.

He dropped the lighter one. They watched it plink into the water. He ran his fingers over the surviving stone, and Katie waited for him to skip it.

"There's more to it than that."

"Not really. Sorry to disappoint. Like I said, it's simple. Sad as hell for sure, but, you know, so it goes. Or something."

He dropped the rock, almost a throw. Its entry noise was louder and echoed longer than its forerunner's.

Katie watched the ripples for a moment but managed to regain her strength. "You wouldn't have agreed to come here if you didn't have more to say."

"I agreed to come here because you're a friend and because I want to make sure you're not bugging out or something about what you saw. You shouldn't have to be involved in any of this, Katie."

"I'm still not sure what I saw."

"C'mon, I'll give you a ride home. Tour of the old neighborhood. We don't need to stand around out here."

He didn't wait for her reply. She questioned if her bike would fit in the car, but as she neared it she saw a rack and remembered how much Eric had liked to ride as a child, always the first to suggest it when other beach activities had run their course or when the weather worsened and their unripe minds thirsted for speeding through the rain. She could halfway picture what must have been the last ride she and Ryan had shared with Eric, one that came a thousand summers before, at dusk after a shouting match on the Clarke porch.

When they were little, he had ridden more confidently than his neighbors, more sure of his abilities and more trusting of the cars that passed them. Katie had usually played the role of time monitor when Eric rode with them because he hadn't minded the dark or his parents' scolding. J.J. and Amelia had never biked much, as far as Katie could remember. Maybe Amelia had when she was younger, but she was busy with other things by the time Katie was old enough to keep up, and she never sought out a spare hour with J.J., especially one away from the friendly confines of home.

He unlocked the car and tossed some wrappers into the backseat.

"I really don't mind riding home. The streets are pretty empty."

"I don't think it'd be very safe. It's going to be too dark for cars to see you soon. Not going to leave you and find out you ended up smashed in the middle of the road. I'll drop you off a couple blocks from your house."

"I'm not embarrassed to ride with you or anything."

He paused, then laughed.

"Well, that's good. I'm not embarrassed to ride with you either. I just don't want to run into my parents. Neither should you."

He strode over and took the bike from her, walked it to the back of the car, and stowed it. His familiarity with the rack made her think he must still ride. Did he do so with the same unfettered motion he had possessed when they were young?

They rode most of the way in silence, and it struck Katie that their meeting hadn't provided her with any new information about any of the parties involved in Tim's death, and she was sure Eric contained more than he would say. But she felt comforted by him, confident that his perspective, which so painfully didn't square with that of his parents, was a judicious one for a scenario like this, one that Jamie and Anne would have refused to face.

There was fear in his eyes, but it was too dark for Katie to see it. It was the same fear, all grown up, he had worn when they rode beside the canal in seeping darkness, loving the wind in his hair, dreading the yawps and strikes of his parents.

July 25

We used to play a lot of basketball during the summer. I don't think we were ever as good as we thought. The outdoor courts at Regional were nice but it wasn't worth the trip unless we knew we had a game set up. Usually we ended up at the courts near my house. One of the hoops was good. One wasn't.

Paul Saunders could dunk in ninth grade but he was a dumbass. The rest of us all wanted what he had but then he barely played at Regional. I think he quit before his senior year.

I went over there to shoot a couple days ago but it felt wrong. It's hard to tell which hoop is the good one now because they're both sagging and the rims are unforgiving.

Going to the Regional games was a good time when we were there.

My hands aren't shaking as much.

15

"What time did they start?" Anne examined her watch, a garish silver thing Jamie had given her for a birthday in some other decade.

"Kevin left around seven thirty, but I'm sure he was planning for extra practice time. He was afraid of making a fool of himself in front of your boys." Beth didn't mean to enjoy her husband's insecurity so much. The words left a sour taste.

"I think their tee time was eight fifty. They probably still have a bunch of holes left." Katie understood the course and its rhythms better than the older women.

Kevin and both Jamies were playing a round at the Dunes. A friend of Jamie Jr.'s filled out their foursome. Kevin was a competent golfer but didn't play often, and he dreaded the possibility of playing terribly in front of Jamie Sr. Impressing him would earn Kevin an invite back and make him feel a little closer to belonging whenever their conversations on the porch or beach turned to golf. On the other hand, Kevin didn't care much for Jamie Jr. or his showy friends and thus wasn't concerned with their reactions to his play.

As their wives and daughters speculated, the older golfers were in fact playing quite well. Jamie was in line for his best round of the summer. Kevin had started the day nervous, worried about his clothes and his technique after a disheartening session on the range, but a handful of pars on the front nine left him swinging more freely. He knocked in a fifteen-footer on the eighth hole and fist-bumped his host, who was also serving as his partner in a match with the younger boys. It had remained good-natured for three of the competitors, but for Jamie Jr. the frustration of his round prevented him from expressing any goodwill toward his teammate or opponents. A missed putt from five feet on the eleventh green led to his third club slam of the day, this one with the putter. He tended to swing harder as a round spiraled away from him. By the time they reached the twelfth tee, hitting the fairway was out of the question; by the time they reached the fourteenth, he and his friend were delaying the group as they flagged Cassie down for another round of the day's choice concoction.

"They gave you today off, Katie?"

Katie thought Anne sounded a little more real in this setting, like she had been able to shed a few caked-on layers of pretense since her holiday get-together.

"Yep. They try to give us a couple days here and there depending on how busy it is. There's another girl driving the cart today."

"And Ryan's out there caddying?" Anne adjusted her sunglasses as she spoke, fiddling with them until they sat exactly as they had before she lifted her fingers.

"Should be, but not for those guys."

"Believe me, that's for the best. Kevin doesn't need another set of familiar eyes watching him swing today. I think he was watching videos last night to work on his form."

"Does Ryan play? Should've had him play with them."

"No, doesn't play much. Just likes the money and the exercise." Beth spoke with some level of admiration for her son.

"Not the worst two things to like."

They sat on the Clarkes' back porch and enjoyed the cloud

cover. Bagels and muffins sat in baskets on the table. Only Amelia and Katie had touched them, and the former had taken only half of a blueberry muffin, which sat mostly uneaten on her plate. The beach below was already crowded, as they expected on a July Sunday, but the direction of the wind shielded them from the sounds of families cavorting. Katie tried her best to not participate. Both mothers' voices grated on her. Nate and the kids were riding bikes or doing something else that kept them away.

"Katie, did you hear Anne's question?"

"No, sorry. Was listening to the water. Mind's wandering."

She tried to recall the last sound she had heard, but her mind was blank. She saw white and made out only a soft ringing.

"That's okay. I said did you know the boy who died at all? The one who overdosed at Greenstone?"

"Oh, no. Never met him."

Katie hadn't been listening to the water, but she had zoned out as she heard the conversation near this topic. Her mind had drifted but proved unable to find a suitable distraction, so she simply fumed, angry at herself for still being dragged down by this story but also angry at them for discussing it in the way they did—as an afterthought, a breakfast accessory, a back-up plan when other wells ran dry.

Anne wasn't as bad of a gossip as many of the adults Katie dealt with at her parties and the course, but for now she sounded like them. "I haven't heard any updates on him. They must not have been able to find more information. It never seemed like they had the full story. Poor boy."

"Do you even remember his name?"

"Pardon, Katie. What was that?"

Anne had heard the briskness of the question but was slow to perceive Katie's indignation, the redness of the girl's face perhaps obscured by the tint of her eyewear.

"Do you—"

"Katie, don't talk to Anne like that. We're just having a conversation."

"His name was Tim McNamara, and he died in the middle of the woods because no one cared if he did or not."

Katie watched as Anne and Beth inhaled quietly. Amelia became reinterested in her muffin, the only one of the three to intuit who Katie was really talking about, at least the only one to let on at first. But Anne got it. Katie saw it creep into her face. She was simply skilled at conveying blankness with the timing of her batted lashes, her calculated half-squint to the horizon. Katie could tell her mother was on edge but potentially oblivious, her tenseness a direct result of her daughter's forward talk. Katie had watched her spend two decades so determined to belong on porches like this one that she had trained herself to push aside the people or topics that didn't. It was, evidently, fashionable to discuss the crisis from time to time, but Eric was something else entirely, an aberration. Beth wouldn't speak of him until her host did. Katie's intrusion wasn't a proper invitation, and Beth wouldn't treat it as one. Katie sensed that she had made her feel responsible for putting this fire out, for ensuring that her girl didn't spoil brunch for the Clarkes.

"I'm sorry, Katie. You're right. We should take time to think about him and his family more. It's such a shame how, well, not rare these stories are over there." Beth's nerves caromed between each word.

"Over there? What do you mean, Mom?"

"Worona. It's been a big problem there for many years now, Katie." Anne thought she was helping by jumping in, but the sight of the outrage in Katie's eyes floored her.

"It's not just there." Amelia spoke curtly but looked at her fingernails, which were painted a bright red that clashed with her violet top.

"Of course not. You know what I mean, Millie."

Katie warmed at the thought of having Amelia on her side but wondered why, if she still had this righteousness in her, she hadn't gone out of her way to help her brother. She was old enough now, Katie thought, to step out from under Anne's umbrella. But Jamie and Anne had imposed their sovereign rule many times. Rattling the cage must have been daunting when evidence suggested the zookeepers wouldn't hesitate to banish an unruly inhabitant. Surely she feared climbing or fighting her way out. "It's not just there" was a two-handed smack on the fence, nothing more.

"It doesn't seem like there was much of an investigation. Have you seen much on the case, Beth?"

"I don't think they spare much time for drug addicts." Beth said it with disdain, target unclear.

Something about the phrase infected the conversation. To this point, Tim had been a lost boy, a Worona casualty, a body on the ground that they were all quietly thankful wasn't Eric. Calling him what he was, or one part of what he was, reminded them that his affliction was not an isolated case and that his death wouldn't be the last of its kind. *Drug addict.* The next death was a matter of when and where and whose son. All four knew what had killed Tim. None of them wanted to guess if Eric used it at present or if a death like this would make him stop. Katie was pretty sure he did, and couldn't.

Anne squirmed in her chair. Her glasses mostly hid her emotions, but her writhing lips betrayed her. Katie wasn't sure if the repressed woman could even process her bottled feelings. Some had been buried, deemed unnecessary or meant for someone else. She was an elegant woman, well-dressed and prettier than her contemporaries, but Katie felt she had aged quite a bit in the past year or two. Her hands were still tan and manicured but closer to leather. The skin on her face was clear but not as taut as it had once been. Her arms and shoulders didn't fill out their space as neatly as in summers past. She pursed her lips and wiggled her toes, free of any summer whimsy.

"I don't think it's such a bad thing. Moving on, I mean. I have to think Tim's parents are ready to stop spending every second of their lives thinking about him dying."

The emphasis she placed on *I have to* softened Katie's heart momentarily. For the first time, she saw a mother distancing herself from her son not out of hatred or self-preservation, but so that when the implosion came, she wouldn't be close enough to shudder at its reverberations, at least not those of the immediate blast. Katie thought she even saw her hide a sniffle under those glasses, and a weight lifted when she realized how little she knew about the Clarke family, or about how much time and energy they had given their youngest child in the years since he had first started to stray. Katie puzzled over the idea that they might have been right to cut him out, if he had in fact exhausted them and their generosity. Her only access points to his missteps were secondhand recollections, vague allusions to his fallibility, delivered in offhand tones that reinforced her alliance. He hadn't been around, but this had somehow made her more sure of his innocence.

But this moment didn't last long, and as Katie saw the first two tears welling in Amelia's eyes, the rage returned. She confirmed then that Anne wanted nothing more than quiet, that Eric was, in her mind, not a source of day-in-day-out pain but a distraction, a blot on the escutcheon. She assumed that the Clarkes' standards for parenting had been skewed by the reassurance that they were doing an adequate job—it came with being able to provide for and spoil the kids. The first two had complied well enough to convince them the third was a rogue. His deviancy was best treated with a few years of discouragement and a rehearsed set of three lines about him getting his life turned around so that he could move in the direction they were sure was due north.

Katie wasn't positive the problem was specific to the Clarkes or their caste, but she was sure that it plagued the demographic: they could converse with archetypes of human beings but lacked the skill needed to treat people as individuals, to display at least an awareness of their idiosyncrasies. Maybe this was fine on the golf course or for hosting the party, but it was absolutely deadly when they were looking their son in the eyes and immediately turning away, refusing to acknowledge his despair.

"I think they might wish they had spent a little more time considering the possibility before it was too late." She looked at Anne while she said it.

If Danny's Greenstone words were to be believed, the McNamaras weren't so different from Anne and Jamie, even if their house was smaller. The things their meandering son distracted them from were not as glitzy, but they were hardly innocent, impossible to absolve.

"I'm sure it was a complicated situation."

Katie resented her mother for seeking an easy way out of the conversation. Beth's face pleaded with her daughter to stand down.

A complicated situation. A Bethism Katie knew well. A substitute, a stopgap. Sometimes Katie was happy to hear it. More often than not, Katie wanted something else from her mother. Something to suggest she understood how much the situation in question mattered to her daughter, understood the toll its complexity was taking on her. Beth was used to pushing conversations like these aside. Maybe she was willing to answer some of Katie's questions, to address concerns related to young womanhood and her path forward, but the younger Murray had long since resolved to stop asking. They didn't need *a complicated situation* anymore. Both parties were usually willing to abandon any talk before it reached that point. Katie couldn't remember the last time they had shared a chat that could be classified as a "heart-to-heart." They played their parts, smiled when they encountered high-school classmates and parents around town, stayed cordial in the kitchen and living room, managed to keep their voices down when one of them grew frustrated and stormed out of the room. Either party was welcome to enter the other's bedroom, even after the door was flung shut. But they chose not to. They reserved their act for other sets of eyes. They had nothing left to prove to each other, nothing of consequence. *A complicated situation.*

Katie waited for her mother's eyes to return to her. When they did, they didn't plead. They warned and, after a torrent of blinks, demanded.

August 5

It's been a month.

Restless on the farm.

It's been a month but if someone had woken me up this morning and told me it'd been a year I'd believe them. I wonder if it felt like a month to Tim or anything at all. Might still be on his way. But I don't think so.

Down, down, down.

Things come to me in pieces but I don't know how to assemble them so I leave them be and they go away.

August 10

They're afraid of me and they should be but I shouldn't have hit anyone this time. He's on my side for now. We want the same thing.

This should be getting easier now that more time has passed but I'm only getting worse. I don't know if it's guilt or just not being sure about what's going to happen to us.

I'm not sleeping a lot. I wasn't eating much from the start.

He didn't put up much of a fight. I guess he didn't want to hit me back. Me and him have never gotten into it before and I don't think this even counted. He's not that type of guy. He's not really like any of the other guys we run with and I don't think he's really like any of the people over there either. I've caddied for about a thousand SoMo assholes. Some of them are fine. Eric's good.

Growing up in Worona you learn to hate the Monomos. South more than North. No one tells you you have to. You just kind of do. My parents didn't say much about them.

I don't get how Eric doesn't hate them. If he does he doesn't talk about it. We drove over there a few weeks before all of this. To the road where his family has all the houses. Sat at the top of the hill and I watched a ship get tiny on the horizon. He was the one driving. He brought us there and then acted like it was a bad idea so we backed up instead of rolling down to the bottom of the road.

One time on a different ride he asked us if we hated him a little bit because he didn't grow up like us. We pretended to be offended and asked him how he thought we grew up. He laughed a little but I could tell he didn't think it was very funny. He said he wasted a chance. I think he did too but a chance to do what. End up like his fucking asshole brother. I met him once a few years ago but most of it I just hear from the stories. I'm not saying I'm happy I didn't grow up in their houses in their towns but I'm saying it wouldn't have mattered where he lived. He doesn't seem like a product of his environment which is what they call people like us when we do something wrong but not too wrong. What I did is too wrong so I don't know what I am.

I think I'm closer to hating him now.

I might sound calmer than I am. Not like writing this down calms me down. It just doesn't sound like how I feel. Because there's still a good chance no one finds out about what we did. And I think I can live with that if I don't think about Tim for too long.

I was on edge when I asked him about Katie asking for his number. That's why I hit him. It didn't take much to set me off. It's never taken much.

Stevie pulled us apart. That gave Eric a chance to talk more and I listened. He's known Katie for a long time. She was worried about him but not because of all this shit. She just knows we hang out together. He said she texted him because his family was acting weird when she asked them about him. I believe that. He said he didn't say a word about the Fourth. I believe that too. The problem is I need to believe he won't say a word. Ever. And I don't believe that.

I need both of them to lie low. It feels like we're close to getting away with it. Getting away with it makes it sound bad. We're close to moving on.

That's why I made them meet under the bridge by the canal. To relax them. To remind them that the hard part is over. People will stop looking for answers. Most already have.

I made Eric get up after I hit him in case someone random came riding by. I got a little bit of his blood on my hand. I wiped it on the graffiti.

At this point Tim's dead forever. There's no way for us to go back and stop what happened. I don't see why we need to suffer if we learned our lesson. We didn't even need to learn it. We already got the point. We just fucked up.

16

One day in their wise adolescence, Katie and Ryan had studied a phenomenon that they felt occurred every summer. Not everyone experienced it every year. They weren't sure if more official names for it were circulating out in the world—"Summertime Sadness" might have come close. They couldn't find an uncrude way to say it: sometimes the summer just fucking dragged.

This sensation wouldn't have been as painful if it wasn't almost inevitably followed by a wave of regret at one's failure to make the most of their summer days. If it hit them in the heart of the summer, when the days were fully canine, there was no out.

The blight manifested itself in different ways, but some symptoms were common. The afflicted complained constantly about the heat but insisted that the water was too cold for swimming and that the air in the house was no salve; they turned to a book to alleviate their pain only to remain stuck on the same chapter or page for days and weeks, citing the brightness of the beach or the eerie quiet of the house as reasons to use the novel as a pillow. Really the sickness looked to them, in a lot of cases, like a sort of mild depression—or maybe a Seasonal Affective Disorder.

The virus looked different for everyone but tended to be clusterable by age. Parents felt it differently from their young, the gap between their suffering wide enough to make them oblivious to the fact that the kids were experiencing the same thing in another form, clueless that they could have provided guidance.

In the Murray kids' experience, some people grew to like their condition. They reveled in the darkness; they let it consume them, redefine their homeostasis. These people looked normal. They acted normal. They were just more comfortable in their ennui than everyone else, and they knew it. The uninfected looked strange to them, masked and peculiar.

Katie wasn't a regular victim of the phenomenon but had experienced it before. The summer she turned fifteen had begun as one of promise and new love, but the boyfriend she had clung to for most of the school year declared it was better that they part ways just a few days after she relocated to the Cape.

Ryan had never faced any major strain of the sickness. Most people at least had an unlucky summer or two mixed in during their teens or early twenties. He figured his circumvention had something to do with his intelligence, given that his was not quite as sprawling as his sister's. They had established brainpower as a fairly reliable predictor of the disease's onset. In fact, they decided that if Einstein or Newton spent a summer in present-day Monomo they would have been, in Katie's words, "terribly fucking unhappy." This analysis may have been way off course; Ryan had suggested they would perhaps not have had time to succumb to this dread due to the stream of shocks to their systems resulting from encounters with marvels like telephones, airplanes, and the electric toothbrush. He beseeched: "If Martha's Vineyard looks bizarre to the average citizens of the world, God help Sir Isaac Newton."

So what Katie was feeling as July crept to its end was in many ways typical but nevertheless deeply unpleasant. Ryan was experiencing no existential discomfort whatsoever. His summer couldn't last long enough, as he was making good money, happily wasting time with friends at the club, and putting off any thoughts of the real world.

Katie had started to feel it more in the last three or four days. The beach was too hot to read or lie on, the house was stale, and the hours in the cart were longer, the golfers inexplicably less skilled and more demanding.

There had been little talk in their neighborhood of Tim Mc-Namara. Katie had been able to block the night out of her mind for hours at a time, increasingly confident that her silence wouldn't hurt anyone but still weighed down by her knowledge of Eric's involvement. She considered contacting him on four different occasions but always concluded that doing so might reopen wounds. She wasn't sure if those decisions reflected sound logic or cowardice. The fear that lifted the hair on her arms each time she saw Danny at the club suggested the latter. She did what she could to avoid him.

Every day, she expected to hear some breakthrough in the case, something that could either put her in danger or ease her mind, but no news came. For the common citizen, the case was closed. Tim's fate had been sealed for some time. Katie tried to convince herself of that last part every night. Sometimes Tim crept into her dreams, speaking in a voice of her creation, a pitch and set of words from inside her head based on the three pictures they had cycled through on the news in the immediate aftermath of the Fourth.

The bike ride on this day was joyless for Katie and not much better for Ryan. His mood could be traced not so much to summertime sadness but instead to the eighty-four percent humidity and lack of breeze on that Monday when the club was closed, the beach had run its course, and cruising on the bike seemed like a suitable way to burn some calories. As they walked to the end of the driveway, Katie asked Ryan where he wanted to ride, hoping he had some new exciting route in mind but too worn out to offer one of her own. She was disappointed to hear "Let's just ride along the canal. Should be cooler there."

There was a breeze once they reached the canal, but it backed off as they rode. Katie stared down at the unusually calm water, forced to veer back into their lane at the insistence of passersby on three separate occasions, each one closer to disaster than the last. She rode behind her brother, so he didn't see either of the first two readjustments, but the third was violent enough to send her skidding into some dirt beside the path. She stayed in her seat, but the sound of the skid alerted Ryan to her predicament. He looked back at her and slowly U-turned, rolling past her as she looked at her feet and closed her eyes.

"What happened? Did they cut you off?"

"No. I, um, just drifted over."

He inched toward her. "What's the matter? You want to turn around? You look a little out of it. We can turn back."

"No, let's keep going. I need some more fresh air." Katie looked up to the light.

"What are those guys doing up there? Weird place to fish."

Two shapes stepped carefully down the bank toward the water, a hundred yards ahead. One let the slope take him, and he stopped a few inches short of the canal before turning to watch his partner, who chose each footplant patiently and held his spot a dozen feet above the tiny beach. Ryan rode in the opposite direction while Katie gathered herself, taking the second position as she rolled back onto the path and waited for the faces to come into focus. The figure on the bank turned toward her before she could identify it, making its way to the path as she approached.

"Hey! Hey!"

Katie veered for the fourth time as he stepped onto the path and tried to block her. She tried to keep pedaling but had to stop. Ryan halted behind her, thinking they had narrowly dodged an accident.

"Watch it, man!"

Ryan wasn't angry but felt he had to defend his sister. He regretted his tone as soon as the boy's bulging eyes turned his way.

"I know you guys." The boy pointed, first at Ryan, then at Katie, and let his finger hang.

Ryan's confusion was genuine. He didn't notice Katie's look of shame. "I don't think so. Uh, we work at the Dunes. Maybe you've seen us there."

"No, I recognize her. I've seen her somewhere."

"Okay. Just be careful. The path's kind of small. I don't think you'd enjoy getting run over by one of these things too much."

Ryan thought they were on their way and started to move around the roadblock, but as he did the boy grabbed his handlebar with one hand and steered him into his sister.

"It's you. You were at Greenstone on the Fourth. I saw you there."

"No, I wasn't there." The lying was no longer easy for Katie. Her voice would have shaken if she had needed another word.

"Katie, wh—"

"Yes you were. I saw you. It was you, wasn't it? You were there, and then you were running. Hey, man, it's her, right? Eric?"

Eric had ducked his head down as soon as he recognized the bikers but now turned slowly and started his climb. Halfway up, the sun caught his face and revealed two cuts running down to his chin from below his left eye. Katie assured herself that the three of them could overpower this interrogator if it came to that. She wondered why Danny wasn't with them. Who was hiding? Maybe Danny was long gone, but she gathered that people like Danny seldom got very far. If he wasn't here, he was still close, and this was far from over.

"Eric, you recognize these two?"

"Of course, Stevie. I've been friends with them my whole life." Eric held up his arms as if to hug them from a distance. His beaming smile dropped as soon as Stevie looked away.

"What are you talking about?"

Eric smirked and hammed it up. He sounded for a moment like his brother. "The Murrays. These guys. Their house is right up the street from my parents. We grew up playing on the beach together and everything."

"You know them?"

Stevie didn't look back to his friend. His eyes scanned Katie. She felt them in her ribcage and on the inside of her throat, creeping toward the section of her brain that wouldn't stop broadcasting incriminating transmissions.

"Yeah, man. You still baked? I said I know them."

Katie approved of Eric's strategy, but Stevie's incredulous look worried her. Ryan was dumbfounded and glared at his sister, waiting for her to make things clearer before finally noticing the urgency in her eyes. He realized that his best contribution was silence.

"She was there at Greenstone. On the Fourth. It was her. I didn't want to tell you guys, but I got a pretty good look at the person running away. I know it was a girl. It was her."

"Katie? Pssh, no chance. Don't you think I would have recognized her? Plus, she's too smart to hang around a place like that. Right, Katie?"

He winked out of Stevie's sight, pulling his cuts up toward his eye, and pushed his hair back so she could see his whole face for the first time. Opposite the cuts was a bruise, too low to qualify as a black eye, and on his lower lip sat a mostly healed split.

"I worked at the club on the Fourth. Is that what you mean? I wasn't too close to the pond, and I don't like being around there at night. Seems like bad stuff always happens around there."

Nothing she said was fully a lie, but she was certain she could conjure something stronger if needed. Ryan now sensed how necessary her performance was. Her voice sounded higher than normal.

She had added some ditz to it and batted her eyes slowly at Stevie, who wasn't stoned but looked not far removed from such a state. Where Katie had previously been surprised by how easily deception came to her, now she was stunned by how much she enjoyed it, how much she savored the look of disbelief on Stevie's face, the bewilderment on her brother's. It wasn't a matter of knowing something they didn't, but rather how small they looked in front of her, three different styles of angst plastered on their faces, three bad haircuts, three little boys unsure of how to be anything other than what they were.

"You sure? You, you weren't there either?"

"No, not that night. We were at Eric's house actually. His parents threw a party." Only then did Ryan realize what they thought Katie had witnessed, what he was now sure she had. They had never kept many secrets from each other, but he figured now that their openness had been a result of having very little to hide. If not, he hadn't paid good attention. He could feel his heart thumping but mustered a yawn, an unplanned side effect of the slow, deep breaths he was struggling to complete. Two fish jumped near their bank, visible only to him.

"Yeah, Stevie. My parents host a big party every year. Katie probably just looks like whoever you saw. You probably didn't even get a good look or anything. I'm pretty sure the girl was tiny, too."

Eric's lies didn't sound as confident as Katie's, but Stevie's reasonable doubt was simple to overcome.

"Yeah, must be. Whatever. Let's get out of here though. Now I'm fuckin' spooked. I think we just have bad karma at this point."

"Okay. Let me just say bye to these guys. Long time, no see. They're pretty much like family, no offense to them."

Stevie walked off. They could see a large sweat stain running from neck to ass on his thin, gray tee. His head was buzzed short and burned, but he carried his Patriots hat. Neither Katie nor Ryan remembered seeing him around. They tended to look away or down when Danny and his crew wandered near. Stevie glanced back, then quickly away as he lit a cigarette. The motion looked natural, genetic. He had lived through more stressful conversations beside this canal.

"Just pretend we're having a normal conversation."

Eric's hands each took a side of his hair, first pulling it gently up before letting it fall softly, more disheveled as a result of his toying.

"I think we're way past that."

"Katie, you don't have to worry. Stevie doesn't know what he saw. I'm the only one who was close enough to see you, and I made sure they don't think I know anything."

Ryan's eyes shot back and forth between them. "Can one of you tell me what the fuck we're talking about?"

"Ryan, be quiet."

His brain sent a signal to lunge for her but caught itself, and he spoke in a prickly whisper.

"Katie, don't tell me what to do. What did you two"—and he pointed at them, an index finger for each—"have to do with Tim McNamara? That's what this is about, isn't it? Let's all stop lying to each other."

"Katie didn't have anything to do with it."

Ryan's attention turned to Eric, and he started to sweat. "But you did? Are you in trouble? You can't let her get roped into this shit."

Eric smiled and looked toward Stevie, who scratched the back of his thigh and looked over his left shoulder to see if something had bitten him.

"It's hard to explain. Maybe some other time."

"What? No. Now."

Eric looked again to his accomplice. "I can't. Stevie is kind of a moron, but he's nervous, and that makes him dangerous for all of us."

Stevie had made it a hundred feet or so and now turned back to wave Eric on.

"Eric, you gotta tell us what happened. Maybe we can help you."

"I appreciate it, Ryan. I'm not going to make you do that. For now, talk to her. Then keep quiet. It's for the best."

Eric patted them goodbye. He jogged to Stevie, hair bouncing on each landing. From behind he was happy and even skinnier than Katie remembered him being days before, as if anything more than his trot could snap either leg in two. But upon closer examination he looked more light than frail, unlikely to break but still too easy to push or cast aside, equally ready to be lifted or, if no one was willing to lift, to float away.

"So are you gonna tell me what happened?"

And she did, but only because she saw no other way, and because she was sure Stevie would eventually realize he was right and seek them out. She didn't know who or what he would bring with him, only that he or it wouldn't be as friendly as Eric. She told Ryan about leaving the car to look for him, about hearing voices in the woods, about hiding behind the rock and stumbling as she ran, and about the kindness in Eric's eyes.

They sat next to their bikes, and the grass left imprints on their hands. She mentioned meeting up with Eric at Bayside Beach. Ryan stood and grunted his disapproval.

"I don't get it. Why would they move the body there? Why did they have to hide it?"

"I think they didn't want to get in trouble for being with Tim when he died. They're paranoid." Katie wanted her words to be true.

"Must be something else, something more."

She hesitated. The suspicion had tried to lodge itself in her mind, but she hadn't let it stay there. Doing so would have made Danny more threatening, Eric guiltier.

"I've been trying to tell myself that's not true. But it's not working. I think Eric's afraid to tell us the rest."

"So who do we talk to? Do we tell the police your story? You're just a scared witness. They won't hold it against you." Ryan was only now comprehending his sister's days of inaction.

"No, we can't say anything."

"What are you talking about?" Ryan scratched his hand while he spoke, a telltale sign of being frazzled usually employed only when someone shared an offensive Boston sports take or probed on what he planned to do with his life after school.

"They'll turn on him and hurt him. You saw Eric's face. Danny or someone else will get him, keep him quiet."

"Katie, I like Eric, and we've known him forever. I get that. But I don't think we should protect him. We should protect ourselves, not some group of addicts and degenerates."

She had grown to hate *addict* in recent weeks. She despised its harshness, its finality. It sounded unnatural, mispronounced, not applicable to anyone in her orbit. It was a word meant for generalizations.

"Eric's not that."

Ryan let out a frustrated sigh. "Yeah, he is. Doesn't make him a bad guy, but we need to look after ourselves. He had chances to figure it out, didn't he?"

"You sound like his mom. Like our mom. Did you see how scared he looked?"

"I think he just looked kind of stoned, Katie. Like he hasn't slept in a month." He walked across the path and kicked pebbles toward the water. Most clung to the hillside, saving their descent for a later date.

"You think maybe he has some reasons not to sleep?"

Katie didn't hate her brother, not then or ever. She didn't even blame him for the narrow vision he articulated. It came from some-where or someone else, and he wanted to keep her safe. He valued her over their otherworldly neighbor. But she needed more from him, more than she would get from anyone else, and she wasn't sure how to pull it out, or if it was inside him at all. As they rode in silence, the wind still unwilling to blow, she daydreamed scenarios that ended with Danny in handcuffs, Stevie seated beside him, and Eric on the beach. But it seemed clear that Eric was unable to escape, that his current life was the hideout and that the one from which he hid would never welcome him back. It would rather hand him over or watch him burn, whichever would leave its hands unscarred.

And she appreciated that Eric would be too kind to Danny and Stevie. To turn them in or do anything other than preserve their tenuous existence would go against everything his soul told him. She could see it in his eyes—on the banks of the canal, in the dark at Greenstone, on the beach when he first made trouble years ago— the unwillingness to throw anyone into the grasp of the misperceiv-ing world that had excommunicated him. He would let his new world swallow him up before he pushed someone into the old one.

Her instincts told her that he would die rather than take the other side. To take the side that had shoved him headlong onto the battlefield would be treasonous. In the taking, he would sen-tence himself not to death but to something slower, venomous. Something like the desolation his would-be allies imagined for him, in the woods and hovels where they envisioned him living, in the patches of filth, waiting to expire.

August 13

Now's not the time for surprises. Stevie texting me wouldn't usually be a surprise but today it is. When I saw he texted me I figured he was just bored or being a little bitch about all this. I didn't like the text I got instead.

Maybe she is a threat. If it turns out she's a threat and Stevie's a liability it's going to be a rough fucking night. Stevie I can control at least. He trusts me.

Should've just told Stevie to run far away and shut the hell up. Him or me.

Him or me.

17

Stevie's boxy physique didn't allow him to walk normally. He lumbered; he waddled; he labored. He wasn't fat, but he was a little embarrassed at how out of breath he was as he stood a tenth of a mile from the playground. Conditioning had never been a strength for him, even when he played basketball and football, both of which he loved but gave up on after eighth grade.

He resented Danny for telling him to meet him here. It was one thing to talk to each other, to break the rules that Danny himself had laid out. It was another entirely to meet at the playground. It was obvious, sketchy. They had both spent many nights there and had, on more than one of those nights, scattered at the sight of cops arriving to break up the party. Stevie wished it was one of those nights, but if they saw cops tonight they would have to do more than disband. His body and mind weren't up for running.

Stevie also wanted to go home. From the fifth of July on, he had spent every night searching for real sleep. Every day passed with his eyes heavy but unwilling to stay shut. He shared a beat-up but cozy rental a mile past the playground with his older brother and three of said brother's friends. The four of them had their own struggles, their own hidden lives, but none of them had Stevie's. He made a point of remembering to ask Danny for a ride before they discussed anything else.

Stevie met Danny in first grade. Danny had always been louder, more social, and quicker to get into trouble. But Stevie had never waited long to join him. They missed recesses and earned detentions, but they did so together and, most of the time, smiling. In elementary school, they challenged their peers to two-on-two (if no takers, two-on-as-many-as-five) basketball for whatever money was in their pockets. Danny and Stevie played rough but fought anyone who questioned their tactics, and members of the faculty were quick to intervene. Middle school was split into phases: learning about weed, acquiring weed, and selling enough weed to earn a reputation, one that parents would have abhorred but classmates respected, an attitude the pair mistook for a sign that they were fitting in. By high school, their attendance was sporadic, though Stevie did manage to graduate; sometimes it involved going to class in secret or rising early to finish homework so that Danny and others wouldn't ridicule the effort.

College and life beyond the Cape had crossed Stevie's mind in the months leading up to graduation, but he never filled out an application or gave voice to his interest. He wouldn't have been the first from his family to go, to leave, but he would have been an oddity. By now, as he continued to lope along the side of the road, where the grass was trampled from batches of kids like him tracing this path, he had accepted that he was destined to grow old in Worona.

He kept waiting to wake up feeling like an adult. The years since high school had passed quickly, and some days he felt he hadn't changed at all. If anything, his decision making was worse, the company he kept more insidious.

Danny pulled up quietly next to him, lights off, in the middle of the empty road, the playground and its parking lot just a minute ahead. He turned off the car and stepped out. They could see each other clearly in the twilight, but Stevie squinted and kept the picture blurry. Blurry was better. They could make out the sounds of arboreous species zizzing, and Danny turned to face the woods, as if to ensure the bugs' attention was elsewhere.

"What's up, Danny? Don't you think it's, uh, a little risky to meet out here?"

Danny let his left hand dance on the car as he moved alongside it. "It's no problem. We can talk quick. I just need to hear what Eric and the Murrays said. You made it sound pretty fuckin' suspect."

Stevie rued his call to keep his friend informed. For some reason he had assumed texting Danny about their accidental interrogation would help solve their problems. Now, as he watched Danny loiter on the far side of the street, he sensed it was already making things worse.

"I don't know, man. It seems like they were being honest. I think Eric was kind of embarrassed that they saw us. But they wouldn't do anything. I don't think they would get us in trouble."

"So you do think they know something? You think Eric is fuckin' lying? Makes sense to me. I think he's been acting weird for the past month."

Danny's hands worked themselves into and out of fists, and Stevie watched them, aware of their thew.

"I mean, I don't know. But it's all kind of weird. That girl looks familiar. What else would I recognize her from? But it could be, like, paranoia or something."

Stevie watched Danny pace back and forth behind the car and didn't realize his mouth was hanging open.

"What is it? Stop staring at me like that."

Stevie closed his mouth but couldn't hide his discomfort.

"Jesus, Stevie, what is it? Fuckin' speak!"

Stevie's hands shot up defensively. "Look, Danny, I'm not trying to start shit, but don't you think we could still just, like, come clean? We could tell them we were with Tim, and he OD'ed, and we freaked out and hid the body. It won't be so hard for people to understand. We'll be able to manage whatever trouble that gets us into."

Danny stopped pacing and licked salt away from above his lip. Stevie had watched him do so ten thousand times but still found it disconcerting.

"What are you saying, man?"

"I'm just saying I think we should tell someone what happened that night. What we did. Not, like, everything. Just enough to, you know, clear us."

Stevie's reflexes forced him back as Danny stepped forward and smiled with something more deranged than simple malice.

"Are you that fuckin' stupid? They're sure someone killed him. They have evidence. It's too late for us to make shit up and hope they fuckin' spank us and let us walk free."

"I know they won't let us walk, Dan. You know I know that. But they don't understand exactly what happened. And the longer we wait, the heavier this shit becomes."

Danny scratched his shoulder. He wore a beyond-ratty Dunes shirt, one that had been roughly four sizes too big when he received it toward the end of his second summer caddying.

"Stevie, it sucks. I know it does. But this, this whole situation, is us. This is our shit to live with forfuckinever. You get that, right? I need you to get that."

Stevie sighed and closed his eyes. He refused to open them. He waited for some force to pry his lids apart and reveal a new world, or even the old one, which on this night didn't sound bad at all.

"I want to have a life, man. Not this one."

"We will. Things will settle down, and we'll be back to the good old days. I'm telling you. Smoking in front of the Silver Fox."

"Shit, Danny. Aren't we getting kind of old for all that anyway?

Can't we do something else? I'm so fucking tired of it."

Stevie's Boston accent usually came and went. Sometimes it got stronger over the course of a night with Eric and like-voiced associates. But it was nowhere to be found now. He spoke with no inflection, nothing tying him to any place in his purview. The night air almost tasted sweet to him.

"Whatever, man. We'll figure it out. Just get in. We can ride around and think about it and figure out what to do next."

"We gotta tell them. We gotta end this now. My head's gonna explode."

Danny faced Stevie, who leaned against the car and looked up. He breathed harder than he had in weeks while his friend closed his eyes and blew out air that would have been visible two months later. He wanted to lunge for Stevie and press this fear out of him, eliminate the threat that had entered his brain.

"Fine. Just get in. We can talk about it. We can't just stand here."

Stevie rolled off of the car and shuffled toward the passenger door. Danny's feet moved before he could finalize his decision. As Stevie's hand reached the handle, Danny struck. Stevie turned in time to see the hit coming but couldn't avoid it. Danny shoved his head into the top of the car, a foot above the window. Stevie's body folded on the ground. He grunted upon impact but quickly went limp.

Danny's heart pushed against every one of his atoms, and his exhales came in quakes. He stared at Stevie and felt the now-familiar rush of blood to his head. He nudged the body forward so he could open the door. Mini heaves of breath served as signs of life.

He reached into the glove compartment and pulled out a gun. Before that summer, he had never held it. He didn't even know the make or model or if those words were appropriate. He remembered only the most basic, necessary information. His dad had owned it as long as he could remember. It had always been stored in a kitchen cabinet, one that was rarely opened, behind a bag of flour, which Danny had never seen anyone use. In his hands it felt heavy, but the trigger was vulnerable, easily manipulated.

The parking lot was still empty, but Danny scanned the rows twice before he was sure. His racing brain seemed to slow as he looked back to Stevie and decided he needed to move him in order to avoid blood spattering the car. He walked toward the body and delivered another blow to the head. Blood leaked out of Stevie's nose. He dragged him diagonally, in front of and beyond the car and across the road, which fell off quickly into dense woods.

Danny figured actors cried in these moments, when their characters were pushed beyond some brink. But he wasn't sure if people did things like this outside of the movies he watched late into the night on the television Stevie had dubbed "Silver Fox" the summer after seventh grade. Either way, he wouldn't cry. He swallowed again and again, each gulp more painful than the last. His hand shook as it brought the gun forward but steadied as he raised it and pointed it toward his friend. For a moment, he wondered if he would be able to do it and how long it would take to muster the energy. He refined his aim, closed his eyes, and pulled.

He fired once and then shook, frightened by how quickly the sound receded beneath the chiaroscuro of the sky. The wound was effective but not neat on the right side of Stevie's head, which had lolled sideways and now rested at an angle that would have been painful for the living. Briefly, Danny forgot Stevie couldn't feel it.

The next thing he knew, he was standing at the side of the road, kicking dirt over the stain of blood that had formed a foot from the pavement. It was dark enough that he couldn't see the body, hidden on the far side of the water. It had tumbled most of its way there.

The creek was low, so Danny had barely gotten wet. The water had been refreshing as it seeped into his shoes.

He climbed into the car, squeezed the wheel, and screamed. The yell had barely made it to the thicket when he took the gun from the passenger seat, got out, and hurled the weapon as far as he could, well past the half-buried body with the face he was already struggling to piece together. He screamed again but cut this one off abruptly.

As he drove past the playground, he waited for sadness to come, for memories of their friendship to beset him, but they spurned him. Maybe people would think Stevie ran off to somewhere else. Maybe they would assume he had found something better than whatever the rest of them were left with. Danny wasn't so sure he hadn't.

August 13

He knew what I would do. Exactly what I would do. Better than anyone he understood what would happen. Fuck.

This time I'm really fucked. Because his brother will notice something's up and then he'll ask me about it. I'm not sure what to tell him. Could put it on someone else. His brother doesn't like me anyway. His brother thinks I'm a bad influence.

Stevie was a little weak. Always was. I got that. He was going to say something. He could tell it was her. He could tell she was lying to his face and he let her. He walked away. She's been talking to Eric. They're planning some way to fuck me. Doesn't even matter what they say. Two SoMo kids against me. Jamie Clarke and whatever he's got against me.

If I hadn't been so distracted in the woods I would've been able to tell something was up with Eric. He saw her. It's obvious he did. He's known this whole time. He's known this whole time but he didn't say anything even though he knew she was the one person who could get us in real trouble. Fuck Eric. Eric and his prick brother and all of them.

Why are they working so hard to protect her? Stevie had never even met her but I could tell he wasn't going to go after her. He wasn't thinking straight. I think I had to do it.

I'm afraid of what I might have to do now.

If Katie saw us and saw what we did then why am I still here? She's *afraid of what'll happen to Eric. She takes him at his word but she'd never give me a chance to tell her what happened. Which is all I need. A minute to talk to her and tell her what happened. If she doesn't want to hurt Eric she won't want to hurt me when she figures out it was all a misunderstanding.*

I'm sorry, Stevie.

Now I'm pretty sure I have to see this whole thing through to the end.

18

Gotta talk to you and Ryan. I'll meet you on Granger

When?

Already in the car

Katie wasn't surprised to receive a text from Eric, but its urgency, two days after they had chanced upon him and Stevie, concerned her. Eric had been in trouble ever since Tim died. That hadn't changed, so either something worse had taken place, or he was worried about them. Katie smiled at the thought of his compassion.

Dodging Ryan's looks and questions had filled most of the two days, and she had been thankful to work a shift that morning while he was home alone. She had thought there was a chance they would never have to confront this again (Danny's continued absence at the club had enhanced the hoping), or at least she had imagined what that would look like, but she knew better than to try to sneak to the beach without her brother in tow. The only way to keep him from going to the police or involving the parents of Seaview was to keep him informed, to assure him that they were not in immediate danger. Now Katie realized that the bluntness of Eric's text served as a warning that this criterion was no longer assured. If Eric suggested they were at risk of attack, Ryan would have to act. She, or at least the Katie of a month ago, would have to take the initiative, too, if she could summon that girl, if she could stomach what that action would mean for Eric.

Eric was already on the beach when they arrived, sitting like he belonged. A black lab abandoned its tennis ball to say hello, and he threw it back toward the owner, who waved her thanks and headed in the other direction. Katie wanted nothing more than to freeze everything around her, to let Eric stay there, unobstructed, the sand cooling underneath him as the sun dipped and the water receding on its way to a low tide. She expected bad news, but she saw no signs of it in his body as he lounged. Maybe he had assumed they wouldn't show. Maybe he had simply grown used to people, especially the residents of Seaview Road, thinking they knew better than he did. Whatever it was, he leaned back on his hands and sat with better posture than his detractors would have expected from a criminal-addict-burnout in the dying light of an August night built for malfeasance. His shoulders relaxed but didn't sag, and his slight tan looked well-earned, more natural than the ones that had crowded the beach earlier in the day and now sailed the boats drifting home for the night.

"Eric? Everything okay?"

"Hey, Ryan, Katie. Sorry to scare you guys. Just wanted to make sure we saw each other in person. Wasn't trying to make you panic."

His nonchalance was out of place but oddly comforting, a reminder of how harmless he was to anyone other than himself.

"No problem. We're happy you're safe."

He regarded the water.

"Beach is nice right now. This is the best time of day to be here. J.J. and I used to play wiffleball 'til all you could see was the ball spinning through the dark."

Katie and Ryan remembered the games, sometimes audible from the Murray porch, often played even as rain poured and lightning cracked. Ryan had played in a few of them but not the ones that dragged on the longest. Those contests usually persisted because tempers flared as the ninth and tenth and fourteenth innings passed without a decisive run, as the prospects of scoring one became grim on the tenebrous beach.

"Eric, did something else happen? Did Stevie say something?"

They let him pause. He kneaded his arms.

"I'm going to tell you guys everything about it, alright? We just need to be careful. There's no point in me keeping stuff from you two now."

"Of course we'll be careful. We just want to help, Eric. We know you didn't do anything bad." She stammered on the last few words and moved toward him.

"I don't know, Katie. I admire the trust, but I'm not so sure I deserve it. It's not for you to say, I guess. You've never done a bad thing in your life, have you? Except that story you used to tell."

She frowned while he flashed his teeth.

"What story?"

"The, uh, red parts. The music class one."

She couldn't believe he remembered the story. Even Ryan took a few seconds to recall it, but when he did all three laughed together at the thought of Katie's misdemeanor. In third grade, her music teacher had given the class a short test. The quiz had been simple. The teacher printed out sheets with the music and lyrics for "The Star Spangled Banner," and the students were asked to fill in fourteen missing words. Now, on the beach, Katie wondered why her schools had devoted so much time to nationalist indoctrination. The twenty or so children sat in a circle on the rug and scribbled in their answers. A few finished quickly. Katie flew through the blanks except for one that didn't jump automatically to mind. Katie never cheated. She was embarrassed to even consider it on the floor of music class, but after two more kids hopped up and handed in their sheets, she let her eyes wander to the floor to her right, where her friend Erin's precocious handwriting had scripted "ramparts" on the first pass. She scribbled it down, the guilt only creeping in when she took her place with the others against the far wall.

Ryan liked this story because he and his parents didn't have much else to rib Katie with, and Eric recalled it from a Memorial Day weekend two lifetimes before when the families had eaten together. Someone had brought up the anthem and the superior songs they wanted to see take its place, which led to a retelling of Katie's misdeeds, embellished by her father.

"You have a good memory."

"That's pretty much all I have at this point." He knocked gently on his temple and smiled, the necessary muscles weary from inattention.

"So now you tell us everything."

"Ryan, don't rush him."

Eric tucked some hair behind his right ear and held up his left hand.

"It's okay. Stevie told Danny about running into you guys. I don't think Stevie knew what he was talking about, but the idea of Katie being there that night made sense to Danny. So now he's pretty convinced she was. I told him that was ridiculous. At this point he's just jacked up from sitting around thinking about what we did."

Ryan clapped his hands and dry-heaved. Katie put her face in her palms. She was surprised to feel so many calluses and such dry skin.

"What did you tell him?"

"Same thing I told Stevie. I didn't get a good look, and I would've recognized you."

"They know you saw someone. They know you're lying. I don't think it matters what you told them."

"Eric, do they know you're here?"

"Of course not."

Ryan paced between Eric's place and the water, trying and failing to find any silver lining in the latest developments.

"So they're pretty much convinced Katie saw you guys with Tim's body?"

"Yeah. I think we have to assume so."

Katie knelt in the sand next to him. Her knees sank quickly. The grains fled before collecting around her skin, tickling her where they were few in number.

"Eric, what else happened? What did you do? You've gotta be honest with us. Everyone wouldn't be this paranoid if all you did was hide your friend. If it was just a regular OD, you guys wouldn't be so worried. Danny wouldn't care so much. The punishment wouldn't be bad enough to scare you guys like this."

Ryan stopped in his tracks. "Katie, don't bombard him. He's on our side."

"Eric hasn't told us everything. Danny did something to Tim."

Eric looked at her. His bruise had mostly healed and was a little yellow, only noticeable from up close.

"She's right, and Danny thinks you know more than you do, so for your sake I have to tell you." For the first time, he looked unsettled. He fidgeted. He cracked two knuckles.

"What happened to Tim? What did you guys do?" Katie's voice shook. Eric fiddled with his hair and grimaced at the utterance of the name.

"I didn't do anything myself, but I was there, and I watched it, and I didn't stop it." Katie waited for his voice to break, but it only grew louder. Each phrase ended with renewed emphasis.

"I'm not asking you guys to understand what happened. You just need to hear the truth."

"What did Danny do to him?"

"I guess the short answer is he killed him."

Ryan's retort came out as a croak. "Now would be a good time for the long answer."

Eric gave it. The night that ended at the pond had begun in a rundown house on Worona's western edge where many of the region's younger delinquents acquired and used their product(s) of choice. Tim McNamara hadn't been part of their plan for the evening, but when Danny entered the house and saw him chatting with a young woman on the couch, plans changed accordingly. It turned out Tim had owed Danny enough money, in Danny's estimation, to warrant being pulled up from the couch by the collar of his shirt and shoved into the wall. Tim's friend scurried from the room, whose only other occupant had floated up into his holy terror a few minutes before and now rested in the corner, unaware of his surroundings. Eric and Stevie leaned against the wall, having witnessed Danny's shakedowns before and expecting a swift resolution. Tim insisted on talking shit to Danny, even after the first two punches, spurred on by the gentler of the two intoxications that would appear on his tox screen the next afternoon. Tim had enough energy to throw a punch of his own but not enough to protect his head at the same time, and Danny's final blow knocked him back onto the couch. Danny then left the room, and Eric suggested that he and Stevie find a good seat, eager to experience the goods with which they expected Danny to return. Eric rested his eyes and sank into an adjacent loveseat until Stevie jostled him awake six minutes later, twenty seconds after Danny had returned and stabbed a vein in Tim's left forearm. He had made sloppy work of it, unlike anything they had seen or done to themselves before, plainly not self-inflicted. Eric watched blood spurt as the contents of the syringe took effect. Next came a surge of panic when the bleeding didn't stop.

Tim didn't die in the dirt next to Greenstone, and he didn't die on the couch where Danny laid him out and stuck him. He died in Eric's car, though his fate had been sealed when Danny and Stevie carried him out the door, looking both ways first, too anxious about Danny's botched handiwork to remember that anyone coming that way at such an hour was already in the house. At some point, the body was moved from Eric's car to Danny's so the ringleader could take control (and leverage his truck's off-road capabilities). Stevie and Eric rode together to Greenstone and parked where the Murrays eventually saw them.

Katie had witnessed most of the rest. What she had seen was indeed discombobulation and fear. Eric remembered the fear and the knowledge even amidst the chaos that he never should have left the couch or laid a finger on Tim, not after Danny had unleashed himself.

Only a nervous gulp interrupted Ryan's hurried breaths. "So Danny thinks we know he killed Tim McNamara?"

"Ryan, we do know it."

Only then did the scale of the revelation bludgeon Ryan. Katie watched him swallow a few times while she waited for the news to hit her harder. She hadn't been sure what to expect of her body, her nerves, but she hadn't considered stillness. The coldness scared her more than the confession.

"What do you think he'll do, Eric? Is he going after you?"

"He's definitely pissed at me." Eric blew out air and rolled his head in a circle twice. "To tell you the truth, I'm not sure what he'll do. He's always been a bit of a dickhead, but this has made him a little more, uh, volatile. I don't think he can figure out what to believe about you, Katie."

It no longer sounded like nonchalance.

"Is he the one who cut your face?" Katie reached toward the wounds, but Eric turned away.

"Don't worry about that."

"I think we need to turn him in. We could all drive to the station together right now."

"Ryan, we can't do that. Danny will just pull Eric into it. He was there and everything, but he wasn't thinking straight. He wasn't even really an accomplice."

Now Eric turned to her but felt further away. "No, Katie, your brother's right. We can end this, and we should've—I should've—a month ago."

"They might make a deal with Eric, Katie. Danny's the one they'll really want."

Katie envied her brother's optimism. She knew how it would play out, how Eric's past and the marks she could see on his arm would collude to align with whatever lies Danny added onto his story. He had watched his friend kill a boy and helped him move the body. He sat in the car while Tim McNamara breathed final breaths, and he kept quiet. Eric would have to fight to have his story heard or understood, and Katie doubted he wanted any part of that affray.

She figured once he ended up in a cell and a jumpsuit he would buckle and accept the unnatural plight bestowed on him. Once there were charges officially attached, labels like the ones his parents already used to keep him beyond arm's length, there would be no fight. Katie could picture Anne crying softly in the second row while Jamie wore a face of stone as the police walked his son out of the courtroom. She and Ryan were left with two options: either they would have to meet Danny and convince him they wouldn't tell the story, or they would have to turn Danny in after sending Eric far away—somewhere for him to hide, again. Maybe he was due for an escape, Katie thought, the one he had sought out across a highway in the next town over. Running didn't sound so bad. No one would chase too hard. Eventually he wouldn't have to hide.

"I don't think Danny will hurt you two. He likes you. He's already lost his nerve about all this, about what he did. There's enough on his mind."

Ryan scoffed and kicked the sand, sending a clump close to his sister's back.

"Whether it's me or Ryan or you or someone else, I think he's going to hurt more people." Katie spoke clearly, her syllables crisp. She remembered how close to breaking Danny had looked the day he left the bag room and declined to hand over Eric's number.

"Right. So I turn myself in, I tell them what happened, and they bring him in. They'll appreciate me coming forward."

"That seems like the best plan." Ryan's eyes pleaded with his sister.

"No." She looked hard at her brother, then back to Eric. The word resounded off the waves.

"Katie, c'mon. It's Eric's choice."

"I know it is, and I think he should choose to run."

"Run? Run where?" Ryan was now incredulous, befuddled by Katie's commitment to the boy with the long hair. He looked so unlike the person they had befriended as children.

"Katie, I don't think I have anywhere to run."

Specks of bitterness touched his words. He sensed someone ready to tell him what to do, where he belonged.

"You're either going to die in that rundown house or in jail or when Danny decides he can't take the risk of keeping you around. Why can't you run? Why can't you leave this place behind you? It's never done you any good. It—"

She had crept closer to Eric, but Ryan pulled her back. She fell into a sitting position and swatted her brother's hands away.

"Katie, calm down. You're being overdramatic."

Her mouth was dry, her words scratchy. "No, no way. He knows it, but he won't listen to himself, and maybe he'll listen to us. You can run. You can go anywhere. There's so much time, Eric. Some-day you'll be half a world away, and this stupid place will be a faint memory, and those spots on your arm will disappear. You don't need any of this. They've all just convinced you that you do, that your decisions led you here and to people like Danny and to places like the house he killed Tim in. But you don't need it. You can run. Someone should've told you to a long time ago."

Eric pulled his knees to his chest and bent his head back to look up at the sky, mostly dark now but its stars still obscured. Katie wiped away tears that had barely come, her red eyes dried out by the ocean air.

"That's nice of you to say. Maybe someone should've said it soon-er, but they didn't. It might've been someone's else's fault at some point, Katie, but I don't think I can point fingers anymore."

"Fine, then I will. I'll point fingers at the house right fucking there. They did nothing for you." She did point, but she lacked the energy to keep her finger lifted. Eric looked back at the house, in awe of something immaterial.

"Maybe. Might be right. I don't remember them being so bad, though. Just scared, I think. They were afraid of what I could do to them. Like Harry Potter at Six Privet Drive once Hagrid told him he was a wizard." Eric laughed at his own comparison and the power he had assigned to himself, ready to take it further but slowed by the trepidation glued onto Katie's face.

"Why are you so calm? Why are you talking like it's all been decided already?"

"The expansiveness of the universe."

"What?" Katie was sure she had misheard. Ryan flinched at her volume.

"It reassures me. Makes me feel big. Ask Neil deGrasse Tyson. He knows what he's talking about. Sometimes. Part of something.

Our atoms from the stars above us."

Eric exhaled, and Ryan laughed. Neither looked Katie's way. Despite his smile betraying an awareness of how much of a stoner—as opposed to an addict, an important distinction for Katie—he sounded like, Eric seemed sincere. He liked to read. He always had. It was easy for Katie to see why, easy for her to discern the sense of membership in his voice.

"Eric, we need to focus."

"Sure, but then you go read about the universe, about what we know about it and how much we don't. It's this unfathomably large . . . thing. There's no unit or measure that captures the enormity of what's out there. None. And it's expanding and expanding, so that makes us smaller with every passing second, but it also means that we're part of something bigger every day. It's a statistical certainty that there are planets out there like this one, better, free from our mania and our destruction."

Katie wondered who he got high with now that this fuck-up had pushed Danny away. He was still using. Nothing he had said or done suggested otherwise. She sensed where he would go that night if it was anywhere but the police station.

Katie was startled by her brother's attentiveness. She could see that Ryan liked what he heard, that he was allowing himself to drift away and forget why they were there in the first place. He couldn't stop looking up, blowing air into the atmosphere until it turned into words. "What the hell have you been reading?"

"Ryan, both of you, Jesus. We need a plan."

"I'll go to the station tonight. You two wait there until they find Danny."

Eric stood carefully as he spoke, attempting to convey finality. But he didn't like being in charge. He was used to submission, and his order rang hollow.

"No."

Ryan simmered. "Katie, it's the only way." Begging now.

Katie walked several steps down the beach. She shortened her strides as she went, eventually shuffling and turning to face the boys.

"You sure Danny won't come hunting us down? He's not going to come get us in the middle of the night?"

"Pretty sure, yeah. I think he's smart enough to try to keep a low profile, and he doesn't know for sure."

"Then we wait."

"Dammit, Katie, wait for what?"

She looked at Ryan, took in his disorder. "Just more time to think. More time to get Eric out of this."

Ryan woke from his daze. He looked pained as he gestured toward Eric but let his arm swing to his side.

"Katie, if Dann—"

"If Danny comes for us, if he even thinks of coming near us, Eric is going to go to the police and tell them what happened. Right, Eric?"

"Right."

Ryan threw up his hands. Eric shoved his in his pockets.

"But what's Eric supposed to do? What if Danny comes for him?"

Katie could imagine how Danny must have felt in the woods, controlling the scared boys in front of him. Powerful but agitated. "He won't. We all have the right idea. He's crazy, but he's a kid. He doesn't want more blood on his hands."

"You might be underestimating him. If he hasn't snapped yet, he will soon." Ryan had seen him come close at the Dunes. It wouldn't take much.

"We'll take our chances."

The iciness of Katie's words struck both boys. They abandoned their cause. She walked away and left them scrambling.

Ryan and Eric walked side by side, five paces behind, slowly gaining ground. The light was on above the Clarke porch, but no one sat outside. Some teenagers, too old for wiffleball, yelled beyond the next jetty. A voice answered them. One of the boys yelled back, but his friends had already started to leave, pulled in by the unseen call, sure of its maternal power.

Katie stopped when they reached the parking lot and turned to face her pupils.

"Eric."

"Yeah."

His shoulders slumped, but he still towered over her wiry frame. His shadow enveloped her as he bowed his head to listen.

"You can't go near him. You can't go looking for him. We'll all get hurt that way."

"I won't. I know how to hide."

They started to move.

"What does it feel like?"

She blurted the question loudly enough to alarm her charges, but Eric's look told her she wouldn't receive an answer.

A white car approached from their left as she turned around. It paused, and the passenger window rolled down. Jamie waved to Katie, but at the sight of her company his face froze, and he lowered his hand. He didn't look away. They could see him swallow twice and tighten his grip on the wheel.

"Hey, Dad. Have a good night."

Eric walked to his car without waiting for the response he was certain would stay lodged in Jamie's throat, if it ever got that high. He backed out and drove off, something from the '70s blaring out of his window. Jamie released the brake and rolled into his driveway. He went to the trunk but stared up the street long enough for Katie and Ryan to pass him.

"Hi, Mr. Clarke. Have a good one."

Finally he popped the trunk, pulled out three smallish bags of groceries, and, after a minute or two, made it inside.

A little while later, Katie looked back from her porch. Would he say anything to Anne? For an instant, she feared him telling her own parents, but she decided he wouldn't. The only reason to speak up would be to warn the Murrays of the company their children were keeping, to admit out loud what Beth and Kevin had known for years, that Jamie was ashamed of Eric and better off when he was out of the way. Katie was willing to admit she couldn't really understand how Anne or Jamie felt about their son. What had he done to them? Anything at all? Had they gone to great lengths to keep him close at some point when she wasn't watching? She couldn't determine what their cores were made of, if they were more substantial than the golf talk and porch parties led her to believe. She had no idea if Eric was hard to corral, if he ever listened to anything they told him, or if anything they ever told him was worth listening to.

But Jamie had looked straight into his boy's bruised eyes. He had recognized his son and chosen not to speak. She could guess that Jamie had gone to the store at Anne's behest. Listening to his classic rock Sirius station there and back. He had silently watched Eric back up and pull away and drive off. She couldn't predict where Eric would go for the night, and she wasn't convinced it wouldn't be his car on the side of some deserted road, but she knew where Jamie would be. She imagined him putting away the groceries, the fruit in the middle of the kitchen island and the milk in the fridge they had installed the summer before and the pretzels and cereal in the tall, white pantry next to the window that looked out to the porch and the water beyond. If the nights she had spent in that house, staying up late playing cards and proving she was one of the big kids, were

any indication, Jamie would go straight to sleep in the master bedroom above the den. The bedroom down the hall, the one closest
to the main staircase, would be empty and stay that way, even if he
found the words for his son, even if he remembered where to look
for them.

August 15

Murder is a weird word and doesn't describe what happened to Tim. Was he killed or did he die. I've been reading about premeditated. I should delete my search history.

Mom and Dad liked most of the same movies but never agreed about music except for Bruce Springsteen. After dinner if they were in a good mood they would start singing along and I would yell at them to stop but they would just sing louder and they could tell I loved it.

Debts that no honest man can pay. Good thing I'm not honest.

That's what I'm telling myself.

19

The next twenty-two hours of Katie's life passed quickly, devoid of the epiphany she had hoped they would include. As she sat in the cart, camped in the shade, her book unturned, she ran through the places and people to which and whom Eric could run, but none of them made sense, and she questioned his willingness anyway. She wanted him to choose but wasn't sure what would happen if he did. For so long he had been trained to believe his choices were wrong.

She sat on the porch for an hour after getting home. Ryan showered and joined her and kept quiet, tacitly deferring to her judgment, trusting that she would have an answer by the end of the night. If not an answer, at least a decision.

Kevin wanted pizza, which was true most days. Beth was around, and whenever she was his desire was less likely to be fulfilled, but today she was busy in their home office and uninterested in arguing for something healthier. He lamented his dying summer, now at the point where he had to devote a small chunk of each day to school-year preparations, not as arduous as they had been in his greener years. But he had always felt in touch with the rhythms of the season's length. Whether he was or not, pizza nights were special occasions; he remained his quiet self but added a boyish smile, delighted by what he was getting away with. His family members weren't usually interested in joining him to fetch their dinner. He liked the quiet ride, the smell and staff in the unassuming store, and the excitement on the kids' faces when he reappeared at the top of the porch stairs, excitement that had once been so easy to induce.

Katie's interest in joining him on this night was disorienting, but Kevin thought there was a chance the offer was a reflection of her maturation, of an appreciation for the father-daughter bonding that the growth had nurtured. Or maybe she was just feeling nostalgic and wanted to soak in a family night together, anticipating that they would be harder to come by in the summers ahead. The last thought saddened him because she was right to think that, if she did think it. He wasn't the type of parent to weep at the thought of his little girl and boy all grown up, but estival air had him in an unusual state, from which Katie roused him with a "Let's go" on her way to the stairs. As he unlocked the car and opened his door, he realized her presence could hinder his ability to sneak the extra slice or sandwich his trips always included. He reminded himself that her company was more gratifying than a slice of pepperoni or a chicken parm sub, still hoping she wouldn't object to either.

They made small, forgettable talk on the way to the store, which was a longer drive than the closest option. Kevin insisted that the extra distance was worth it over his kids' gripes that the pizza was merely ordinary at both shops. He had expected Katie to be more talkative given her enthusiasm for the trip, but he didn't dare push her; too scarce was the opportunity to coexist.

They made it to Tocci's without Katie broaching any of the subjects she wanted to cover. As almost always, Kevin hadn't called in their order ahead of time. Unless the family was in a rush, he chose to order at the counter and enjoy his bonus snack in the corner underneath the television, or at a table closer to the counter if the staff members were in a chatty mood. Katie declined to join in on the appetizer order and picked out a table. From her side, she could see the television clearly. A reporter talked inaudibly about a house fire in North Monomo and smiled a bit too hard for Katie's liking as the segment concluded. Her father sauntered to the table with a soda bottle and a bag of chips and checked again if she was sure she didn't want anything.

"Begging for diabetes, Dad."

"It's a cheat day."

She feared that once she broke the ice they would both fall, and the frigid water had already pulled enough people into its depths. So she scuffled as she looked at the screen, where a Red Sox highlight played and the sports reporter's vapidity came through even without sound, and then spoke cryptically about, in so many words, the meaning of life and asked her dad what he valued most, what he found the most rewarding.

"What do you mean, Katie?"

"I don't know. How you define success, how you measure your happiness."

"Oh. Well, no better place to discuss this than over a slice of sausage and peppers."

She tried not to look at the grease spilling onto his fingers and the paper plate below them as he ate the pungent triangle, chewing most of a bite before speaking again.

"You've probably heard me mock your mother about the 'brochure life.'"

"Not really, no."

He wiped his hands. "Well, you get what I mean. People who want the new house and the nice car, expensive but not over the top, the big yard, trendy clothes, no obstacles or anything in their way. Spend their time laughing and chatting like still-lifes in some ad for a retirement community."

She took a moment to consider the words, which he had delivered quickly.

"And you make fun of Mom for wanting that?"

He paused with the slice halfway between the plate and his mouth, realizing the need to choose his words carefully, though he reckoned Beth didn't need protecting from Katie, who had already penetrated her mother's last nerves.

"Not so much now, I suppose. When we were younger, a little more often. There were times where we fought about things like that, whether life was just about ticking boxes and moving along on some track until you can retire and sit on the beach down the street from your summer home."

Katie hesitated. "But, I mean, you did kind of do that, didn't you? You bought the summer house and had your kids, and soon you'll retire and sit on the beach as much as you want."

"You kidding? I'll work until they drag me out of the classroom," and this time he didn't do such a fine job of chewing before speaking. He wiped his mouth with a napkin already stained orange.

"You know what I mean, Dad. You guys do sort of have a brochure life. You chose to follow that path. I'm not saying it's a bad one."

"No, it's not. Maybe we could've done different things or pursued other lives. I don't know, honey. This life brought us two perfect kids and a rich, peaceful existence. Maybe there's more than that waiting for some people, but it's hard to complain. I guess the issue isn't, well, ending up here. Pursuing it, relying on it as your sole source of satisfaction and purpose is the problem."

Katie reached for the soda without asking, and he slid it to her. She felt the fizz before she tasted anything sweet. Once she did, the liquid's tang struck her as man-made and lingered on her tongue. Kevin watched her sip and chuckled at the burp that followed.

"Why are you asking about this? One year of school and you're already considering life's heaviest questions."

"I don't know."

He wiped his hands and mouth, then wiggled his fingers over the second slice, which he held up for Katie to try but happily indulged in as soon as she turned it down.

"I've just been thinking about Tim McNamara. I saw them talk about him again on the news a few days ago. The kid who died last month. The one at Greenstone?"

Kevin had considered a number of topics Katie might want to address on the ride over, but somehow the dead boy from the next town hadn't crossed his mind. He had committed a fair number of hours to thinking about Tim, but he hadn't taken one minute to consider how the death might be affecting his daughter. He and Beth never spent much time worrying about Katie or her ability to weather adversity. Beth sometimes complained about their friction, but to Kevin that didn't sound like concern.

When he did worry about his daughter, it had mostly to do with loneliness. She had always possessed the ability to blend in. He accepted that she didn't mind being alone. She was better suited to it than anyone else he knew. She got this from him, as she did so many other things. Most notable was the curse of overthinking, for her not a case of indecision but rather a nagging contemplation of her life, founded in logic. Logic could take people in different directions, toward alienating truths. Kevin's truths were bitter. Maybe Katie's were different. Most of his involved silence and rumination, so he hadn't thought to ask her. If he had, he would have assumed she preferred not being asked.

"Of course. What about him?"

"Just, um, what do you make of the trend? All these kids my age around here. There are a lot of them."

She comprehended how much it hurt him to think about it, and she expected him to meet the question with silence or a throwaway answer. He chose the former at first, chewing slowly, biding his time, but as she prepared to abandon her plan entirely, he spoke up.

"It breaks my heart. This Tim kid, but every other story, too."

She resolved to keep him talking, moving toward a fix. "Why do you think it happens so much here?"

"Hard to say. Quiet towns, seasonal lives, young people who are impressionable and vulnerable and don't see ways out or ways to escape, even temporarily. I don't know. I don't think it can be simplified or easily explained."

"Brochure life doesn't sound so bad to kids like Tim McNamara."

"Maybe not."

Katie didn't cry often and didn't cry now, but her eyes revealed enough. She sniffled, aware of her visible emotion and hoping one hard snort could hide it all so they could carry on and forget this conversation had ever taken place.

"Katie, what is it?" He was yet to determine the gravity of the interaction, or at least the source of that gravity.

"I think there's more to Tim's story."

"More than just another victim? Well, you're absolutely right. We shouldn't treat the kids lik—"

"No, more than you've seen. Some people are in trouble."

Kevin put his slice down and ensured no one was listening. Customers chatted loudly at two tables halfway across the room.

"You and Ryan. You know something. You saw something that night after you left the party?"

She nodded, and the movement almost turned into shaking, but she caught herself and took a deep breath while her father's red face slowly returned to normal, still moderately colored by the sun.

"Can you tell me?"

"In the car."

"Sure."

Three minutes passed awkwardly before the pizzas and garlic knots arrived. Kevin was a little too eager to grab the boxes and leave, but the server turned away without a second thought.

Katie followed her father, still unsure of what benefit telling him could produce but positive that another night of keeping these secrets would make her sick. Even if Kevin didn't have a perfect solution, he would provide affirmation. He would protect her. He tossed the food into the backseat, where it landed safely and upright despite his lack of care. She opened her door slowly, and he gripped the wheel in the unstarted car.

"Can we talk here? Do we need to leave?" Kevin glanced around outside the car and looked behind them to check if anyone was prowling.

"No, Dad. This is fine. You have to promise to just listen for a bit."

And he did listen. She couldn't have forgotten a detail of her night at Greenstone or of Eric's story if she had tried, and she shared every one.

Kevin started to jump in several times but always stopped himself, his vise grip on the wheel taking the place of interjections. He wanted to hold Katie, to hug her, but she spoke as if in a trance, as if someone had injected the story and the crimes into her blood, and he didn't want to disrupt her as it finally left her system. They weren't a hugging family anymore. Most of their embraces came at funerals and weddings, and they didn't have many weddings to attend. When she finished, she was crying, and Kevin pulled her close, neither one of them minding the gearshift jabbing their ribs.

"Katie, where's Eric now? What happened to him?"

She sniffled. "I don't know. I haven't talked to him."

"You and Ryan were just going to let this go? Were you going to tell anyone?"

She didn't mind his mistrust. Still, she spoke in an exasperated tone. Her voice broke but quickly regained its footing. "That's why I'm telling you. I don't know. I don't know if I should go to the police or to Eric or let it all play out."

"Katie, we have to go to the police. We can go right now."

"No."

He reached for her hand. She let him take it. Both were clammy. Four motorcycles passed on the road behind them. The leader revved his engine.

"Katie, I do—"

"We can't. Not yet. Eric won't have a chance to defend himself. He won't be able to tell his side."

He brushed hair out of her face. "Yes, he will. His family will make sure he gets the best situation possible."

She puffed.

"It's sad if you believe that. I don't think you do. Mom might not know better, but you do." She spoke through gritted teeth to the windshield before peeking his way. He studied his feet.

"I know it's hard. He's your childhood pal. But they have to be held re—"

"No, he doesn't deserve it. He doesn't deserve to get dragged down in this."

"Deserve? Tim McNamara didn't deserve to die, Katie. His parents didn't deserve to bury their kid. Worona doesn't deserve to have crap like this happen to them over and over again. They killed a boy, Katie. They watched him die. Am I missing something?"

He spoke with passion but didn't raise his voice. Katie had always liked that about her father: the privacy of his rage, how seamlessly he contained it.

"Eric didn't kill him. He didn't. He was there, but he was scared and alone. All he could do was watch it happen. What else could he have done?"

Kevin let her words hang for a moment before proceeding. He saw that she had given the matter weeks of thought. "He could've run and called 911 or . . . I don't know, I don't know. We can't let it slide just because we like him and live down the street from his family."

"His family that pushed him away and let this happen."

Now they both looked forward, exhalations synced. Kevin had stained his shirt near the shamrock on his chest, and a sweat blotch had started to form below his neck.

"What did you want me to say when you told me? What did you think I was going to do?"

She sniffled, then looked up. "I wanted you to say we could help Eric."

"I don't think he can run from this, sweetie."

They both hated his pet name as soon as he spoke it. Either the look on Katie's face or the earnestness she had displayed throughout the conversation wore Kevin down, and he let go of the wheel and pressed back into his seat, bumping his head gently on its rest as he did.

"What were you hoping for? We toss Eric in the trunk and drive him to Oklahoma?"

She didn't respond to his puzzled smile. He put it away quickly. "Just forget it. We can go to the station now."

"Maybe it can wait until after pizza. Mom will be mad if we don't bring dinner."

Katie looked at her father, who now closed his eyes and stretched his hands behind him, interlocking them behind the headrest before lifting them until they struck the roof.

"You think I should tell Eric to run?"

"You didn't already?"

"He could use some more motivation. Maybe if you told him."

She wanted to pass the burden, shed the weight.

"I don't think so."

"So what? Just go to the station tonight and hope for the best?"

He rolled his head to the right to look at her, his hands still locked. "Eric knows he can run. He's had weeks to leave. He put you and your brother in danger. He understands what you have to do, and I think he wants you to do it."

"Maybe."

"Okay then. Tomorrow. You and Ryan go to work, and I'll pick you up, and we'll go to the station together. You two tell them everything you saw and everything he told you, the whole truth, and we go from there."

Most of the scenarios Katie had unwound in her head for that night ended with them at the station. None of them ended with Kevin telling her it could wait until tomorrow. She sensed that he, too, hoped Eric would split. She wasn't sure if Eric would even try to. She hoped he had already started.

"Sounds like a plan."

"Call in sick if you want, if you think it's safer."

"It's fine, Dad. We haven't seen him around the club. I don't think Danny is showing his face around here anytime soon."

But here was Danny's face. Right then, right there. He appeared from the end of the row of storefronts, on their left, turning the corner and then into the convenience store next to Tocci's. He wore a vintage Red Sox hat pulled low over his forehead and a solid red shirt with jeans, stained around both kneecaps with paint. Kevin was already backing out when Katie spotted him. Danny never looked in the car's direction, peering only at the ground and then at the little neon sign showing the jackpots for Mega Millions and Powerball that hung to the right of the door. Katie waited for fear or anger to rise inside, but only pity came.

His face was smooth, his jeans an inch too short, the shirt worn at the collar. He was skinny, pubescent. Above all else, he looked small in the doorway, lonely against the backdrop of cars and shoppers and the girl who held his life in her hands.

Or maybe it was just another kid in a baseball hat, and her mind was only superimposing Danny onto this boy. She thought, only for a second, that maybe Danny would have run by now. But he wouldn't leave. This life was all he had, all he was allowed.

She wondered what Danny would do in prison, if he would be able to pull off the bravado and douchebaggery that had been his signatures until the early hours of the fifth of July. She doubted he would because there would be a hundred Dannys, each older and stronger than the last, ready to put him in his place, infuriated that another Worona boy—and for every hundred Dannys, she conceived one hundred Woronas, some on the water, some in the woods, others in distant states and territories—had fallen into the trap, or not fallen so much as failed to escape from it; these traps had been laid down years before, camouflaged enough to remain unseen until boys like Danny sped into them for the first time and felt them draw warm blood. She bet he would be quiet around men like that. He would follow their orders, and they would absorb him into their ranks. Katie couldn't imagine his worst-case scenario and didn't want to, though she suspected it was on its way. Or orange might suit him, and he would get clean, see the error of his ways. Her picture fizzled first around the corners. There was no worst-case scenario, no spectrum of outcomes. His lot was set. All that was left to settle was who would go with him and whether they would resist.

The boy left the store less than a minute later, gum and cigarettes in one hand and an orange soda in the other. Kevin had already steered them away. Neither one of them spoke during the ride's first half.

When the silence broke, it was only Katie reminding her father not to say anything to her mother. They both agreed that was the best way to approach the situation, considering Beth would be at the station or hunting Danny and Eric herself before Katie could get a third of the way into her side of the story. They didn't discuss how they would handle telling her or others what they knew once they had gone to the station, and they didn't lay out exactly what Katie or Ryan would say to the police, though Kevin assumed Danny's associates would go unmentioned.

They watched the Red Sox while they ate. Katie nibbled on a slice and went to bed. Kevin watched until the end and fell asleep in his chair, from which he could see the door.

August 17

I bought a soda because I thought it was too hot for beer and because it reminded me of stopping here when I was little. Stopping with my dad. I'm not sure what the store was on the way home from but he told Mom it was on the way home. I let Danny get a treat on the way home. We grabbed a bite on the way home.

I think he liked taking the long way. They weren't mean to each other but they also did better when they spent some time apart. They probably did better when I spent some time apart. I'm not what they had in mind.

I liked riding in the truck. He played Johnny Cash CDs but he never explained what the songs were about. I had to find out later. I liked them but I never listened to them when I wasn't with Dad. I haven't heard them in a while. Time keeps dragging on.

I'm wearing his jeans. Mine now. Mine for a long time and I don't know how long he had them. Long enough that the stains look like they came with the pants. I actually bought a couple pairs on sale a couple months ago. With birthday cash. Doesn't seem right to wear the nice new pairs when it's hot like this though. I'd rather save them. Make them last.

I'm not sure what I think they're lasting for. They're not going to let me wear them where I'm going. They're going to pick my outfit for me.

I'm starting to think it might not be worth fighting. Or running. I don't want to tell them about Stevie but I want them to punish me for it.

I didn't usually get orange soda when we stopped here. Maybe I never did. We got root beer. That was the deal. He said go in and grab a root beer and get one for me too and one for whoever finishes theirs first. Sometimes he wanted a Twix or peanut butter crackers too. When I won the contest he would tell me to save the extra one for home. Just don't tell your mother you already had one. One's enough.

Stevie didn't come to my house and I almost never went to his. We always met somewhere. At school or the fields or in town. I think he liked just riding or walking so he could be away from them because they were mean. Mine were never worse than sad. His were mean and loud. They yelled.

I've been avoiding the club but I think I have to go back. If I'm going to get to Katie it should be there. Away from her family. I don't want to think about the families.

20

By the time Kevin stirred, NESN was showing a condensed replay of the baseball game, which had ended four hours earlier. He had been dreaming. The memory of the dream tried to come back to him, but it ebbed away, save for the image of Beth standing at her desk, in the home office, telling someone to "get fucking serious." Now, sitting up in the chair, he wasn't sure if it was part of the dream or just a misplaced segment of memory. Either way, she must have known the person on the other end of the phone well. She didn't curse very often. She almost never said "fuck."

His memory failed him plenty. Beth tended to grow frustrated when he could summon only shadowy recollections of events she recounted for him with barbed precision. But he remembered the first time he heard her say "fuck" to him, and it wasn't sexy. The conversation, whatever distorted version of it his brain permitted him to access, played in his head as he flipped away from NESN in search of something live.

"This is ridiculous. Every time I so much as hint at having ambition—for us, for me—you shut me down. You remind me how stupid I am and how stupid I sound."

He let SportsCenter highlights wash over him. He was pretty sure he had her words right. They had lived in a tiny apartment, too cramped to escape a fight like this one. The words played again, and he could picture her stance as she delivered them: arms crossed, eyes toward the window, too angry to acknowledge his seated form at the snug round table. He supposed he had looked to the window too.

"You can't possibly think I think you're stupid. For one thing, you're not. Second of all, why would I still be here with you if I didn't think you were incredibly smart and kind?"

"There's the million-dollar fucking question, Kevin."

Even now, two kids and almost three decades later, the word startled him. It didn't bother him, though the depth of her rage had caught him by surprise. SportsCenter updated him on the Padres and Dodgers as they entered their sixteenth inning. Even the anchor sounded bored.

In his version of the apartment fight, he had let her "fucking" hang. He had allowed her to think on it, to decide if the night demanded it, to consider the possibility that he was simply not right for her. She continued, and he could tell she despised his silence.

"Well? Are you going to tell me I'm misguided? Go ahead, and then I remind you that there's nothing evil about making money and wanting more. We make money and have kids and grow up. That's what we do. I'm trying to be an adult. We're not twenty-two anymore."

And then, after his brief foray into "there are more important things than money" territory, she said it again.

"Kevin, don't you think I fucking picked up on that by now? Don't you think I got it the first three hundred times you mentioned how you grew up rich but are worldly enough and special enough to be disillusioned about it?'

The ESPNer looped him in on the latest NBA free agency news. He didn't recognize most of the names they mentioned. The big stars had finalized their deals weeks ago. In front of him, on the coffee table, his glass of skim milk had reached room temperature on its coaster. Condensation soaked into the cork. He reached for the glass but didn't drink, choosing instead to go to the sink and empty it. He rinsed it three times, filled it halfway with water, and swigged.

He didn't trust his mind to provide an accurate memory of how long the next silence had lasted. It seemed eternal. It only broke when he tried to call her "honey," and she snapped.

"Don't call me that."

He couldn't even pretend to remember what he said next, but he could picture her telling him it wasn't as profound as he wanted it to be. The lifetime of evidence since the fight suggested she had been right.

He filled the glass all the way with water this time. He leaned against the sink. A commercial previewed an NFL preseason game. He wondered if his friend in the math department was running the fantasy league again and if he was invited. As he lifted the glass to sip, some water splashed over the edge and onto his chest. Droplets ran down the outside of the surface. He saw tears in them. She had cried in the apartment. Tears of exhaustion, of stalemate. Kevin had no idea how or when he had moved, but she said the next part close to him, cowering against the wall, her breath warm on his chin.

"It's like there's a side of you I can't ever be a part of. There's another person inside of you that doesn't want any part of this, of us."

She was right, of course. It wasn't a secret, the hidden side. It wasn't even taboo. They had simply, and silently, agreed to leave it be, to trust that he had come to terms with whatever mistakes he now chose not to discuss. The agreement lasted. It was still in place as he returned to his chair and placed the glass back on the coaster, the ring of wetness on the cork of a slightly greater circumference than the glass itself.

"Beth, I'm just saying the type of life you're picturing for us doesn't always work. It just seems like something to aspire to because you see it in the other people at work or in people like my parents. We can have more than that. Those other people aren't spotless. And they're made of glass. They're fragile."

He doubted he had been that coherent. He had probably mumbled a bit or rambled on. But he had reassured her, convinced her to meet somewhere in the middle.

"As long as you don't talk down to me."

She was sound asleep now. He didn't have to check. When he fell asleep in the chair in front of the Red Sox or in some other unforgivable place, she left him there. She would ask him if he had learned his lesson the next morning when his back was stiff and his eyes drooped. He would smile and take his mug from her and stretch while she sat at the table separating the sections of the paper she wanted from the rest. He was good about telling her how much he loved her. He had been back then, too.

She had worn her reading glasses while they fought in the apartment, simple and thin but for him a reliable turn-on.

"I love you more than anything in this world, Beth. I mean it. I was in a bad place before we met. You know that. Born into the brochure life, and I still ended up there, still went rogue. That's all I'm saying. There are no guarantees. We have to be careful."

"We will be."

The anchor warned him a SCORE UPDATE was on its way. The Padres had ended the game with a walkoff single, a bloop to shallow left, innocuous if not for the circumstances. The game-winning run trotted in from third, his arms raised in triumph, his teammates galloping to him before they made a beeline for the hero rounding first.

He smiled at her when she reached out and gripped his forearms. She looked at the ground but only because she was tired. He felt her soften.

"Did our fight get you riled up?"

"No. You smell like shit. I'm going to bed."

21

Eric got high while the Murrays ate pizza. It was the first time he had done so in several days. He didn't do it alone, though the faces around him were unfamiliar and the couch he collapsed into only hazily recalled. He hadn't made a plan to do it, but as his day wore on the thought of doing it crept toward the front of his mind. He wasn't sure if he could ignore the urge anymore. He couldn't remember if he ever had.

For most of the afternoon, he wandered on and near a beach. After a few hours of walking and swimming, he sat and then stretched his full length on the sand, packed firm beneath him. He closed his eyes, letting the sun warm his face, and waited to open them until clouds relieved the heat. He questioned why he needed the drug at all when there were moments of Zen like this one naturally occurring in the world. But then he considered whether this table scrap of Zen would be that much better with the drug, with the high, and the thought crept that much farther along. He stayed in his spot a while longer, then got up and walked the beach until he came to a decision. His next stop, once he got in the car, would be the house with the exotic faces, the house he trusted enough. No one watching him there.

He didn't mean to push thoughts of Katie and Ryan and Tim out of his mind. They swirled in the background, but he couldn't focus on any one of the three long enough to forge a plan. He knew he wanted to protect them, to do whatever remained of right by Tim's family, and he understood Danny should be punished. Regarding his own fate he was blank. Once he turned himself in, he wouldn't have the means to stave off the penalties and condemnations. He wasn't sure he wanted to sidestep the retribution. Some days he did.

On the days he awoke ready to give in, Eric didn't think much about the future or prison. Mostly he tried to remember the hours before Tim's death, not the one or two immediately preceding it— those he remembered well—but the three or four before those. His best efforts produced some strands, pieces of a late lunch he had devoured and a ride along the water that he was starting to think was just a composite of other sequestered afternoons. His wish was that a faultless recollection would divulge inflection points, moments at which he could have curled away from disaster. The presence of such points would suggest his current position was not destined but was instead the result of choices made in moments of reverie, made in detestable places, on the banks of his Styx.

Before the high, before he could feel nothing other than the inside of his own mind, he smiled at the thought of his environment—the grungy music, someone trying to reinvent the good stuff rather than the good stuff itself; the slumping bodies; the squalid house—and how well it mimicked any random outsider's assumptions about a person like him and a place like that. The circumstances were easier to picture than understand. Eric himself rarely understood them, but at least he possessed the sense not to pretend he did. It was safe to assume many were like him, running away but too afraid to go far, like puppies staying in an owner's line of sight. The crowd he mixed with skewed male and young. The older addicts and tag-alongs preferred the quiet of other hideaways. They had left the fear behind in another era.

Eric was eager to hear their stories, though most weren't willing to share. Those who did tended to talk in circles. He didn't mind. It was clear they liked having someone listen. Everyone in the room was some form of alone. Matching his brand of isolation with someone else's had proved difficult, but there were worse ways to pass the time.

Eric still felt the high. Some of the lumps around him were only there to stop their aching. He hadn't reached that stage. He was nodding within a minute, somewhere between awake and alive, nine hundred pounds light and extraterrestrial. He wasn't forgetting Katie or Tim. For now he had never heard those names, never felt anything heavier than a gentle pressing on his chest that was commanding but not forceful. This wasn't bliss. It was something weaker, laced with dread. The dread, the paranoia, had oozed into someone else, the boy in the corner of the room next door, who promised to hold it for Eric until he returned. People in the house were always willing to share their burdens or hold a friend's for safe-keeping. They trusted the favor would be returned, that night or the next, by a body new or known.

So in the hours the house was awake it ran like a machine. A stream of twitching, lifted souls leaving their cargo at the door; the parcels sometimes latched themselves onto someone headed willingly across the threshold.

But no one could take Eric's dread that night. It clung to him, to the back of his shirt, never detached. It watched him float away, unfazed because it was sure he would return in short order, plenty patient enough to watch his flight and the others throughout the terminal, some longer than others but all landing with the same dull thud. It was polite at first, looking over Eric's shoulder. It didn't reenter him for a few minutes, giving him space and time to re-member its presence, to dream it had been banished in the midst of his slumber. Eric would have liked to shoulder someone else's lesser burden, but that would have meant leaving his ordeal for someone unprepared, so as it crawled up his back and peeled the skin at the top of his spine, he let it in. Then he calmly rose and crossed the room, stepping over an entwined couple, to splash water on his face until his eyes adjusted to the light.

He didn't know what constituted the ideal length for such a respite, but he was sure he had surpassed it. His body creaked as he stepped outside and felt the air, yet unwarmed by the incipient sunrise. Three sedans sat in the driveway. Another lounged behind his on the street. He looked back at the house, sure there had been more than four cars' worth of people in the basement. He had no inkling of who lived there. Discussions of homeownership didn't come up often in the catacombs. Whether he was leaving a crowd of six or forty he was unclear. Numbness roiled the memory with each step toward the car, the line between the corporeal beings that had surrounded him and the spirits that he reckoned lived in the walls blurring as he yawned in the driver's seat.

The radio jumped into something like the selection he had heard in the crypt. He hadn't changed the station or adjusted the volume in weeks. Usually he rode with the windows down, eager for the smells of beach, gas, and forest. But he never shut off the music. When the wind died down, the silence needed filling.

He drove three miles before he encountered anyone. It was a runner waiting to cross a quiet four-way, so he waved him on and admired his gait and wondered if this pre-dawn riser crashed early each night or had simply been programmed for longer days than the average person. He didn't have to wait as long for the second, third, and fourth. They biked together, two in neon green shirts and the other in a flatter yellow. They looked professional. The leader gave Eric a friendly wave as he passed, but by the time he saw the hand there was little point in returning the favor.

Mornings like this had unfurled often enough for Eric to develop habits, serene regimens springing forth from insidious dawns. If he awoke alone or in the proper company, he would drive far away for breakfast, riding until an exit enticed him. He would find a diner or corner store that offered decent breakfast sandwiches, but he wouldn't stay long, eating in his car unless a companion insisted on staying inside. The people were almost always pleasant, despite the hour. Eric could tell they were used to opening early and serving the same fourteen patrons with coffee, a bagel, or the newspaper. They noted Eric's newness but never thought of him again once the bells over the door signaled his departure. If he returned at a later date he was still new, and they smiled warmly when they took his order.

This morning's ride took him a few exits toward the full ocean. He noted the convenience store advertising breakfast just off the highway but held out for something heartier. By the time he found it in the town's center, the well-behaved had started to rise, so he hurried out of the cafe as a short line formed behind him. He wanted to steer clear of the glances of the waiting, mostly parents who looked unbothered. His sandwich was delicious, and he wished he had saved a sip more of iced tea to wash it down, but to head back in and purchase another would have been a violation of his best practices, so he rode into the next town and found somewhere quieter that also sold his favorite chips.

The thought of driving away, for good, crossed his mind as he ate them, but he had no destination selected. Whatever he chose would be no good. The place would pale in comparison to the trip, and he couldn't drive forever.

Pleasing his parents had never been his priority, but he never meant to hurt them, except for a night or two that had gotten away from them all. They wouldn't worry if he fled, and their tears at the news of his involvement in the boy's death would be spotted with relief, with a sense of vindication, if they believed the account he expected Danny to dream up. They would believe it because believing it would produce a faster resolution, once they convinced the cops they knew nothing of his whereabouts. He doubted Millie would believe Danny or the news, but he was sure she wouldn't fight the lies. She was busy and outnumbered, in his mind not at fault. He thought about writing a letter, a note to leave behind for Katie so the details would be clear, but he was confident she remembered them. No one could learn she had associated with him. She had to be guarded, or allowed to defend herself.

He drove until he needed gas, filling up at a station he remembered passing once before. He paid with cash and pulled back onto the road, closer to congested than abandoned, his car unexceptional among the others, all headed east, in one thousand different directions.

22

Katie had expected her nerves to be worse, but they were only a minor distraction as she and Cassie rode around the course, emptier than it had been in weeks, its grass browned on the holes most exposed to the sun. It wasn't yet noon, but she could feel a burn forming on the back of her neck and beads of sweat fattening at the base of her arms. Cassie went on about a handful of job opportunities for the fall. Katie didn't listen.

She didn't burn as easily as Ryan or Beth. Kevin rarely wore sunscreen. He told them he didn't like the way it mixed with his sweat on the tennis court. One summer, at a restaurant some friends had suggested for a double date, another patron mistook him for a Native American, citing a resemblance to a close friend of the family. Beth intervened before he could play along or say anything offensive.

Katie's neck and shoulder tops were more sensitive than her legs and forearms. She was fairly diligent when it came to applying lotion in the cart. Cassie was a bad influence. She tanned as a matter of principle. She saw it as a vocation, but she didn't use that word.

Katie didn't know the name of Cassie's brother, the one who died in a house that didn't belong to him.

Ryan's side of the plan was simple. He was to meet Kevin in the lot once he had finished caddying and corralling his sister. Ryan's nerves were as bad as he had expected. Thankfully, the two members he had been assigned to for the morning didn't ask much of him, though he was moments away from reaching the sixteenth green and realizing he had left one player's gap wedge on the eleventh, a minor inconvenience made major by the layout of the course and the timing of their arrangement. He had finished his second Gatorade on the thirteenth hole. He worried that he would have to speak, that Katie would look to him for backup. He was ready for the summer to end, ready for heat sickness to afflict him before he reached the clubhouse.

Eric had been sitting in his car in the row closest to the putting green and the pro shop for some time. He split the minutes between a pit of doubt and the brink of revelation. He thought of leaving, yet he trusted Katie to keep both of them safe, to share the truth and his story, which he hoped were the same and believable. Each time he considered retreating, he pictured Katie standing at the bag rack in front of him, arms crossed, lips pursed, satisfaction discernible in her eyes.

It would be nice to hear a goodbye, just this once. Once he heard the word, he would never need to hear it again, at least not for a long time.

Most of his life's episodes hadn't ended with goodbye. They had ended with incomplete assertions of faith on the part of those supposedly closest to him, half-assed attempts at willing his fortitude into existence.

Goodbye would be nice. It would be honest. People didn't like to be honest around him. Their statements weren't always lies, though; sometimes they were aspirations bequeathed to him. Sometimes the lies were better, less suffocating.

After a sweaty, white-haired man bought their last bottle of water, the girls drove down the eighteenth, Cassie at the wheel. Behind the hole, the path sloped and turned around the putting green. Katie looked over in time to see Eric's car and him waving at her from within it.

"Cass, can you let me out here? I need to go talk to someone."

"Mmm, a boy coming to track you down? Don't take too long. You can tell me all about it." She pulled them over. Katie stepped out before they had come to a complete stop.

"Don't count on it."

Katie walked on the regular turf above the practice surface and checked to make sure the car hadn't attracted any attention. Two older couples walked toward the club's front entrance, and a group of early starters chatted a few rows away while one of them changed out of his golf shoes in the bed of his pickup. Eric gripped the wheel lightly as she approached, but the car had been off for several minutes, since his last fancy of flight.

"What are you doing here?" The question carried an edge, but she liked seeing him. She could reach out and touch him if she needed to.

"Not sure I have a good answer for you. Car sort of just, uh, ended up here."

"We're going to the police today. In a little bit."

She opened the door and stood for a moment before sitting. The seat had baked in the sun. It singed her thighs.

"That's good. They'll move fast. No one wants to drag this out, including me." He squinted hard while he said it. Katie had never seen him do that.

"I guess so. What are you going to do?"

He took a deep breath. "Working on it."

A car pulled up behind them, waiting for another to back out of a spot farther down the row. Katie kept her head pressed to the seat. Eric looked out his window. He could see the main building, the pro shop, and, in the distance, the first two of six outdoor tennis courts.

"You look exhausted. Is everything okay?"

"All good. Just a late night."

She didn't want an alibi. She feared he would be forthcoming if she asked for one.

"I'm afraid of—"

"You shouldn—"

"I'm afraid for you. Afraid of what Danny could do or say, what you could do to yourself."

He looked away to shake his head. "You really shouldn't waste your time worrying about me. I don't waste mine."

More than any of the fragments churning in her mind, this one she wanted to discard, but she couldn't. She believed him. She blinked off a tear.

"Aren't you scared? You could end up hurt or in prison or . . . dead. Every time I see you, I expect you to be falling apart."

Now he looked to his right, directly at her, and he was certain her goodbye was worth the detour. The care in her voice reverberated around the car, infiltrating every one of his pores. Her eyes, now watering, turned away from his.

"I hope not. But maybe. Maybe dead." His mouth was dry, which added fragility to the final word.

"And that doesn't terrify you?"

He started to shrug but stopped. "Sometimes it does. Sometimes it's a comfort. I think mortality may be the best thing we have going for us."

Katie shifted as she took in his peculiarity. He was different without pretense. He was, in so many ways, an alien. That he was alone was no longer a surprise, if it ever had been at all.

"How do you figure?"

"We need it. If it wasn't there, if it wasn't haunting us every day of our lives, we'd have no excuse. There would be no reason why we couldn't do more, learn more, find more answers."

The slow pace of his speech made him sound more confident than he was. She could tell but didn't want to uncover him. He would have made a wonderful ambassador to worlds beyond their own. Non-threatening at least. Patient.

"It's an escape pod."

He smiled. "Something like that."

"Could use one of those right now."

They spoke in hushed tones. Eric's came naturally, Katie's from a place of unrest. She realized how softly Eric spoke, not just then but in each interaction that had transpired between them over the course of the summer. He sponged up others' volume, their force, but didn't return it. He spoke on the lower frequencies to which no one, as far as she could tell, was tuned, audible for those who remembered where to listen and were willing to act on it. Plenty of people had either the knowledge or the will necessary to listen to him, but Katie doubted that anyone other than her had both. Surely he wouldn't be alone if the right people turned the dial. They knew the station. Perhaps they assumed its location had changed over the years. It hadn't.

What would happen if he did release all the force he had stored up for so long? Would it explode out of him? Would he have control over it? She didn't know if it was even still inside him. She suspected he found it safer to allow it to leak out in small doses.

"So you're going to run?"

"I guess so."

"I wish I could go with you, away from here."

He rested his head in his left hand. Knuckles tapped the glass as he wiggled their fingers. She felt like a character in a lightweight movie, something written for girls half her age with low standards. She waited for profound words to reach her lips, but they received only spit, which frothed as they parted. At least the lightweight stories had happy endings.

"No, you don't."

"I do. I've had enough of this bubble. That's what it is. They all live in a bubble. Sometimes they go to the edge of it to golf or eat, or they slip outside just to, well, get into someone else's bubble for a night. It's mind-numbing."

Eric laughed fully, shaking loose some hair. Even his laugh was quiet. In better settings it was contagious, not because of the noise, but because of the way it took over his face. He was blind, deaf, and dumb while he laughed. He was impenetrable.

"And so what? You think life's better outside the bubble?" She wondered how old he perceived himself to be, how old he wanted to feel.

"Maybe. Must be."

"The bubble isn't so bad, Katie. You can live a good life inside of it. As long as you remember there are people on the outside. As long as you pop it now and then."

He bit his lip. He wanted to convince her but intuited she wasn't in the mood to be swayed, so he didn't prod.

"Didn't work too well for you."

"C'mon, you're smarter than that. What I've done isn't my parents' fault or society's or anyone else's. I settled on that a while ago."

"Then whose is it?" Her softness was gone, her words closer to a prayer than a question. She wouldn't look at him, so Eric looked forward to the putting green.

Jamie had brought him here a few times, long ago, usually to hit on the range and grab lunch. Once or twice they played nine holes, just the two of them. Eric had shown promise, enough to compel his father to buy him a new set of irons, but he only used them once. Afterward, Jamie leaned the bag against the back wall of the garage, excited for their next round, sure that Eric was on the verge of scoring in the eighties if he took the time to practice. The clubs hadn't moved since, and a mess of other equipment crowded around them, behind the bicycles, beneath the shelves lined with cans of tennis balls and boxes of trash bags and toilet paper.

Eric had almost made a hole in one the day he debuted the irons. The ball hit the pin on the second bounce and settled three feet away. He missed the putt. Jamie joked about beginner's luck. They laughed together at the statistical improbability of a novice getting his first ace so quickly beside someone who had played so many rounds without one. Eric ended up happy he had missed out. He didn't want his name on the board in the clubhouse. He didn't want his dad to have to see it on his way to the locker room.

"I don't think it matters. I don't think it helps to say who it belongs to. Or if it belongs to anyone at all."

Her eyes closed. She let them. Closed for the asking, for the hiding. "Can I ask you something more personal? You don't have to answer."

He nodded, and she sniffled, and they looked out their windows while she mulled over if she really wanted his explanation.

"What does it feel like?"

He wanted her to mean something else, but she didn't. Tears replaced sniffles, flowing gently, steadily down her face. No one else had ever asked him. No one else had ever asked anything other than why, for which he had no answer. More than anything, it felt lonely, or at least he had come to associate every stage of feeling with the loneliness that accompanied him from the first time a needle perforated his skin. The loneliness wasn't always bad. Sometimes it felt good to unhitch himself, to separate from the people around him and those who refused to be. He didn't mind lonely. He had grown used to the sensation at an early age, and he recognized it in his parents and siblings. They were all different kinds of lonely but afraid to describe their personal strain. They each dealt with it in different ways or ignored it altogether until they could mold it into something more acceptable, something easier to tuck away from prying eyes. He had always thought that was too bad, the tucking away, given the potential for salvation if they had recognized the similarity of their ailments.

What does it feel like? It felt heavy. He felt heavy. He felt anchored, like his immobility was justified, out of his control, for as long as the spell held. Being held in place was far better than merely staying in place, and to have such an identifiable source holding him was a relief, though by now the relief came in tortured fits, shorter each time. That's why he needed to run, not because of Danny or Katie or the McNamaras living and dead, but because he needed to go forward, even if forward was not the same as away, even if putting distance between himself and this place failed to erase a thing. The relief had shrunk down to nothing. He was now the sole anchor, his metal wearing away, his chain threatening to untether a ship already taking on water, out of sight of the people on the shore and their porches overlooking the sea.

What does it feel like? Good. It felt good, still. It had taken him a long time to separate the pleasure of good from right and to accept that pleasure was fleeting no matter what. What does it feel like? It felt like delaying something, like pressing pause on every emotion and the stressors behind them. When the time came to resume, he had to generate the stress himself. If he couldn't generate it, he would slip away.

What does it feel like?

"Not good enough."

She let the answer hang. She didn't need to know anything else about it. "What do you think's going to happen? You think Danny will run?"

"Mm. I don't think he'll get far. Just a matter of how bad they want to find him."

Two men walked in front of the car and waved without looking, maintaining the appearance of knowing everyone at the club. Katie noticed her hands had balled into fists. She loosened her grip and felt a twinge in her forearms.

"Maybe he won't give them your name. Maybe you can come back."

A hand through his hair once more, tracing a line down the center of his head. "I don't think so. I'm better off never seeing this place again."

She let out a deep breath, unsure of how long she had held it. Months or eons. She thought if she closed her eyes and inhaled, held the air, she might never have to open them again.

"Probably."

"At least I've convinced myself that's the case. Isn't that enough?"

He looked forward but hoped she would look over. She watched a boy step onto the putting green and roll three balls out in front of him. His putter was too big for his body, and he had little feel for the speed of the green. He looked around to make sure no one was watching but couldn't see them in the car.

"I hope so."

Katie had never hugged him before. Years earlier, at the beginning of summers, Clarkes and Murrays would hug whenever whoever showed up second arrived, but Katie had been young and awkward and only hugged Jamie and Anne, and even then she embraced begrudgingly.

She hugged Eric now. He hadn't felt one in a long time, based on his initial recoil. He wouldn't have to wait so long for his next one. The thought comforted her—that Eric could have a new life, that he might hold someone or be held and feel less alone—so she squeezed him tighter. He would chase the feeling somewhere else, somewhere where being anchored wasn't so bad, where staying put wasn't a mistake because the place had been carefully selected. Made to feel like home.

Katie didn't say another word as she let him go and fumbled with her lock, but she waved from outside the car and again as she turned to track down her brother. Eric waved back the first time. By the second, he was facing the other way as his car inched toward the row behind them. Then he took off.

August 18

I don't want to hurt her. But I think I have to scare her at least. Do what it takes. Eric must've told her everything. Or close to everything.

She asked me about him at the club. I guess I should've been paying attention then. There are a lot of things I should've noticed. It shouldn't have been this big mystery. We should've grabbed her in the woods that night. I should've. Could've left her with Tim. Left them lying there for the world to make assumptions. Made it look natural. Or maybe like Tim did it to her. Case closed.

I'm sitting in my car right now. I'm parked at a gas station a mile from the club. She should be working today but I have no way of checking.

If I can scare her enough maybe I can just leave her. Scare her and run somewhere. Drive for a while now that the tank is full. Delaware or some place like that. Nice beaches. Different but nice.

Based on what I know about her I think I'm going to have act crazy. She's not going to be scared of me. How to get her alone is the problem. I think I'm going to have to wait until the end of the day when she goes home.

If Ryan's with her I'm going to have to live with the collateral. Do what I have to. Too bad because I think Ryan is down to earth. A regular guy. But I have to do it if they don't listen. Then it would just be Eric left and he won't hurt me. He wouldn't hurt anyone. He had the chance to.

I wonder how long it will take to feel normal if I have to get rid of her and Ryan. Tim fucked me up and I'm still thinking about Stevie. But I think it's getting easier. Easier to function at least. Still hard to sleep. Hard to picture what life will look like in a month. A year.

I think I would get over them quickly. Two Worona kids are dead because of all this. Two SoMo kids would even it out.

And then after that it might be Eric so three SoMo kids. Because I have to.

That's what I'm telling myself.

23

Katie didn't get far. She reached the sidewalk and watched Eric's car weave its way to the exit. As she turned away, another car's racket captured her attention. It whipped around the second row and skidded to a stop, slanted haphazardly across two spots in front of her. She froze as Danny's head emerged. He stood next to his open door. He wore a Red Sox hat but not the one she had seen the night before. It cast a shadow on the bags under his eyes.

"Katie, I need to talk to you. Need to ask you some questions. Can you get in the car? No one's getting hurt. It's just talk as long as you listen to me. I need you to listen to me."

He moved forward as he spoke and wiped his unwashed brow, but she didn't back away. One of his heels dragged as he walked.

"No."

He grabbed her left arm and pulled her toward him. She slapped his hand away.

"Danny, I'm not going to say anything. Leave me alone."

"You know I can't do that. I need you to get in."

"I'll scream."

He was close enough to see her shiver. She had never noticed how many freckles he had before. They gridded his face, densest on his cheeks.

"I wouldn't."

"You deserve to get caught. You killed a kid, Danny."

He grabbed the same arm and shoved her at his car. "What the fuck did you just say to me?" Her back hit the side at an awkward angle, and her knees buckled. Danny backed away and held his hands on top of his head, frazzled, still flammable.

"I didn't try to kill him. I didn't understand what I was doing. Can you just get in? I need you to get in. I need to tell you what happened. We can talk about it."

Katie tried to catch her breath as the pavement scorched the undersides of her arms. Danny paced behind the car. Somehow their scuffle hadn't attracted any attention. She guessed the boy on the green had walked back to the pro shop. His balls remained on the surface, inches from one of the fun-sized flagsticks. Members had vanished inside in search of air conditioning. Katie calculated Ryan's timing in her head. He should have been done, should have been looking for her by now. Her father was on his way. One of them would be there soon, in time, if she could keep Danny talking, if she could avoid getting in his car.

"Danny, you don—"

For the second time in as many minutes, the sound of tires squealing cut into her. From the ground, she could see a car moving between the rows behind them but couldn't make out the model. Danny turned around and looked up but had no time to avoid the strike. The sedan took out his legs. The back of his head hit the hood as he collapsed. His groaning body crumpled a few feet in front of the car as it broke. Eric left it running and opened his door.

Danny winced as Eric closed in. Katie saw Eric's right arm swing forward, and for a moment she expected him to help Danny to his feet. Then the fist clenched and wound up, and Eric unleashed six vicious punches, the whole time holding Danny up in a defenseless position with his non-striking hand. What looked from the outside like ruthless, efficient strikes were in fact wild swings, each one more powerful than the last, fueled by years of mistreatment.

Katie prayed her eyes were deceiving her. A stranger had happened upon them and taken action. Eric was miles away by now. This man looked nothing like him. He circled Danny like prey but kept his distance, waiting for a sign of life.

A member ran up and shouted, "Someone call the police," and Ryan, right behind him, out of breath, was first to dial. Eric wore a soft green shirt and Danny's blood, which soaked into the fabric in dots at the front of his shoulders. His car chugged behind him, loud in the stillness. His hair stuck to his forehead and the back of his neck. Katie was crying once again, slumped next to Danny's car, and didn't catch sight of Eric looking her way, as if for guidance. She looked up in time to see him kneeling next to Danny's unconscious body, and she feared he had given in. She feared his rage had already acceded to sympathy's pull. He lifted the body gently, letting the shoes drag, and leaned it against the curb. He stayed hunched over it. Katie waited for someone to tear him away, but the member who had called out for someone else to make a move waited bashfully next to Ryan. The others were still outside the pro shop, pointing to the lot and waiting for someone else to guarantee their safety.

One motion seemed to carry Eric from crouching to moving to driving. He sped off faster this time, barely slowing as he neared the exit and careened onto the road. He was out of sight in seconds. Katie tried to send a message to him, to warn him to slow down enough to avoid suspicion. She shut her eyes. He would outrun them.

"Did someone get the plate on that car? They'll have to track him down." Another member ran up to check on Katie as he shouted the words to the crowd behind him, which hadn't sought a vantage point that would have allowed for such close inspection. Katie sat up and leaned against Danny's car. Ryan knelt beside her and swept the hair out of her face. She shuddered. The words came in a rush.

She lost air quickly as she tried to drive the member away.

"I got a clear look at him and the car. We're going to the police anyway. I'll tell them everything. He's the one they want. Trust me."

She gestured weakly at Danny's form to punctuate her final words. She fell away from her brother, but he caught her head before it struck the ground. He laid it down and whispered to her. Her lips and tongue moved but produced nothing. He removed his caddie bib and folded it into a pillow, the damp side facing the ground. Her hand squeezed his but without much power. He let it go and watched it fall limply to the pavement. He checked her head for blood, his heavy breaths like steam on her face.

Sirens wailed louder and louder. Three cruisers screamed into the lot. Kevin pulled in behind them and parked as close as their blockade allowed. He opened his door and leaned on the top of it, surveying the scene and the officers' approach until he spied his daughter and sprinted to her.

"Katie, Katie, Katie. Ryan, what happened to her? What happened? Is she hurt?"

"Dad, it's okay. I'll explain it. Danny—"

"He's here? Is that him? How did—"

"Dad, is that you?" Katie spoke softly. Concussion and sun schemed to weigh down her eyelids. She lacked the strength to lift her head. It didn't rise high enough to hurt on its way back to the ground.

"Sweetie, did he hurt you? What happened?"

The name sounded fine now. She almost smiled.

"Da-Danny showed up. Then Eric showed up."

"Okay, okay. Take it slow. You can tell us the whole story later."

Ryan's call had been detailed enough to focus the cops' initial offensive on Danny, but now one came over. Paramedics followed him.

"Dad, keep them here."

"What? Who? What do you mean, honey?"

"Don't let them go after Eric. Keep them here."

He understood, but his look apprised her of their reality: the matter was out of their hands, for good. "They'll do what they have to, just like he did. I'll be right here."

He stepped aside for the paramedics. "These people are going to help you now. Ryan and I are right here, Katie. Tell them everything they need to know."

"But nothing more."

She mouthed these words. No one read her lips as she began to receive medical attention. Two officers stood over Danny, who stirred and yanked himself aware of his handcuffs, too disoriented to look in Katie's direction. The blood was already starting to dry below his nose and above his left eye. The right one was swollen almost shut. He could move his legs enough to inspect the scrapes. His right foot was bare.

The back of the ambulance was bright for Katie's eyes and aching head. She had never been in one before and found herself surprised by the space, cramped but not claustrophobic. She wanted to ask someone to adjust her angle, to let her sit more upright, but she couldn't summon the energy. Two new faces peered down at her. Another officer stepped in and called for them to slow their departure. Katie could hear voices muttering about waiting until they reached the hospital to debrief.

"Katie, we'll talk soon if that's alright with you. You'll tell us what happened here."

"I'll do my best" went unanswered. She wasn't sure if it ever made it from her brain to her lips. Someone brushed hair away from her forehead, and their hand held her shoulder. Unprompted, an attendant shifted her slightly, allowing her to look out the back of the vehicle. A small crowd had formed. Most wore golf shirts or attire befitting the semi-formal outdoor patio overlooking the middle of the front nine. A few breathed heavily in sullied work-out clothes. No one said a word as the doors shut, and she let her eyes close.

August 19

Deserved to get hit. That's what I'm telling myself. Got what was coming.

Didn't think Eric had it in him.

My dad used to tell a joke that my mom didn't like very much about a priest and a horse that ended with a line about asking for forgiveness instead of permission. I think someone told it to him at work. I didn't think it was that funny even when I was old enough to understand it but he liked it and I let him. One time he said I was kind of like the horse in the joke but now I don't remember what the horse actually did. Kicked the priest maybe. Walked into a bar. That's a different joke. I laughed at that one even when I was too old for it. Why the long face.

That's what I'm telling myself.

That's what I'm telling myself.

24

Katie dreamt of Eric her first night back from the hospital. She watched him writhe in pain. Her mind refused to wake her until she was beside his impervious body and could feel the vapor of his screams running up her neck as she leaned over, unable to touch him. She jolted awake but then tried to return, shutting her eyes and striving to remember. Only the outlines of their bodies and the room came to her, and her heart pounded too hard to fall back asleep.

Katie recalled Harry Potter saving Mr. Weasley after a similar vision in *Order of the Phoenix* and wondered if Eric was in pain somewhere far away in a room like the one she had seen. Could she go there? She remembered his mention of the Boy Who Lived. He hadn't grown up in a closet. No one had come to take him away. Win some, lose some.

She hoped he wasn't screaming, wherever he was, and she suspected that whether he was or not, he didn't want to be found. As she settled, she realized she had no sense of what his scream sounded like. She had never heard him yell. He smiled and forced laughter for the most part. Maybe he had yelled at his parents when things got bad, when he strayed from their lines. Maybe, more likely, they had yelled at him or talked in their stern voices, the ones Katie used to hear a few times each summer, in tones that were somehow more cutting than the yells.

Yelling wasn't so bad for Katie. Yells were filled with raw emotion.

The yeller couldn't help but yell. Stern voices were measured, calculated, intended to puncture. Sometimes the stern speaker couldn't help but speak sternly, but more often than not they schemed. Katie didn't yell much, either. She left that to some of her more obnoxious floormates and her mother, whose yells were unstoppable and on occasion preconceived. Her father used a severe voice when circumstances demanded one, usually at Beth's request. It was hard to picture him yelling at a student or colleague. They were fragile, some of them. He didn't allow many things to upset him enough to yell. Katie didn't remember him yelling for her in the parking lot, but he must have, and he would have yelled more at the hospital had he not trusted her.

The plan itself, although it had not included encountering and getting concussed by Danny, had turned out to be a good one. Once conscious, the police had endless questions for her. She steered them in the direction she preferred, the one that largely evaded the subject of the second car and the boy driving it. That subject wasn't hard to drop, not when The Cape's Most Wanted was sitting in their station and unable to credibly deny Katie's account, unconcerned with filling in the missing pieces, accepting defeat.

She had worried that the police would lambaste her for waiting so long to share what she had seen, but mostly they seemed relieved to have lucked into what they viewed as good news. For the first time, she appraised their undertaking. She pitied them.

She dreamt of Eric again the next day, this time during an afternoon nap. Doctor's orders were to keep her in the dark and to rest, and Katie lacked the energy to counter. He didn't scream this time, but he wasn't comfortable. At first, she thought he could see her. She thought he looked at her and smiled, but it must have been a coincidence because he didn't acknowledge her thereafter. He only talked to someone behind her, out of sight, the words muffled. Eric's shirt was ragged, his left sneaker had a hole above the big toe, and bruises covered his right leg. He didn't move much. When he did he limped until he could find something to put his weight on. Katie trailed behind him as he progressed but couldn't see beyond his hunched frame. Eventually, they reached a door. It seemed Eric knew it well or had at least expected to find it. He shoved it forward. Light streamed in. Refused to yield.

Sunlight through a windblown curtain nudged Katie awake just as Beth entered her room and sat at the end of the bed, iced tea in hand.

"You okay? Have to make sure you stay hydrated."

Katie nodded and accepted the glass. Beth rested a hand on the foot of the bed, unsure if she should take a seat.

"You sure you feel alright? You look a little overheated. I can turn the fan on."

She started toward it, but Katie signaled to leave it be.

"Just a bad dream. I'm glad you woke me up from it."

Beth smiled but let it fade quickly as she reached the door. Katie wiped the remnants of open-mouthed sleep from her lips and drank from the glass.

"Mom?"

"Yes?"

"You can stay in here if you want. Play a game or something. As long as I don't have to look at a screen."

Beth kept her hand on the doorknob. She hadn't brushed her hair or showered, but she still looked prepared, ready to stave off any potential embarrassment or disruption that the day might hold. Katie didn't want to play a game. Not even a little bit. But just sitting there sounded nice. If they sat there long enough, Katie propped up against her pillows and Beth leaning against the railing at the foot of the bed, they might talk, maybe even about the complicated things.

"That's okay, Katie. You should get your rest. I'll check in again soon."

25

The Clarkes' end of summer get-together was impromptu, tame compared to their typical programs. They had drinks to spare and waning days, so they invited some neighbors and friends, but the crowd was far smaller than the one they had hosted for the Fourth. Dread of the calendar's imminent flip colored the atmosphere on the deck; for some attendees, the revelation that a murder had taken place roughly five miles away deepened their somber outlook. Some people shirked the subject. Most had simply grown tired of the case and the momentary warmth it compelled them to find. Local news had moved on after an initial onslaught of renewed interest.

Katie managed to avoid the spotlight. Only a handful of people were aware of her role. She imagined word would eventually trickle out. If it already had, people were kind and didn't bother her. She was easy to not bother. She didn't work; she mostly stayed inside; when she did go out, she waited in the car while a parent or Ryan ran an errand. Headaches still popped up but less frequently every day. She put up a brief fuss when Beth suggested she try attending the party, but once she acquiesced she grew intrigued. It was a shameful excitement. It stemmed from the thought of Jamie and Anne standing in front of the crowd and her calling them out with a rant that made everyone in attendance squirm. By the time they arrived and she and Ryan took their places in a remote corner, she had lost her gusto.

Ryan ate cheese and crackers like an unthumbed toddler next to her yet kept mercifully quiet as she massaged her temples and sur-veyed the ongoing conversations. Jamie Jr. and Amelia spoke to an older couple neither Murray recognized. They were out of earshot, but Katie could tell the chat boiled down to knowing J.J. and Millie since they were little and being so proud of the young man and woman they had become, so amazed by how beautiful the whole family was from the hosts down to the grandchildren.

Jamie and Anne stood in the middle of the deck, leading a circle of eight in conversation, telling a story in tandem, dreadful to be-hold. Kevin and Beth were two of the eight but had heard it before. They had been quiet ever since Katie came home. The whole house had been. Ryan worked, Beth too, and Kevin kept Katie company, finalizing his syllabi while she rested or joining her on walks short enough for her to handle, out of the sun.

Jamie wrapped up their story with a mimed tennis swing and a smile. His audience met the conclusion with more-than-polite laughter, and he joined in. He reached for a glass on the table behind him and clinked it, though most of the bacchanals were already within arm's reach.

"I want to thank you all for coming. It truly fills and bursts my heart to see so many lovely faces, faces so dear to us. We are sad to see summer end, but we are delighted to have been given the chance to savor it. This toast is to summer, to companionship, to the love of family and friends. May all three last forever."

Katie seethed. He kept talking to those around him. A breeze distorted his words. He hugged Anne around the shoulders with one arm and held his glass in the other hand, touching it to that of the man across from him, who whispered something apparently worth a chuckle in his ear.

"Katie, did you hear me?" Ryan sounded far away.

"What? No."

"You want me to get you something? They're putting out some of the dinner food."

"I'll come with you."

Amelia and a friend were unveiling several tins, brimming with pulled pork and cornbread, that a Clarke had ordered from a well-liked barbecue spot in North Monomo. "Too worn out to cook."

Ryan waited awkwardly by the plates and silverware, but Amelia urged him to be the first, so he filled his plate quickly and slathered a mix of two sauces onto his pork and bun.

"Been waiting for this all day."

Katie took some chicken without a roll, cornbread, and mashed potatoes, which looked good enough to prompt her brother to circle back to the tins. Ryan wanted a stable eating surface and chose one of the tables next to the chatting circle, which began to break apart as its members saw others walking by with aromatic entrées.

Finally, only the Clarkes and Mrs. Heffernan remained. The Heffernans had sold their Seaview house several summers before so they could build something larger and more private in Barnstable, but they remained close to the Clarkes, and their children's ages aligned almost perfectly. Katie remembered them playing together when she was little. The friendships had always seemed convenient, not affectionate. Mr. Heffernan drank too much. It wasn't a secret. He kept out of real trouble, but approximately sixty percent of the parties they attended ended with Mrs. apologizing for his unfiltered speech or dragging him to the car. She looked happy to catch her friends without him around. She had told the Clarkes he had an event to attend in Barnstable, and no one involved was insulted by the flimsy alibi.

"Jamie, you have such a lovely way with words. Simple but so moving. What you said about family is so true. It's no wonder this one is so strong. I wish we could be your neighbors again."

"The guest rooms are open anytime."

Katie sat with her back to them but could hear clearly, and she ate more aggressively as Mrs. continued singing unwarranted praises. Ryan went back for seconds as most of the crowd scooped their firsts, leaving Katie alone at the table, which could have seated five. Mrs. Heffernan backed up and into Katie, knocking her toward, but not quite into, her potatoes.

"Katie, is that you? I'm so sorry. I am a total klutz."

Jamie stepped over to assist but found no use for his generosity of spirit, so he patted Katie on the shoulder.

"How are you feeling, Katie? Your parents say everything is almost back to normal. I'm so glad to hear it."

"I'm not sure about that." She barely made eye contact. Mrs. Heffernan didn't seem to take heed.

"Well, Katie, Anne and Jamie told me you've been very brave. Doesn't surprise me. You were a strong lady even when you were this high."

She gestured vaguely, barely high enough for a garden gnome. Katie swallowed potatoes and smiled without her teeth.

"I was just telling these two that they're still the best hosts. Aren't they just the perfect neighbors?"

Katie sympathized with how difficult Mr. Heffernan was and liked Mrs., but at this moment she snapped. When she had fantasized about this moment—and it had been at times a fantasy, albeit one tinted with furious red at its edges—there hadn't been a crowd. She didn't need one. She wanted only to look Jamie and Anne in the eyes while she spoke. Sometimes during naps she imagined going after them; getting close enough to glimpse their irregularities and their nervous swallows would be ideal. It wasn't all rage. At times, Katie felt sorry for them and their lack of a panacea, how wholly oblivious they were to the need for one. But it always ended in rage. It always ended with thoughts of Eric and the empty room upstairs.

Rage wasn't so dangerous when it was allowed or forced to burn out quickly, but Katie's days were passing slowly in shady nooks not cool enough to extinguish the fuel. In her normal life, her past life, she controlled her rage. She ran or worked or wandered until it was safe to return. Now? She couldn't run or work; only her mind could wander, and it was solely interested in fury in the moments it wasn't longing to know where Eric was.

So Katie's snapping wasn't surprising to her. Part of her had hoped she would avoid it, but from the second she stepped onto the deck she knew it was likely, maybe predetermined. She snapped for a number of reasons, not all of them manifest—not to her, probably not to the people on the assault's receiving end.

"They're better neighbors than they are parents."

"Pardon me?"

Mrs. Heffernan was too confused to be upset. She was too used to these parties and families to expect anything disruptive. She was far enough away from her husband to trust that her evening would be pleasantly uneventful.

"If only they were as focused on their kids as they are on their parties."

The Clarkes were quiet. Only Jamie's eyes met Katie's. While they filled with a separate rage, they didn't object. They didn't dispute the accusations levied upon them. Beth walked over with a plate and prepared to sit across from her children. She apprehended the trouble. Her heart raced as Anne spoke.

"Katie, I know you're upset. You've been through quite a lot this summer."

"The issue isn't me being upset. It's how the hell are you not?"

Beth quickly put down her food and grabbed her daughter's shoulder. "Katie, that's enough. Now's not the time. Ryan, maybe you two should head home."

"When was the last time you saw your son? When was the last time you saw Eric?"

Anne shifted uncomfortably. Jamie blinked until his eyes closed. Katie hoped he was picturing the night he saw Eric, the night he couldn't find the words.

"Katie, we appreciate that you care about Eric. It means a lot. We do, too. We love him. Sometimes things are too complicated to—"

"You're watching him die. Your boy. No, not even watching. Letting. You're letting him die. He's out there. You don't know where. You're letting your son die slowly because he doesn't quite fit inside your world, and you won't bother to make room for him. He's got a needle in his arm as we speak, but God forbid we think about anything other than this cornbread and how nice the breeze is and if the thunderstorms will hold off. He's in a basement somewhere, but you don't like to think about that."

She shoved her plate across the table. It stopped just short of Beth's. Katie stood. Jamie turned to let her pass between them. By now the crowd had adjourned to listen in. Most had missed the beginning of the exchange. Katie turned back to Jamie and Anne and stayed still, out of breath, ten sets of eyes on her, the other ten waiting for a Clarke to speak.

"Katie, we all want the same thing. We all want our boy to come home."

Jamie almost stumbled over the last few words. He got them out before tears began to run down his cheeks. Anne's face was dry. She struggled to lift her gaze from the floor.

"Only way he comes home is if you bring him."

Katie felt no satisfaction as she walked off the deck and toward the street. None of it had gone to plan because there had never been a viable plan. She had trusted that improvisation would facilitate honesty, or at least an admission of cowardice. She doubted they wanted him home; she questioned if she did. It was impossible to know if he was better off here than wherever he was, if the gleam of Seaview Road was any brighter than the glare she had seen in her dream, the luminescence he walked into without hesitation. Here or there, Eric was in someone's crosshairs. Either way, he made for an easy target. His only hope was for someone's finger to slip off the trigger and wait for him to run.

Maybe that was just Katie's hope. For all she knew, he was waiting for that finger to pull, waiting for the distant sound of the firing that would reach him just as the metal did. That's how he wanted it: in someone's else's hands. Katie pictured him waiting, always waiting for an outside set of hands to smother him or pick him up because his were trembling. He didn't know whose appendage to expect or if he would have to pass over before feeling its touch, its hold. The power rested elsewhere. She hoped she was wrong.

Katie wasn't supposed to drive, but she grabbed the keys from the bowl next to the entrance and headed back outside, catching the swinging screen door before it closed. Ryan and Kevin walked slowly up the street, so she waited next to the car.

"Mom's still down there apologizing for you." Ryan couldn't hide his smirk. He was on her side but also enjoyed the spectacle. It was her fight.

"Why don't we all find a movie to watch?" Even Kevin didn't sound attached to his idea, which the kids met with silence.

"I was going to go for a ride."

"Where?"

"Anywhere."

Kevin stopped walking and turned slowly to look back at the Clarke tract. Hands on hips, he used a dour teacher voice, one they couldn't take seriously.

"Fine, but take Ryan with you. You're on parole. We're going to have to talk about this. All of us."

Ryan took the keys from her and got in the car while Kevin smiled and waited for her to join her brother. They drove up Seaview and away. Katie provided no destination, and Ryan never asked for directions. For now, away was enough. They would have to come back soon.

Ryan parked them at a convenience store along a side road, forty minutes' worth of Cape towns away. Katie said she didn't want anything, but he returned with Swedish Fish in addition to his selections, citing his disinterest in having her take any of his snacks.

From their spot beside the store, they could see everyone who entered or exited. For a few minutes, one person left every thirty seconds, almost exactly. They had the data because Ryan tracked and announced the procession. The first three were men. Two were young. The third looked to be in his sixties and lit a cigarette in the doorway, his lean suggesting he did this often. He was still there when two women passed, either sisters or a daughter with a mother striving too hard to look young. The man smiled at them, and they said hello. He offered the mother-sister a cigarette, which she took happily. They walked away. The man spent the next minute drifting from the door. He crossed the street and pulled headphones from his pocket. Ryan made some guesses at what he was listening to. Katie didn't play along. The women walked down the street. They stopped at a crosswalk too far away for Katie to see them clearly, but she could tell the younger one adored her companion. They reached a car across the street and hugged goodbye.

August 23

I told you I'd give my side because I was afraid no one else would. I'm sure no one else would. But I probably made things worse.

The cops weren't as mad at me as I thought they might be. I think they were just happy to put this story in the past. I knew one of the guys at the station. He was a few years ahead of me at Regional. Smoked with him once but he didn't usually hang around those types of places.

I told them it was all my fault. I didn't say anything about Eric or Stevie. I didn't have to. They could tell I was too tired to be upset so I think they could tell that I'm not a monster. They probably see guys worse than me all the time.

Someone will find Stevie eventually and it won't be hard to tie him to me. I was thinking about that last night. That I'll be back in the news some other time in the future. That made me a little sad but it wasn't as bad as realizing that when that happens and they ask my parents or Stevie's brother or anyone else if they could imagine me hurting Stevie they'll all say yes. If they pause before they answer it'll just be because they're protecting me a little bit. And themselves.

I bet some smartasses might even get a little mad at those people. They'll say if it wasn't surprising that he hurt Stevie then why the fuck didn't you say something. How did you ever let it get to this point. Two boys dead in the woods. Weak boys but innocent too.

I told my side because I have no idea who's going to tell this story and where I'll fit into their version. If they do talk about me just trust that they didn't really know me. Might not have known me at all.

They're guessing. That's what I'm telling myself.

I'm guessing too sometimes. Just trying to remember how I felt or why I hurt people.

Let that lonesome whistle blow.

For a few years my dad worked nights a lot and when I got sad about him not being home for dinner sometimes my mom would take me to the Ocean View Diner in town. They called it that but you couldn't see the ocean from anywhere inside. One time I asked the owner when he came to our table to say hi why he named it that. He laughed and took one of my fries and said if you climbed on the roof and stood on your tiptoes and looked to the east and the waves were big you might be able to see the water. He said he had never tried it.

Most of the time I ordered grilled cheese and fries and I dipped both in ketchup. I told my mom I wanted to own a diner or a restaurant when I was older. She said it was a good idea as long as I worked hard. Then she said guys like Ronny the owner were good at the job because they were people pleasers. She knew then that I wasn't one but it took me a couple more years to figure it out. After I figured it out I didn't dream about owning a restaurant anymore.

In sixth grade they told us to write about what we wanted to be when we grew up. I didn't want to own a restaurant anymore so I said I wanted to work in a store that sold music and movies even though there weren't a lot of them around.

I said those stores were my favorite even though I'm not an expert at all about songs and movies because I liked the way the people that worked in them talked. They talked like the rest of the world outside the store didn't matter. A whole different language. About the things they loved and hated.

There used to be a store like that on South Street called Cape Cod Entertainment but it closed when I was in fourth grade. We bought DVDs there and Dad told me about record players. We didn't have one but he still liked to look at what they had and pull out the best albums. I don't remember the names of most of the bands he said were his favorites growing up. Mom didn't like the store because it was a little dirty and the guys behind the counter usually smelled like weed.

I said I would tell my side. That was some of it. There's not much point in sharing the rest. It would just be a stack of papers in the cell. They would throw it out when they find me tomorrow.

If they did it would be okay. I can't write for shit and my story belongs in the garbage. Even if I told them everything about me they'd just remember me for killing Tim. And then for killing Stevie when they find him.

I'm sorry for what I did. How could someone not be sorry for doing what I did to Tim and Stevie. My best friend.

I've never thought about what will happen after I do it. We never went to church and no one ever asked me about it. I don't think I'm going anywhere. If I am it's somewhere worse than where Stevie and Tim went and I'll be alone.

I hope I'm not going anywhere because I'm already alone. So there wouldn't be much point in doing what I'm going to do tonight if I'm just going to go somewhere else and want to do it again.

I think it will hurt for a little bit and then feel like falling asleep. It'll *be scary at first but it'll feel good when I break the skin. Endorphins or something. Then I'll feel light until my head gets heavy. And I'll sleep.*

That's what I'm telling myself.

26

A somber end to the story of Tim McNamara, who died at Green-stone Lake last month. Eyewitness testimony helped the police identify McNamara's killer as twenty-three-year-old Danny Moreland of Worona. Last night Moreland, who confessed shortly after his arrest, took his own life in the cell where he was awaiting trial. He told police he acted alone and that McNamara's death was an unintended consequence of a misunderstanding between two friends. The McNamara family has not commented on recent developments and has expressed a desire to maintain their privacy.

It's hard to imagine what they have gone through over the past month and a half, Stacy. While the circumstances of this case are rather unique, we cannot help but count these deaths as two more added to the toll of the opioid crisis. Two young men, gone far too soon, one by the other's hand. As vacationers prepare to make their exodus, full-time Cape residents are left to reckon with what is, in no uncertain terms, an epidemic. Solutions remain elusive. Parents continue to grieve. Next, we'll speak with leaders from CPOC, Cape Parents of the Opioid Crisis, about where we go from here and where exactly 'here' is. Back after this.

27

"Damn. Almost two minutes this time. Things are slowing down." Ryan played with the stopwatch and tried to land on an exact second.

"That time of year." Katie's attention was elsewhere. Her words snuck through the hand covering her mouth.

"That guy looks familiar."

Ryan looked away quickly and waited for his next mark, but he was right. The young man's hair was short, fresh-cut, uneven in the back. He held a bottle of Coke and a bag of chips and wiped his free hand on jeans that were worn but fit him well. Despite his posture, he was handsome. Sunglasses covered his eyes. The frames were small, maybe a prescription. He wasn't smoking anything but pressed himself on the wall like a man who was. He opened the chips. Katie could see his jaw work on a generous handful.

As a woman and her toddler opened the door, he backed away and smiled, but he had lowered his head too far for them to see it. Ryan said something about him not drinking the Coke, which he had placed on the brick ledge behind him. Katie didn't listen. She closed her eyes to find Eric, waited for a hint regarding his orientation, half-hoping it wouldn't come so she could interpret the radio silence as confirmation of what she wanted to believe about the boy in front of her. He finished his chips, tossed the bag, stepped forward, took out a cigarette, fumbled with his lighter, and made sure his smoke blew harmlessly away from the foot traffic around him.

He had forgotten the Coke. Katie reached over to lower her window. To alert him would require a yell. He noticed before she could produce one and squeezed the bottle into his back pocket, where it stuck out at an awkward angle. Katie thought it must have chilled the skin beneath the fabric.

He turned and inhaled deeply as he moved. A cloud of smoke formed and quickly dissipated. They could see his shoes now: unhip, white and chunky, something like the ones Kevin and his doubles partners wore for the sake of traction and ankle preservation. Maybe he had bought them cheap, or maybe they had spent some years untouched in a closet or garage. He moved well in them, light on his feet as he stepped out of the way of a man headed for the trash can. He tinkered with the sunglasses. Katie didn't think he wore them often. She considered asking Ryan if the store sold them. They looked inexpensive, like they could have been spinning on a rack until minutes ago. Ryan wouldn't have paid attention to something like that. It wasn't worth asking. She preferred not knowing. The boy kept working on the cigarette while he leaned on a mailbox and checked his phone. Katie surmised that he had owned his shirt for a long time. The short sleeves crept up, closer to the intersection of his armpit and shoulder than his elbow. When he slipped his phone back into his pocket and stretched an arm overhead, she could see the skin of his lower back and the top of a pair of plaid boxers.

She had Eric's number. She could call him, just to see if the boy picked up. It wouldn't put Eric in any danger. But if this wasn't him there was a chance he was far away. Even if it was, there was a chance he was far enough.

He put out the cigarette and opened the Coke. He took a long sip and twisted the cap on before starting to walk. He progressed with his back to them and took long strides, passing the Coke from hand to hand as he did. His gait was smoother than Eric's, more sure of where each step would land. He stayed in her crosshairs as he continued. The sidewalk was empty ahead of him, so he walked in the middle of it. His journey carried him east. Ryan pulled them out of the lot and turned in the opposite direction.

They had driven half a mile before she turned to look down the street. The sun had snuck over the trees in front of them, which rose higher than the stores and homes. The light stung her eyes. Dots of purple and green hovered before her as she looked back. The street was almost empty for the season now. Ryan picked a preset that came through fuzzy this far out. He let it play and flipped down his sun shield. Katie looked up and let the light in once more.

The station crackled to life in time for a commercial advertising a weight-loss program. One of the morning show hosts sang its praises. Katie didn't know what the host looked like. There was no way of evaluating the program's efficacy without seeing her. Listeners had to take her word for it.

The Camry in front of them obeyed the speed limit. Ryan grew impatient, but it turned at the next light.

Soon they saw the sunset, pink and blue and orange, almost kaleidoscopic. It revealed the sky's expansiveness, and Katie daydreamed about the other places over which it hung, the ones she could not and would never see. They looked welcoming in her mind's eye, and largely unoccupied.

It was nice to know there were still places to run to. It was pleasant to think they were hard to reach. She wondered if someone else was watching the colors mix from their car or porch or beach and picturing what rested under the sky directly over her and Ryan. Perhaps they ached to hide inside of it.

She shuddered at the thought. She wanted gray skies and summer thunder, whatever it would take to keep them away, to save them.

Epilogue

I've always found that people don't like to move all that much. Some of them are proud, some are lazy, and some just think there's no other option. It doesn't matter which group they fall into. Staying is staying.

The Dunes membership has been working hard. While there's some paperwork left to do, permits and the like, it looks as if their first United States Golf Association event is coming in a few years. The U.S. Senior Amateur. Quite a victory for some of the committee members that have fought so hard over the years. The tournament won't attract a big crowd, but it should serve as a bit of a test for attracting loftier tournaments, they figure. The club will have to shut down the course for about two weeks for the practice rounds and maintenance and the tournament itself. The members won't mind. Some of the best players in the country, of a certain age, will be there.

The Monomo Whalers managed to make the CCBL championship for the first time ever last summer. They were led by two players, one a pitcher from Cal State Fullerton and the other a shortstop from Duke, who went on to be first-round picks in the MLB draft. Chatham swept the Whalers, outscored them 19-5 across the two games. But Hutchinson Park hosted the second one. Biggest crowd they've ever had, and they cheered straight through the ninth, after which the players strolled out of the dugout untucked, eye-black smeared, and thanked the fans.

Barbara Mullens died a few years back. That probably won't surprise anyone. Her family said she went peacefully, full of love. For them, for her community, for the Cape. Now the oldest resident in town is only ninety-six, and he doesn't get out much. He doesn't participate in any parades or festivities.

Seaview Road pretty much looks the same now as it always has. There's been quite a bit of construction on Squall Lane, but Seaview's gone largely untouched.

South Monomo put in new parking signs on Seaview last summer. A few residents spent years complaining and writing letters about how crowded, dangerous even, the road got when beachgoers lined both sides of it with their cars. They can still park on the bottom section, closest to the beach. But if they go any higher they'll get a ticket or—and this has happened a few times already—the police called on them. The officers on the scene are usually interested in resolution more than anything else. They've had about enough of the calls from the Simms residence.

Worona is about the same. South Street's seen more retail turnover of late. They renovated the middle school, though that was a matter of structural decay rather than popular demands.

Otherwise, Worona's no different from what it's always been. It's between destinations. You have to get close before the highway signs alert you to its presence.

It's still just a few miles from Seaview Road to Worona, but the number of people making the drive has shrunk with each passing summer.

There aren't many people who leave these towns, not really. Worona, the Monomos, or otherwise. They pass down their houses; they buy one down the road or across town from their parents; they hold onto them even when they start to fall apart or go unused. Something makes them want to stick around, or at least have the option to return. It's rare to find a family that's truly left this place behind once they've stayed a while. Some of the summer set might move on after just a year or two because an opportunity arises on Nantucket or the Vineyard. But they were never really here.

A lot of the people who do stick around, I find, are the same ones who insist a place is just a place. This happens to be the one they picked or the one that an ancestor picked for them. Whether they hate it here or sought this location out, most of them say the same things. For them, their place is a random circumstance. Happenstance. Who they are led them to where they are, not the other way around.

Somewhere, they know better. I'm sure of it.

Acknowledgments

Seaview Road wouldn't exist without the hard work and support of a number of people. Lucy Davis: equal parts patient, incisive, and benevolent. My family and friends: the early-reading, blindly-lauding lot of them. The wonderful teachers and professors (English and otherwise) of Wellesley High School and Georgetown University: I was taught well, so I have no excuse. There are too many of you to name everyone on this page, but for this time around the warmest thanks to Christine So, Brian Hochman, and Paul Esposito for their generosity and zeal. Mirabile dictu.

Emma Olivia McMahon and Bumper McMahon: the best friend and most useless assistant anyone could ever ask for, respectively.

Author Bio

Brian McMahon is the author of *Seaview Road* and a reader of other books. He is currently working on his second novel, but for now this one in your hands is all you get.

He lives outside of Boston with his wife and their dog, who is a good boy.

To learn more, visit BrianMcMahonWrites.com.

CPSIA information can be obtained
at www.ICGtesting.com
Printed in the USA
LVHW020338010620
656996LV00003B/197